THE ATONEMENT

The Book Class

Honorable Men

Diary of a Yuppie

Skinny Island

The Golden Calves

Fellow Passengers

The Lady of Situations

False Gods

Three Lives

Tales of Yesteryear

The Collected Stories of Louis Auchincloss

The Education of Oscar Fairfax

NONFICTION

Reflections of a Jacobite

Pioneers and Caretakers

Motiveless Malignity

Edith Wharton

Richelieu

A Writer's Capital

Reading Henry James

Life, Law and Letters

Persons of Consequence: Queen Victoria and Her Circle

False Dawn: Women in the Age of the Sun King

The Vanderbilt Era

Love Without Wings

The Style's the Man

La Gloire: The Roman Empire of Corneille and Racine

The Man Behind the Book

The Atonement

AND OTHER STORIES

LOUIS AUCHINCLOSS

Houghton Mifflin Company

BOSTON   NEW YORK

1997

Copyright © 1997 by Louis Auchincloss

Library of Congress Cataloging-in-Publication Data

Auchincloss, Louis.
The atonement, and other stories / Louis Auchincloss.
p. cm.
Contents: The atonement — Ars gratia artis — The last great di-
vorce — The Maenads — The foursome — Lear's shadow —
The hidden muse — Realist in Babylon — Geraldine
ISBN 0-395-86826-2
1. Rich people — United States — Social life and
customs — Fiction.
I. Title.
PS3501.U25A9   1997
813'.54 — dc21   97-14570   CIP

Book design by Anne Chalmers
Typeface: Linotype-Hell Fairfield

Printed in the United States of America
QUM 10 9 8 7 6 5 4 3 2 1

FOR

ED AND EVY HALPERT

CONTENTS

THE ATONEMENT

The Atonement

—— ᧁ ——

SANDY TREMAIN had a pardonable vanity about his good looks; they expressed the amiability of character and equanimity of temper that had been his valued trademarks for a near half-century of life. Of course, as everyone was always saying in the early 1980s, people were living longer; one's middle forties were really almost a part of youth. And he had lost none of his silky brown hair; the few wisps of grey could be passed off as distinguished. But if he weighed only ten pounds more than a decade back, it was also true that his creamy skin was not quite so creamy and that the luster of youth which had once so illumined his features that friends had joked of a movie career, was now only a cherished memory. Oh, he was still well enough — far above the average indeed — and he was fully aware that his grey-blue, amicably gazing eyes inspired both trust and affection and that the easy movements of his lissome, well-coordinated and well-clad limbs were the admiration at least of female observers. Sandy knew that he could always count on his charm, the charm of a seemingly controlled laziness, or rather of a seeming laziness that was really a mask, but a mask put on not to deceive but to reassure, to allay anxiety, to make people as comfortable as they should be — why not? His demeanor put the world on notice that it could relax, because there was nothing to be gained by being on edge, because, whatever tumble lay ahead, one would break fewer bones in a graceful spill. And at least one would not have looked a fool.

But why, he found he was now irritably asking himself, did it always have to be *his* role to put people at their ease? Was it a must that he should maintain forever the image he had once created of the wizard investment banker who made money as easily as he spent it and who scorned the vulgar habit of touting his work hours? Why was it incumbent on him to play the lead in a parlor comedy, night after night? Who had written the play? Who was even directing it?

That objects which seemed to glitter in the shop window should lose half their gloss when taken home was a truism of which he had no need to be reminded, but now even the shop window had lost its sheen. Take the penthouse into which he and Amanda and the two girls had just moved. Thirty-three stories above East Fiftieth Street, it commanded a 360-degree view of the city through huge glass panes opening on a terrace that surrounded it like a moat. Shaving in his bathroom, Sandy could look north to the George Washington Bridge and infinite stretches of the Bronx; Queens and the East River greeted him from the french windows of the drawing room; the Verrazzano and Staten Island were seen from the dining hall; the mighty Hudson rolled before Amanda's boudoir to the West. To contrast with the modernity of the panorama, the décor was antique and choice: a Louis XV parlor, an Inigo Jones library. Yet "this majestical roof fretted with golden fire" was no more to Hamlet-Sandy than "a foul and pestilent congregation of vapors." He felt like the mad Ludwig of Bavaria, who had dotted the countryside with his crazy castles to make the world seem something it wasn't.

At breakfast, on a weekday morning, his daughters, Kay and Elise, thirteen and fourteen, large, pale-faced, with long blond hair parted in the middle, their eyes solemnly fixed on nothing, were silently eating cereal. Sandy had to remind himself that at their ages one could tell little of their future; they might yet be beauties. Amanda, who always rose in time for the meal, was still in her dressing gown, but it was the beautiful kimono that he had brought her from a business trip to Tokyo. It looked very well on her; she had a figure for clothes. But she was sipping her coffee too audibly as she studied what he assumed was the editorial page of the *Times* to cull her opinions for the day. Amanda prided herself on having moved to the left of her admired father's extreme right wing; she was a fan of Adlai Stevenson. She had met the former Illinois governor and been charmed by him. She was very proud of that. She talked a lot about it.

And why, pray, was he having such snippy thoughts? Was she not exactly the wife he had expected she would be, sixteen years back? Perhaps the filling out of her round cheeks had made her dark eyes seem closer together; maybe her abundant black, stiffly curled hair gave her a bit of an air of rigidity, of premature middle-age set, but she was still a fine-looking woman at forty-one, and she was as brisk and enthusiastic as ever. More so.

Yes, that was it: too eager, too avid, too quick to extol the many blessings she had never questioned. It was not that he hadn't suspected, in the core of his wife's being, a hidden panic that she might be deprived of some of the glittering externals of her life if she did not keep crying out her appreciation, that the Santa who had regularly visited her hearth from earliest childhood might be capable of bounding back down the chimney and snatching away his toys. But in the past year she had seemed to have laid that old ghost, if indeed it had ever haunted her. She now appeared to take even her beloved husband for granted. Sometimes at night when he wanted to make love, she, who had once been so eager, would object: "Heavens, what's got into you, bozo? We did it the night before last. Do you mind terribly if I slip off to sleep?"

Had the world of her lunches at the Colony Club, her charitable committees, the Kip School fund, of which she was chairman, her constant calls on her mother and aunts, begun to take precedence over love? And why should he resent it if it had? Was he such a Romeo?

But she was not, after all, reading the editorial page. She suddenly folded the paper and looked down the table at him with an air of disgust. "Oh, Sandy, here's another of those terrible cases!"

"What cases?"

"Another of these insider traders. Really, one begins to wonder if any of the firms are free of it."

"Are you beginning to wonder about mine, my dear?"

"No, of course not. But don't you think something must have happened to our moral standards when there are so many of them? What is this consuming greed? Where does it come from?"

"Your father says they're all Jews."

"Oh, Father. Well, you know how he is. We needn't go into that. Of course, it does seem odd that so many of the men indicted are . . ."

Elise interrupted her. "Ellie Kneller's uncle was indicted,

and he's Jewish. But Miss Pringle says it's unfair to make a point of that."

"And Miss Pringle's quite right," Amanda agreed hastily. "And speaking of her, it's time you girls were off to school."

Sandy submitted benignly to the demonstrative osculations of his daughters and watched them as they left the room. But he had no intention of dropping the subject.

"You know, it wasn't so long ago, Amanda, that any cautious investor, even a fiduciary, was *expected* to use all the inside information he could get his hands on. It was even considered a duty when he was acting for others. The only odium incurred was by men who listened at keyholes or opened other people's mail. I remember the story of your maternal grandfather, who discovered that a man in his office was sweet-talking his secretary into letting him peek at her boss's market orders. So he kept secret the big sale of a stock he had reason to believe would nose-dive. How he must have chuckled when the poor sneak lost his shirt!"

Amanda looked puzzled. Was he criticizing her ancestor? Her family had always revered Grandpa Burrill, a tough old trader of the twenties and thirties, and they disliked any comparison of him with what they called the "whiz kids" of the current market. She, of course, had married a whiz kid and had accepted the compensations, and she tried to be fair about it. Oh, yes, Sandy conceded, she really did try! But he still suspected that she had never been able to convince herself that his earnings were quite the same, quite as "solid," as Burrill money.

"Well, didn't the man deserve it?" she demanded. "No gentleman would flirt with a secretary to find out things he wasn't supposed to know."

"I agree. But a gentleman like your grandfather might have obtained his own information as a member of one of those secret pools he was so adept at organizing which would trade a stock up to a dizzy price and sell out just before its inevitable crash."

"And wasn't that ordinary business, in those days? Wasn't it simply being smarter than the next guy? Wasn't it what free enterprise was all about?"

He smiled. "A good definition, perhaps. And now, presumably, it isn't free anymore."

Amanda's brow was still puckered. "What are you trying to tell me, darling? That there are laws today that make it illegal to do what it was perfectly legal to do in the past? Isn't that obvious?"

"But your tone, my dear, implied that you were talking more about morals than law. The moral issues are not always so clear. The law tries to put all investors on an equal footing. That may be commendable. But isn't it always true that one man is better equipped to make a choice of securities than another?"

"Well, you can't expect lawmakers to equalize brain power!"

"No. They're trying to establish an objective standard of what does and what does not constitute privileged knowledge. The rules, as always, seem arbitrary. A cautious man does not consult his conscience as to whether he may make use of a particular piece of information. He had much better consult a lawyer."

"I don't see what you're getting at."

"Simply, my dear, that you are making stringent moral judgments in matters that are not quite so clear to others. Take this case, for example. Suppose I suspect my partner of using insider knowledge in purchasing the stock of Company X."

"*Have* you suspected one of your partners?"

"How like a woman at once to reject the hypothetical! No, I suspect no one. But let us say in my example that my firm has been retained to finance the take-over of Company X by Company Y."

"One of your raids." Amanda's lips were pursed in faint distaste. Her father deplored such things.

"Exactly. A hostile take-over. Very hush-hush. The moment the tender offer is made, the stock of Company X will soar."

"Why? Isn't it the victim?"

"But the tender offer will be higher than the market price. Our firm, however, is legally forbidden to buy. But take that partner I said I suspected. Say I have a hunch he's buying up X stock and keeping it in the name of a friend. What we call 'parking' the shares. What should I do?"

"Well, isn't it clear? Go to the partner and tell him to stop!"

"But, Amanda, my dear, he'd simply laugh at me! Of course, he'd deny the whole thing. And the parking friend, if I pushed the matter so far, would assure me he was buying the stock on his own account."

"Couldn't you go to the police?"

"You mean to the Securities and Exchange Commission? Or even to the United States attorney? I could do that. It might be difficult to prove. But suppose I *could* prove it. What would be the result? A partner disgraced and perhaps jailed. Our firm suspended from trading and possibly bankrupted. Myself impoverished and no doubt reviled in Wall Street as a whistle blower. Haven't I paid a rather stiff price for my squeamishness?"

Amanda was giving him her total attention now. "I suppose if the situation became too painful, you could always resign from the firm."

"And live on your money?"

"You know, darling, you're always welcome to it."

"We'd have to go begging to your parents."

"Sandy, you're talking nonsense! What makes you think you couldn't get another job?"

He felt with a sudden grimness that she was slipping from his trap. He reached almost fiercely to pull her back. "But not one where I'd be making the kind of money I'm making now. Where would your school pledge be?"

Amanda was chairman the board of her and the girls' school, Kip, once more elegantly known as Miss Kip's Classes. She was heading the drive for the renovation of the building, to which Sandy had pledged half a million. Her features drooped.

"Would we have to renege?"

"Most certainly. But that's only half the story. We are on the verge of a boom market the like of which has never been seen. If I stick where I am, I may very well in a couple of years be able to raise that pledge substantially."

Amanda allowed her mouth to gape. "How substantially?"

"Maybe to a million."

"Oh, Sandy!" The mist of their discussion of morals had melted away before this vision of a glittering city of golden turrets under the bluest of skys. "And of course you said this whole business of the partner was only a supposition?"

She stared at him, but he would not answer her. He could only smile at how desperately she reached for the edges of the tent of hypothesis that she had so rashly collapsed and endeavored to pull it up again.

"Of course it was!" she replied for him. "How silly of me; how like a woman, as you said, to take things literally. And I should remember what Daddy told me about a wife not interfering in her husband's business matters." She glanced at her watch. "I must get dressed. I'm due at the dentist at nine."

She hurried from the room, leaving him to wonder what else he might have told her had the crazy mood lasted.

❀   ❀   ❀

Sandy had furnished his office at Monroe Ritter & Co. as differently as possible from the trading rooms and other spaces of the firm, and his door was always closed to muffle the mellifluous hum of the business machines. In what he liked to think of as his carved niche of tranquillity amidst the chaos of market transactions, his chairs were English Regency, his desk a huge boule table, and his walls were arrayed with five master drawings of the Italian Renaissance, the principal one a portrait sketch of the strong, knobby features of Leo X, who had exclaimed, like a true Medici: "God gave us the papacy; let us enjoy it!"

That morning, on entering, he picked up his telephone and told his secretary to ask Mr. Brandt please to come in as soon as he arrived.

He then sat down to his mail, already sorted and opened in a neat pile before him. But he reached for none of it. His attention was fixed on the silver-framed photograph of Lenny Brandt to the left of his blotter. It was larger than the one of Amanda and the girls to the right. It depicted Lenny's big stocky figure and broad grinning face in a triumphant pose, rifle in hand, over the carcass of a Cape buffalo.

It was perhaps slightly odd to keep on one's desk the likeness of a partner whose office was only two doors down the corridor. It was perhaps equally odd that there should be on Lenny's desk a photograph of Sandy on a pier by the body of a suspended tarpon. No doubt an occasional office boy made smutty speculations on the relationship of the two.

But Sandy made it a point to himself to emphasize openly the role that Lenny had played in his life. Lenny had been his closest friend since Yale; Lenny had introduced him to the active life and the active mind; Lenny had lured him from his law firm and initiated him into investment banking. Lenny had damned him.

He was different from any friend Sandy had had before. To begin with, he was Jewish, though his rather "butch" blond looks suggested another ethnic origin. There was, however, the occasional gleam of an eagle in his small, sparkling, grey-green eyes and aquiline nose which might warn a keen observer that here was a much more complicated character than the rather coarsely joking and sports-loving individual who presented himself with such easy, near-arrogant assurance. Lenny's family were related to the great German-Jewish banking clans of Manhattan, but they had had reverses, and what money was left, in his Yale days, though artfully spent for the best show, had been strictly limited. The Brandts were not Orthodox, and Lenny himself was a cheerfully avowed atheist, but he was also extremely proud, and quick to resent the smallest hint of anti-Semitism, with which at college he had had some experience.

He was an existentialist, as well. He believed that a man was wholly in charge of his own destiny and responsible to no one but himself. As a boy he had suffered from rheumatic fever, but had rigorously trained himself to be a football player at high school and at Yale. In this he liked to compare himself to Theodore Roosevelt, who had found his manhood in the West, but he scornfully rejected the twenty-sixth President's sentimental moralism, which Lenny claimed was only the mask of a superior ego. He stoutly maintained that people who professed to "live for others" did more harm than good and that the great deeds of history, like the great works of art, were the results of enlightened self-interest.

Lenny at Yale had had, or at least had shown, no interest in penetrating the smart prep school crowd of which Sandy had been a natural leader, but Sandy, without in any way resenting it — indeed, being rather flattered by it — suspected Lenny of wanting to show the world — or himself — that he could pluck the juiciest apple off that still green but already withering tree. Lenny could never bear to concede that anything was beyond his reach; he had to prove to himself that he could become the best friend of the most socially eligible member of the class. He did not want Sandy's friends or Sandy's fraternity or even, ultimately, Sandy's senior society. Sandy's head alone, so to speak, on his watch chain would suffice. Which did not mean, either, that he and Sandy would not be the best and truest of friends. They had been. Presumably they still were.

The door opened, and Lenny stood there. He did not enter, but waved a hand in a cheerful salute. "What's up?"

"Come in, please, Lenny, and sit down. I have something serious to tell you."

Lenny, expressionless, walked slowly to the seat before the desk and eased himself into it. For a moment he looked gravely at his partner. Then his lips parted in a small, perfunctory smile. "You want out."

"Out of what?"

"Out of our little game, of course. What else?"

"How in God's name did you know that?"

"It's written all over you. You've been stewing about it for weeks."

"How have I shown it?"

"Well, not to everyone. But, my friend, I read you like a

book. You WASP intellectuals like to kid yourselves you've got away from your puritan heritage. But you never do. You've got a conscience like the chain on Marley's ghost."

"And you haven't?"

"Not one like that, anyway. Because it's basically the kind of thing I live for. The game. The sport. It's a bullfight, man. You're out there with a red rag between yourself and the raging beast."

"And yet you're always telling me it's so safe!"

"We try to *make* it safe. That's the game."

Sandy gazed curiously at his partner's square strong face. Except for the nose, the features were rounded and hard. Yet the eyes had a hint of friendliness, just perceptible behind the guardedness, the suspiciousness. A bullfight? Was that it? Because a man risked his life, did it have to be a man's game? Was that really enough for Lenny?

"You sleep at night, then?"

"Tessie tells me I even snore."

"No bad dreams?"

"Look, Sandy. My father was a good man. None gooder. You know how his father lost our share of the Brandt fortune. But it wasn't enough for my old man to start out without a penny. Oh, no. He had to take on Grandpa's debts. Every fucking one of them. And he spent a good part of his working life paying them off — paying off a bunch of usurers who were little better than crooks. Eventually he got out from under and made a little dough for himself and his family. But nothing to what he would have, had he not been such a white knight. And who really paid for his high morals? His wife and kids. When we were on scholarships, wearing hand-me-downs, my poor thirsty ma wasn't even allowed a cocktail before dinner. 'While we accept help in tuition, we can have no liquor in the house' was Pa's pious precept. I tell you, there were times when I actually hated the guy!"

Sandy, of course, knew all about old Mr. Brandt. Lenny had talked obsessively about him. "But you haven't been bad, surely, just because your father was good?"

The twinkle in Lenny's eyes was extinguished by a momentary glare. "So it's bad and good now, we've come to that."

"Oh, yes, very bad. Wicked, if you like."

"Words, words, Hamlet."

"Tell me something, Lenny. What's your real goal? You don't spend it all, the way I do."

"No, I haven't a society wife."

"You thank your lucky stars for that?"

"Not necessarily. I like Amanda. I even forgive her that 'some of my best friends are Jews' attitude. I can see she tries, which is more than so many of her class do. It's true I put my money away. Most of it, anyway. Oh, I buy Tessie everything she wants, but she's a reasonable girl. And of course I like spiffy foreign cars and my little shooting spot in Georgia. But I could swing all that, and more, and still be legit. Frankly, Sandy, I don't quite know what I'm after. I sometimes get a dark little feeling that I shan't keep it long anyway, so there's one solution. But you were speaking about dreams. I do have some."

Sandy shuddered. "So do I."

But Lenny for once seemed more interested in his own reactions. "I sometimes feel I might be like the great Schliemann. He made a fortune, mostly in Russia, I believe, and not too scrupulously, either, so that he could finance his excavations in Troy and Mycenae. Well, you may hear someday Leonard Brandt has dived to the bottom of the ocean to bring up the lost island of Atlantis."

Sandy was struck. "I'd like to think that. That you might be able to make up for what we've done."

"Hell, no. I'm making up for nothing."

"Well, I'm still through. I mean it, Lenny."

Lenny stared. "You're not thinking of leaving the firm!"

Sandy shook his head. "No. At least I don't think so. Not yet, anyway. I mean I'm through with what you like to call our little game."

Lenny was silent for a moment. His face told nothing. But he was used to crises and dealing with them. At last he nodded. "Very well. But what about the Ruark shares?"

"You keep them."

"Half are yours, Sandy."

"I don't want them. Save them for Atlantis."

"I'll hold them for you in a kind of trust. Your kids may need them someday."

Sandy shrugged, and Lenny embarked on a final plea. "Look, Sandy, you know everyone does it!"

Sandy jumped to his feet at this. "I do not! Do you think a single one of our thirty-eight partners does?"

Lenny rolled his eyes to the ceiling. "Oh, I imagine Tim Doyle uses a few tips now and then. And I can't think that Max Segal lets *all* his opportunities slip by."

"And that's all you can mention? Two? And you don't even know about them!"

"Know? How am I to know? People don't talk about these things. Have you and I? To anyone else, I mean. When did we start this little game? Five years back? Whom have we hurt? Oh, maybe a handful of greedy traders have had to pay a little more or take a little less for shares because we've had the inside track on a dozen or so take-overs, but what the hell? It's dog eat dog in this market. And most of those traders, I'll bet, had their own scoops."

"I'm still through, Lenny."

Lenny sighed as he gave it up. "Very well. And maybe you have a point. Maybe it's time. Quit while you're ahead."

"Oh, Lenny, would you quit, too?" Sandy was surprised at the sudden clutch of emotion in his own tone. Lenny had turned to the window and was gazing out over the harbor. It was a splendid view, but, as he used to say, what could you do with a view? It was suddenly vividly clear to Sandy, from the quick beating of his heart, that if he and Lenny were really one, both had to renounce if either was to be truly free.

"Oh, I might," Lenny said at last. "Just so long as something too juicy doesn't come along. What did Wilde say? That the only way to get rid of a temptation was to give in to it?"

"Lenny! Do it for me!"

"Well, if I did it for anyone, it might be for you, my friend. But as Hamlet said to Horatio: 'Something too much of this.' See you at the firm lunch. But don't make any announcements!"

The door closed behind him. Sandy knew he had failed.

⸙   ⸙   ⸙

Sandy had heard Lenny, to the point of ennui and exasperation, expatiate on the virtuous misdeeds of his father, but it was significant that, for all the intimacy of their relationship, he had never confided to his partner his resentment of his own sire. For he had not relished the idea of the parallel that Lenny might draw between the two. The senior Brandt had evidently been something of a tyrant who had imposed his moral standards — or at least the burden of bearing them — on his descendants. Foxhall, or "Foxy," Tremain, on the other hand, seemed never to have thought that the straitjacket of his own pure thoughts and deeds should be strapped on shoulders other than his own. The god who watched over him so strictly had apparently a more tolerant eye for the rest of humanity, and Foxy matched his own eye to the deity's. However stern his principles, they applied only to himself; his smile and his twinkle went out to all. Lenny may have hated Mr. Brandt; Sandy loved Foxy. Did his father return that love? Did Foxy really love anyone, or just mankind? That was the question.

He and Emily, Sandy's mother, still lived up at Averhill, north of Boston, in a small, retired-master's cottage at the boys' preparatory boarding school where, as a student and, after college, as a teacher, Foxy had spent his whole life. Even at seventy-five, like his son, he enjoyed youthful looks, but they were of a very different kind. Foxy's thick curly grey hair, his long thin lineless face and skinny strong figure suggested an asceticism that he did not, however, practice; one could imagine a Tintoretto or even an El Greco using him as the model for a monk with pale hands clasped and eyes rolling heavenward. But if this was a role he *might* have played, very different was the one he had: that of a master ever popular with boys and parents, an always encouraging athletic coach, an enthusiastic if simplistic teacher of English classics, and the man who more than any other had become the living spirit of the Averhill legend.

There had never really been very much besides Averhill in Foxy's life. Even Emily, his plain, practical, commonsensical and always adoring spouse, admitted this. "Oh, compared to the sacred school, you and I and even his beloved poodles could jump in the lake," she had once told Sandy, not perhaps the thing to say to a child, particularly an only child. But then Emily seemed to feel so little resentment of Foxy that she could hardly imagine it in others. To her it was quite natural, even fitting, that a man should have a love beyond his love for wife and family. Perhaps she even thought it was the way a man *should* love, as in the Miltonic phrase: he for God only, she for God in him. Except that she was never too much for the God in Averhill. She used to joke that the Protestant church school was the conscience of capitalism. But that was all right with her. Capitalism *needed* a conscience.

Sandy sometimes wondered whether his father's decision to return to his school after college had been idealism or evasion. Had Foxy, at Yale in the 1920s, seeing — as who could not? — the discrepancies between an era of reckless marketing and the lonely Christian ethic he believed to be enshrined in the school chapel, hesitated on the brink of that suddenly sinister world and turned back to the protected innocence of Averhill? He had, in any case, fled back to his boyhood, but he had also made a life out of it. He had become a school institution; he officiated at class reunions; he addressed groups of parents interested in sending boys to the school; he was its ambassador at large.

None of his old classmates ever came back to the school, as reunioners, fathers or trustees, without looking up Old Foxy, hugging him and wanting to know how he kept so young looking — "Have you discovered a fountain of youth?" They saw him not only as a boy, but as the boys they once had been. There he was, after all, still *there,* amid all the red brick and white columns of the beautiful old campus and its shimmering lawns; but was such a vision really compatible with the hard grey world of their own success, or even of their own failure, in downtown streets? Yes, that was it; the world of Averhill was not quite real to them. It was a golden memory, a fantasy, an illusion.

And Sandy had known as a student there that his own

classmates, however fond of his father, however careful (at least as they grew older) not to hurt Sandy's feelings, had not regarded Foxy, as they privately but affectionately referred to him, as quite the equal of their own fathers, who were all bankers or corporate lawyers or business executives, with here and there a doctor or, more rarely, a politician. Teachers belonged not to the managerial class in life, but to the maintenance crew, perhaps comparable to estate managers or the captains of yachts. And on vacations, when the boys all went home, and Sandy had only to walk from his dormitory to his family's cottage on the edge of the campus, he had the desolate feeling that his friends had slipped away from him into the glittering world of adults, and he was left in the nursery.

Sandy, in his prosperity, had never been able to induce his father to accept the smallest financial aid, although he and Emily lived rather sparsely on a school pension. No matter how many times Sandy reverted to the subject, pointing out that he and Amanda would never miss anything that he advanced, Foxy would decline even to discuss it, simply smiling broadly or laughing, as if it were a good joke, and then smothering his son in a bear hug that effectively quashed the subject. If he really loved his boy, wouldn't he have allowed him the satisfaction of giving his old man a small present? Sometimes Sandy's mother could be privately induced to pocket a small check, but he knew she would never dare tell Foxy.

❦   ❦   ❦

In the weeks following his resolution to have nothing further to do with their "little game," Sandy maintained all the outward forms of his old friendship with Lenny. The latter would wander into his office as often as ever for an occasional chat — particularly when he wanted to share the latest salacious or political joke on the street, telling it with his usual hilarious gusto. Lenny never said anything about what they no longer shared, but the inner reference was there in the sudden smile that had no apparent cause, in the occasional gaze a bit too protracted, in the rare motiveless shrug. Did Lenny want to remind him that, however passionately Sandy might wish to clear his conscience of the odium of the past, there was no way he could ever shake loose what he himself had termed a Marley's chain of misdeeds?

Sandy's attitude to his old friend hardened in direct proportion to his efforts to hide it. It was Lenny, he kept telling himself, who had lured him from his old law firm into Monroe Ritter, pointing out that lawyers were only the "ladies' maids" of investment bankers and received, deservedly, only a minor share of the profits. It was Lenny who, after Sandy had made partner, had exposed to him his brilliant secret scheme of buying forbidden stock through a small network of initiated collaborators in different firms, almost foolproof, and at the expense, as Lenny put it, only of other traders who, more than likely, were up to their necks in their own tricks. And it was Lenny who, most damnably of all, had thus placed the necks of himself and his co-conspirators in Sandy's hands without the smallest commitment from Sandy himself, showing his trust, his good will, his simple purpose, at no gain to himself — indeed, at considerable risk — to cut his friend in on a lucrative field of profit.

"It's like Faust and Mephistopheles!" Sandy would moan to himself. "He had no motive but to damn me!"

He had visions of going to the United States attorney and exposing Lenny's little ring. The prospect of public disgrace, even of jail, began to seem like a cleansing north wind on the peak of the mountain of guilt he had scaled. Amanda's horror, the scorn of her parents, the falling off of the friends, old and new, the disdain of the whole hypocritical world, might be a blessed relief, actually a joy to him! He went so far as imagine that he might even relish the contempt he would reap as the betrayer of his oldest friend. It would be like the self-inflicted lash of a monk in the frenzied ecstasy of penitence!

At home now he was short with the girls and rude to Amanda. One morning at breakfast he lost his temper completely.

"Daddy wants you to call him this morning," his wife reminded him. "He wants you to lunch with him at the Patroons."

"But that means I have to come all the way uptown!"

"He doesn't ask it often. I think you might oblige him."

"But what does he want?"

She hesitated. "I think he wants to talk to you about our social life."

"Our *what*? What's wrong with it?"

"He seems to think you and I are not seeing enough of the right kind of people. That we're too . . . well, financial is the way he puts it. That we don't see enough of the people who really make the city *go,* is the way he puts it. You know, the ones who support the opera and the Philharmonic and the museums."

"But that's just the same old social game he and your mother have always played! Who sits on what board. Who dines with Brooke Astor or Blanchette Rockefeller. We all see through *that*. Does he take me for a complete idiot?"

"If you don't want to lunch with Daddy, don't," she retorted, rising now from the table.

"All right. I will."

"I don't in the least care if you do or don't."

But of course he did, and at one o'clock he faced his father-in-law across the latter's usual table in a corner of the great Georgian dining room of the Patroons Club, overlooking the Central Park Zoo.

Douglas Craig, pushing eighty, some dozen years older than Amanda's mother, belonged to a generation where a gentleman — and nobody ever looked it more (grave, stiff, lean and grey, an exterior made to resemble a fort so that when the portcullis fell the charm of welcome was all the more pleasant) — could marry a fortune, entirely comfortable in his sense of giving quite as much as he got. He was too intelligent to have much faith in any political or economic establishment, but also percipient enough to see that the status quo was probably the best that he and his like could expect, and that was enough for him. Sandy had always believed that most men are essentially dead by thirty, that thereafter they simply repeat, in one form or another, what they once *were*. Mr. Craig, he assumed, might have died even earlier, but not before he had learned everything that was necessary for Douglas Craig, president of the Patroons, to know.

They had been discussing, of course, the social life of the Tremains. Showing, as Mr. Craig liked to put it, whom they "played with," Sandy pointed out, a bit crassly, that their friends included some of the "powers" of Wall Street.

"I rather thought I'd done all right, sir, on that score at least."

"Oh, financially, you mean. Yes, yes, my boy. No complaints on that score. Indeed, I should say you'd almost overdone it, as my father used to say about the Vanderbilts. But my point is, you've got into the wrong crowd in doing it.

We all know there has to be a place in the social world for the newcomers, the rough diamonds and all that. Go far enough back in any family tree, and you'll find one. Even in my own. There was talk of a Craig being a pirate in Peter Stuyvesant's day. And in my good wife's family, we needn't go nearly so far back." Here Mr. Craig favored his son-in-law with a conspiratorial wink. "All we really have to do with you, Alexander, is get you back to where you started . . . before, that is, you became quite so associated with market raiders and arbitrageurs and Jewish whiz kids. With the girls growing up, you'll want them to meet a rather different crowd. Oh, it won't take much, given your background and Amanda's. Not even to mention your bank account, my boy. A cottage in Newport for the season, or maybe Northeast Harbor, if Newport's too stuffy for you. Your beloved Hamptons have become decidedly too flashy. If we could get you on the board of the Morgan Library, that would be a good step, too. And I wish you'd let me put you up for this club . . ."

"But I belong to three clubs already, sir!"

"I know. But not the best. I'm talking about what our French friends call *la societé la plus fermée*."

"You don't think that sort of thing is a bit what they call *passé*?"

"Going but not gone. Remember that the Roman Empire took four hundred years to decline and fall. Of course, things have speeded up today, but we still have some time. When people tell me the ticket I'm holding is for a show that's dated and out of fashion, I glance at the box office. If there's a line there, I hang on to it. Well, we have a good-sized waiting list for this club."

Sandy sighed. "Put me up then, sir, if you want."

"Don't act as if you are doing *me* a favor. It's all for your own good. And while I'm dishing out good advice, there's another bit I'd like to offer you. Amanda tells me you haven't as yet made any substantial settlements on the girls. Isn't that a mistake? Have you consulted a good tax attorney?"

"You know, I'm a lawyer myself."

"Yes, yes. But you haven't practiced in years, and you can't be expected to keep up with every last wrinkle in the tax code. My lawyer has shown me how you can save untold sums with cleverly drafted trusts."

Sandy could not but marvel at how easily this man took for granted a son-in-law who could make a fortune and how serenely he felt his own superiority in being able to mould the crude market operator into a man of the world.

"I'll look into it," he muttered, and Mr. Craig, wisely content with the least concession in a delicate matter, changed the subject to the ineffable horror of the city's government.

Sandy was too irritated to return at once to his office, and, leaving the club, he decided upon a stroll in the park.

If he had ever thought of himself as action, force, "downtown," the park surely represented the passive side of urban life, both in its prosperity and its dearth. The children, the nurses, the sleek dogs, the bench-sitting retired couples were the former, and the derelicts . . . well, they were as shabby as the patches of yellow grass without the grass's hope of spring. Did civilization do anything but add riches to rags?

Wasn't that what his father-in-law was? Civilization? Douglas Craig did what a stable society had always done with its innovators: he cleaned them up. The men who had conquered the West, who had covered the land with rails and had flung up skyscrapers, and those who had made mincemeat of any law that stood in their way — did a Craig distinguish between them? — had to be put, so to speak, in striped pants and tailcoats. Their rapacity, maybe even their unscrupulousness, might be deemed essential to the vigor required for their tasks, but they must ultimately learn to put on ethics with their new manners and behave themselves. And in this process the Douglas Craigs were just as important as the pioneers; it was all part and parcel of the same thing. At least one could say of his father-in-law that he engaged in no sentimentality or hypocrisy; he put it right on the line.

Would he care if he knew all about his son-in-law? Probably not, so long as it was kept secret. Would Amanda? Had she not turned her attention away from any discussion of it? Lenny might have been right in calling it a game. If one broke the rules, one went to jail. But there was no real disgrace in it. Coming out, one could write a book about it. Maybe even a bestseller.

He had reached the southern end of the park and could see ahead the newly regilded statue of General Sherman riding on a steed guided by the angel of victory. He laughed aloud. He, Sandy Tremain, advancing to denounce the world! Why not? Why not go to the authorities and tell all? In bringing down the temple, like Samson, he could bury himself in the ruins. For would he not have forfeited the love and respect of both family and friends? It would be an end, a suicide, an atonement, if there could be atonement after the lights went out. It would be a drama to make up for all the dullness that had preceded it.

He hailed a taxi and sped downtown to his office.

But he found the reception hall full of people. A glance told him they were all staff. What in God's name was going on? The receptionist, livid, cried out to him: "Oh, Mr. Tremain, something awful has happened!"

And just then three men strode through the crowd. One was Lenny, handcuffed, unbelievably, escorted by two policemen. When he saw Sandy, he raised his joined fists dramatically and exclaimed, almost jovially: "Behold, Alexander, what an ambitious U.S. attorney will do if he plans to run for mayor! See how he exults in crucifying us Midases of Wall Street! Not too late, nay, just in time for the evening news! What a glorious humiliation!" He lowered his hands and spoke to the men guarding him. "If you please, gentlemen, if such ye be, I would have a word with my partner to convey to my poor wife."

They allowed him to approach Sandy, in whose ear he now spoke in a lowered tone. "I think I can keep you out of this. Just be damn sure you don't implicate yourself. Mum's the word. Don't worry about me, whatever happens. Remember that, pal. It was all my idea, from the start." He turned back to his guards. "All right, fellas, I'm ready."

As soon as Lenny had gone, Sandy and whatever partners were in the office met for a hurried conference behind closed doors. There was general disbelief that the U.S. attorney could possibly have a case against Lenny. Counsel was dispatched to the prison where he had been taken and an indignant statement issued to the press. Confidence in Lenny was warmly voiced and a strong denunciation of the despicable tactics of the government.

But when Sandy got home three hours later he found that Amanda and the girls had gone to her parents. Her note read: "When I saw what had happened on the six o'clock news to poor Lenny, I was terrified the same thing might happen to you, and I didn't want the girls to witness it if they should come to the apartment. Call me when you come in."

Sandy didn't call her. He reflected with a grim satisfaction that the desertions had already begun. But what he didn't like at all was that Lenny's first thought had been to protect *him*. It was in anguishing contrast to what he had planned for Lenny.

❀   ❀   ❀

When Sandy graduated from Yale, it was perfectly clear to him how he should conduct his life. He had certainly no idea of being taken for granted or condescended to by rich friends, as his father had been; on the other hand, he was determined to be as mentally independent and morally free as his parent. The law, as practiced by Wall Street firms acting for clients who ran the nation's major industries, was the obvious choice for a young man of intellect, ambition and the right connections. Indeed, he could hardly fail. He would not only become rich and important; he would be the captain of his soul.

Everything seemed at first to fall into line. At Harvard he made the Law Review and was hired on graduation by what was widely considered the premier firm of New York. It may have had a reputation of monastic severity and prodigious hours of toil, but its partnerships were prized beyond the presidencies of great corporations or even high political office. Yet achieving one of these was a process so laborious that a beginner had at least to consider the risk of failure, for failure might mean, even weighing the high resale value of an ex-associate of such a firm, that one had more or less wasted a half-dozen years of one's life. And even success, the far-sighted Sandy now mused, was not without its pitfalls. As he contemplated the serious, monk-faced partners who worked as hard as their clerks, he began, after the first couple of years in harness, to wonder whether his plan had been the right one.

It was the beginning of the era of corporate mergers and acquisitions, a practice at first disdained by the more venerable firms, as it involved the institution of lawsuits for purposes of harassment and legal maneuvers amounting to deception, but rapidly adopted by all when the profits proved irresistible. Lenny, already striding ahead as a young banker in Monroe Ritter, had been a quick and enthusiastic convert to the new business and had persuaded Sandy to move into the recently established "M and A" department of his law firm.

"Take my word for it, pal, that's the tail that will soon be wagging not only the dog but the whole damn kennel. It's your sure key to an early partnership."

"You don't think you're turning me into a shyster?"

"That, my friend, is a matter of nomenclature."

Sandy took his friend's advice and soon discovered that there were plenty of lawyers in his firm who felt as Lenny did. And he found that he enjoyed the new work, grueling as it could be, far more than he had his old registration statements and recapitalizations. It had the exhilaration of combat: the tense, secret preparations after the target company had been selected by the prehensile client, the piecing together of a master plan of attack, the drama of the tender offer, the race for stock control and the heady moment of victory when the target's management succumbed and bailed out, usually in a golden parachute.

Lenny was delighted at his progress and was soon asking that he be assigned to every Monroe Ritter take-over. Nor was it long before he was actively suggesting that Sandy leave the law altogether and move to Monroe Ritter.

"In this game, why play second fiddle? For that's what counsel essentially are. Sure, they pick up big fees, but nothing to what our boys get. And you know as well as I do that in this racket you and I are basically doing the same work. Why not get paid top dollar for it?"

This point especially worried Sandy. For when he and Lenny worked together on a take-over, they *were* doing essentially the same job. He found himself discussing the question with one of the few associates in his law firm with whom he was really congenial. She was Olive Dean, a female clerk, not in his department but in trusts and estates, then considered more appropriate — as presumably less exacting — for women. She was pale and thin but rather lovely, with a soft voice and long dark hair, tense, shy and very intelligent. They sometimes dined together on nights when both were working late, and she would listen attentively to how he had wrestled with the day's task. She would say very little about how she had wrestled with her own, less dramatic problems, though she could be at times amusing with tales about imperious rich women clients and their wills. Their talk never touched on the romantic, though it was evident that she was attracted to him.

"Lenny works as hard on a job as any of the lawyers," Sandy was careful to point out, "and he's sharp, too. None better. But when the job's done, he takes a break. He goes skiing in Saint Moritz or tarpon fishing in Florida. And he lives it up, too. Last year he got a bonus of fifty g's!"

"But he doesn't have the intellectual rewards that you do," Olive insisted. "To him it's just a quick deal, a fast buck. He's not concerned with the overall economic and legal picture."

"And I am?"

"Of course you are. I mean the whole tangled mess of law and society. How these things work. Or don't work. Isn't that what we're really concerned with?"

"Not anymore. We're just concerned with who grabs what company. For the quickest profit. Who cares if an old business is wrecked and thousands thrown out of work? Lenny has no illusions about it. People are going to do what they want to do, he says, and nobody's going to stop them. So why not pick up a fortune while you're at it? I think he *does* see the whole matter of law and society. As well as I do, anyway."

"You'll do all right once you're a partner."

"But nothing to what I'd do as a Monroe Ritter partner!"

Her intense appreciation of him and his problems inevitably led him occasionally to consider her qualifications, in the strict privacy of his mind, as a life companion. Of course, she wouldn't do much for him socially — nothing to what the hearty and almost breathlessly enthusiastic Amanda Craig, at whose family's hospitable city mansion he was always welcome on his rare free evenings, would do. Olive had almost no family — an old mother somewhere, obscure if respectable New England forebears — but the obvious devotion and loyalty she would bring him as a spouse, her evident ability to make him the focus of her every intelligent interest, was certainly attractive. He could visualize her in a small but impeccably neat and well-appointed flat always ready with a good dinner and a sympathetically listening ear, no matter how late he came home. For that she would willingly abandon her own legal career for marriage, he had no doubt.

And then he would pull himself up. What on earth was happening to him? What did he really know about her? Would anyone who knew him believe that he could prefer her to Amanda Craig, who made little secret of her attachment to the blond-haired and romantically moody young lawyer who was so hard to get hold of for a dinner party? Did he need a vacation? Lenny wanted to take him fishing in Norway.

And then something *did* happen to him. It was on a Saturday night when he and Olive were dining at a cabaret. But they were not going to work afterwards; this was actually their first "date." He had gone briefly to the men's room, and when he returned he was surprised to see a look of something not unlike panic in her eyes.

"Is something wrong?"

"Not really." She picked up her drink and listened for a minute to the music. She appeared to be debating a point. "Well, I'll tell you. Of course, it's perfectly silly. When you went out just now I was perfectly convinced that you were never going to come back."

"What on earth made you think that?"

"I can't imagine."

"Well, as you say, it was just something silly. A notion that flitted through your mind. No telling why or wherefor."

"Except it wasn't just a notion. It was a conviction. An absolute conviction. I *knew* you weren't coming back. I even looked in my purse to see if I had enough money for a taxi home. I didn't. I'd have had to take the subway. Not that I mind that."

He looked at her now in deeper perplexity. "I wouldn't worry about it."

"But I do."

They talked about it. She was entirely frank. But he thought it over morosely in the next few days, and he didn't take her out again. It was, of course, perfectly possible that she suffered only from a mild neurosis that could easily be cured, and he even imagined that the love and security of marriage might be precisely what she needed to pull herself out of her depths and become a wonderful woman. But why on earth should he take the chance of tying himself up for life to the victim of obsessions and depressions? Particularly when a girl like Amanda Craig, rich and aboundingly healthy, had an obvious crush on him?

So Olive turned out to be right. He *didn't* come back. He saw her still at the office, and they chatted in friendly fashion, and he invited her to lunch with him but always with another associate. As he had never initiated anything more serious, there were no steps backwards to be taken. But he could read easily enough the disappointment in her eyes. It made him sad but not sad enough to change his course.

Olive, as it turned out, was the last obstacle to his joining Lenny as the most junior partner of Monroe Ritter. His law firm countered with an offer of partnership there, but the sums dangled by the investment bankers were so much larger that Sandy hardly hesitated. Lenny was delighted and even loaned his friend the capital needed for a stake in the firm. Marriage to Amanda followed, and a life of prosperity began.

It was some years before Lenny introduced his partner to their little game. When he did so, Sandy always conceded, it was with no attempt to lure or inveigle him into something small that would only later turn out to be large and dangerous. Lenny from the beginning had put all the cards on the table and explained exactly how and on what scale and with whom he operated. The only defense he submitted for his criminal activity was that it hardly differed in principle from what he and Sandy did every day legitimately. And Sandy was inclined to agree.

It was what in the end destroyed his equanimity. If wrong

and right were the same, then the world was a farce. Lenny had to be his superior in that he had no conscience.

❧   ❧   ❧

On the night of Lenny's arrest, when Sandy got home to receive Amanda's message, he did not call her. He called his father instead. Foxy had come to town without his mother to attend an alumni lunch for Averhill School and was staying at the Yale Club. He agreed at once to be his son's host for dinner and seemed to sense that a crisis was at hand. Had he seen the evening news?

He had. When Sandy arrived at the club, he found his father waiting for him at a corner table at a comfortable distance from other diners, with cocktails already ordered. He listened without a word while Sandy drank his and then another in quick succession and told him the whole story of the little game. Then, with simply a sharp nod, he suggested that they order dinner, and there was no further talk till the waiter had gone.

Sandy, his mind humming from his rapid consumption of gin, felt a dizzying detachment from the scene. Who was this lean, fine, handsome old man with the gently gazing eyes who seemed not to be shocked or even much surprised by any of the horrible things related to him? Had his father always suspected that such things were in his son, or was he like some wise old Catholic priest who understood that sin was in every man, that only the manifestations were different? And Sandy had a sudden vision of the stalwart nature of his father's character, that he was, and had always been, stronger, much stronger than the world that had presumed to find his "innocence" irrelevant.

When he spoke at last it was simply to ask: "And what do we do now, dear boy?"

"Oh, I guess it's not so much what *I* do now as what'll be done to me. They're bound to catch me once they've caught Lenny. And if I cooperate with the prosecution, which I should, I might get off with a big fine and a suspended sentence. Or maybe even a year or so in jail. Does that matter? The point is, I'll be disgraced, disbarred and unemployable."

Foxy was unexpectedly practical. "Would they take *all* your money?"

"No, I guess they'd leave me something. Some of what I'd honestly earned." Sandy was going to order another cocktail, but desisted when he saw his father's faint frown. Anyway, he was beginning to feel a bit better. There was even a faintly pleasant melancholy about the idea of a future stripped of all the tedious features of his old world. He had a glimpse of himself alone in Rome or Venice or travelling in the East, with time to read, even to write, a kind of lonely poet or philosopher, with a lifetime to see and evaluate what was left of the civilized planet. "I might go abroad. I might paint or draw or write. I don't know. I might even *live,* Dad."

"What about your family?"

"Oh, Amanda's left me."

Foxy fixed him with a long, quizzical stare. Then he uttered a short staccato laugh. It was utterly shocking. "No such luck, my boy!"

Sandy gaped. "What do you mean?"

"Amanda hasn't left you. You just told me she's taken the girls to her family's to avoid some awful scene at home. She'll be back. I bet she's in your apartment right now. And you'd better go home and join her!"

"You really think that?"

"You were talking about what you can *do.* There's not much, I grant you, that you can do for yourself but take it on the chin. But there *is* something you can do for your wife and children. You can see them through this!"

"Dad, they'd be much better off without me! I'll give Amanda a divorce and all the money. All but a pittance. Gladly! She can marry again and change the girls' name to her husband's. They can forget all about me."

"And you can forget all about them; isn't that the point? So you can enjoy your bath of self-pity and see yourself as a kind of romantic international drifter!"

Sandy was able to reflect, even in his initial indignation, how remarkable it was that his father could say such cruel things with love in his eyes. He could only look at those eyes as if hypnotized as Foxy went on: "Your job is right here, my son. And it's going to be a tough one, believe me. So tough that no penance will be required for any wrong you've done. Now go to it, my lad, before you've had another drink. Finish your sandwich and we'll have some hot coffee, and then I'll order a cab and drive you home. Or to the Craigs', if Amanda's not there. But I'll bet my last dollar she's there!"

Only half an hour later, when he stepped across his threshold to be enfolded in the arms of a weeping Amanda, did Sandy realize that if his story was now going to be one without a hero, it might not be one without a heroine. Perhaps, he thought with a grim sigh, that was only fair.

Ars Gratia Artis

LIVING IN THE PAST is constantly derided, particularly by those who like to pride themselves on being abreast, if not actually ahead of, the passing moment, but there comes a time in life for some of us, alas, when it seems the only place where we *can* live; and that is certainly the case of an infirm and antiquated bachelor living alone — except for a loyal caretaker and an uncertain cleaning woman — in his old family stone *gentilhommière* (I'm sorry; I *like* the French term) on the Yorkshire moors. And to make matters worse, far worse, I must add the date: the winter of 1943. Wartime is bad enough for the young, but it's still hell for the old, who cannot help in the fight against the hateful Boches except to observe the rationing rules and keep the house dark in air alerts.

Escape to the past, then, has become a necessity in my long, dull days and nights, but for dignity's sake I call it "writing my memoirs." Should they ever be published, which seems unlikely, as I shall probably not live to finish them, I may call them *In My Father's House,* for there will be a chapter on each of the "mansions" that my old firm either built or reconverted or decorated or even had the wisdom to pull down. But I am making a point of writing each chapter first in a tell-all draft, endowing every face (or façade) with all the warts that I can think of or dream up. They can come out later if anything comes of my project. This chapter, anyway, will deal with the Roman palazzo, more or less modeled on the Farnese, which Alonzo Hawkins erected on "the fifth avenue," as old New Yorkers used to dub it, to house his great collection of art, partly at least put together by the genius of guess-who.

Lovat, Lovat & Speyer (we took Speyer in later), founded by my father, was, of course, a London architectural firm, but in those days before the first war we decorated interiors and bought and sold art as well, and I, though licensed to build, specialized in adorning the near limitless wall spaces of our wealthy clients. In the late 1890s Father established a branch office in New York, which soon became our central one, and I moved to Manhattan in 1904 to dip my cup in the great river of new fortunes that gushed up Fifth Avenue, turning it into a caricature of the Loire Valley, a jigsaw puzzle of derivative castles and palaces. But let me add right here that I am sick and tired of British sneering (including my own) at the vulgarity of the American millionaires of this period. Anyone who will make a fair study of what our British parvenus were putting up at the same time will have to admit that it was quite as bad, if not even worse. Happily, our horrors are all now orphan asylums or sanatoria, un-visited by tourists. We expose only our "stately homes" to the alien eye.

It was in 1909 that my father assigned to me his commission from Alonzo Hawkins.

"The old boy lives in a jumble of mid-Victorian horrors. He tells me we'll have carte-blanche. He wants a new house, new pictures, new bric-à-brac, the works. He may get Horace Trumbauer to do the house, but he wants us for everything else. He even suggests that you pack a bag and move in for a week so that you can get to know all his junk. Of course, he can afford anything he fancies. He's a majority holder of Mohawk Railways. There's only one thing that puzzles me."

"And that is?"

"Why he isn't perfectly happy with what he's got."

"You mean it seems so to suit him?"

"Well, you'll see."

Indeed, I couldn't miss it.

The house was a huge dark cube of Victorian Gothic occupying half a block on Fifth Avenue in the Fifties. The walls of the vast shrouded rooms were entirely covered with ornately framed nineteenth-century paintings by European academic artists. The mansion had belonged to the late Amos Hawkins, father of Alonzo and tough old amasser of the rail fortune, who, according to the legends already clustering around the hull of his unbeloved memory, had treated both his descendants and his employees as if they had been cotton pickers in the Old South. Yet Alonzo himself seemed nothing if not benignant.

Already nearing sixty, though he appeared older, with a gleaming bald head, muttonchop whiskers and a decided paunch covered with a rich velvet vest and a much-fingered gold watch chain, he received me, broadly smiling and snugly comfortable, in a huge armchair by the fire, from which he appeared to have no intention of ever rising. He extended an arm to introduce me to his five children and two in-laws standing around him as if posing for a conversation piece, and to his stout pale-faced wife, who sat opposite him in a smaller chair with a black volume in her lap, perhaps a missal or Bible, in which one felt that she took more interest than in anyone else in the room.

"I was glad you could come tonight, Mr. Lovat. It is not

every day that I have the good fortune to have all my children present. This is my eldest, Amos II, who has just succeeded me as president of the Mohawk Railways and his wife, Ellen. This is my daughter, the countess of Florham, who is passing the winter with us, far from her icy Scotland. This is my second daughter, Mrs. Dorr, who occupies the twin brownstone to the south. And here are my two youngest, Miss Dorothy and Mr. Sylvester, who do me the honor still to reside with me. And I see you have already kissed the hand, in good European fashion, of my better half."

That lady had indeed responded to my gesture as if I had exposed her to a disease. But the others seemed friendly enough. Sylvester, the bachelor son, actually offered me a wink, and Lady Florham received my quick little bow as a peeress should. Amos II preserved his rank as heir apparent with a solemn handshake and an accepting nod; Mrs. Dorr was all smiles, and Miss Dorothy wrung my hand as if to show me she was really a man. Mrs. Amos and Mr. Dorr, as modest in-laws, beamed from the sidelines. If I had an enemy in the room it could be only Alonzo's wife.

"My father built and lived in this house," my host now continued, "until his demise ten years ago. I and my family used to live here with him." I could see, in the faint elevation of the countess's eyebrows, how much *that* had been liked. Perhaps it had prompted her flight overseas. "My dear wife thinks there may be a question of disloyalty in our moving to another home. But I have opted to keep up with the times. I want to pull back our heavy curtains and let in the light of the new century." Here, he gazed about at his family to see the appreciation of the image evoked. "And you are going to help me, Mr. Lovat. I am glad that you have consented to dwell with us for a few days at least. I want you, so to speak, to take the temperature of this house and its contents. I want you fully to assess just what I have and what you think I need. You will be the doctor. I plan to take the doses you prescribe!"

Well, I could only take him at his word. What was it to me that he struck me as the living incarnation of every prejudice and misconception of the Yankee new rich? What he offered had to be grabbed. And I was smart enough to divine, already, that had he been everything he seemed, he might not have offered what he had. Had there not even been a hint of irony in the way he had referred to his consort and offspring? Were they afraid of him as he might have been afraid of *his* father? Ah, there might indeed be depths. I had learned that the greatest mistake that my fellow Brits made in New York was concluding too soon that they had fathomed the Yankee.

In the week that I passed in the mansion I had occasion to study the family as well as the collections, for they all lived in or near it, Lady Florham as a houseguest and Amos II and Mrs. Dorr in abutting brownstones. I was free to roam at will, though each of the five children, concerned no doubt with the effect of the paternal plans on their future inheritance, would, on one or another occasion, find the opportunity to inveigle me into a corner — too often, alas, a "Turkish" one — to edify me with anecdotes of the lovable eccentricities of "darling Papa." They seemed to be putting me on notice of a possible tendency to irrationality. I listened politely, carefully, even sympathetically, but committed myself to no stated view.

What I was having was nothing less than a course in American mores. Here were five human beings desperately if ineptly seeking to fit themselves into a species of new hierarchy in a society whose very Constitution denied the existence of rank. Were they creating a new class or trying to adapt themselves to an old one? Their wardrobe was stuffed with costumes, as if for some gala fancy dress ball (such balls, by the way, were very popular in New York of that day), but they were never quite sure which to don.

The French Revolutionary painter David would have sketched them first in the nude, but as their essence was in their raiment, I choose to be more like Philippe de Champaigne, whose strict jansenism required his models to be covered up, but who was able to express all the power of a Richelieu in the rippling robes of a cardinal. The Hawkins children, God knew, were no Richelieus, but their essential amiability and naïveté were well illustrated in their neatness and finery.

Amos II was the sober heir apparent and undisputed leader of the younger generation. He had largely taken over control of the family rails and terminals; he worked hard and, by all reports, well; his aim was to build for the future, to sustain the family company in splendid permanence, so that the Hawkinses, like the Medici in old Florence, could be a ruling family of the town. He conceived of America as a benevolent plutocracy, guided by an industrial elite born and raised in the tradition of a wise rule. But neither he nor his dour little bride seemed endowed with the smallest gift of humor or imagination. They lived and entertained grandly and joylessly, as if rather grimly accepting the wearying obligations of their social position. At the first reception of theirs that I attended I wondered what would have justified such tedious stateliness but a pair of thrones at the end of their new ballroom for the sovereigns who weren't there because they didn't exist.

Sylvester, the second son, a bachelor who was clearly to remain one, was altogether different. Slim, pale, alert, agile, with long shiny black hair and timid, curious probing eyes, he was the aesthete of the family and would have nothing to do with business. If Amos strove to be Piero de Medici, he would be Lorenzo il Magnifico. His tastes were Edwardian; he collected Moreau and Leighton and Alma-Tadema; he had been painted by Boldini in Paris and sat at the feet of Robert de Montesquieu. He had published a mild medieval romance and a slim volume of sonnets. He was very kind, very dear, very full of himself. He wanted desperately to be a mother's boy, but Mrs. Hawkins, although occasionally flattered by his filial devotion, had too much common sense to play the role so warmly demanded of her.

Mabel, countess of Florham, was partially separated from the cross and dyspeptic old earl who had married her for what earls marry Americans for and spent much time visiting her parents. She was a big, handsome, noisy, splendidly garbed and jeweled woman who trumpeted British aristocratic views in New York and Yankee democracy in London and was accordingly disliked in both places. Like so many American heiresses, she could never see why she couldn't have her cake of peerage and gobble it down with the appetite of a republican. She wanted the best and got the worst of two worlds.

Mrs. Dorr was the one realist of the lot. She, like her sister, was tall and dark and regal of bearing, lending herself to Sargent's type of society portrait (he did her in ruby red against a heavy curtain of gold damask), but she aimed to be nothing more than what she could quite appropriately be: a staid and respectable *bourgeoise,* richer and grander than most but essentially of the pattern, with brownstone in town and shingle in Newport, gold plate, many-coursed dinners and evenings of bridge.

Which leaves Dorothy, "Miss Dot," the old maid. This was not a type often met in Europe, where heiresses find themselves married off even if they are hunchbacks. But in New York I met not a few of them: the names of Misses Frick, Jennings, Berwind, Morgan, Wetmore and Twombly spring to mind. The cause might have been the curious emphasis that even the most worldly Americans place on "true love" and the fear of plain women that they may be wed for their moneybags. At any rate, the unmarried heiress had two options: she could become a saint or a "character." Miss Dot chose the latter. She was big, like her sisters, but stouter and more abrupt, almost masculine. She affected low shoes and suits and liked to walk with a cane, which she needed more for brandishing than support. She made a kind of cult of her father, who seemed to accept her worship in the fear that it might turn violent if he didn't. She loved music, though she had an irritating habit of moving her hands and feet at home concerts in time to the beat. She sat on some charity boards, where her contributions, I was told, barely made up for her bossiness.

All of the children, I learned, had once looked to their parents for guidance, but had received very little of it. Of their father I shall have more to say later, and their mother is soon disposed of. Alfreda Hawkins was the smooth-browed, smooth-haired, plump and placid daughter of a devout Brooklyn pastor, who had never quite come to grips with her husband's fortune or the problems it entailed, and had retired, Bible in hand, to the circle of a handful of pious fellow worshippers. Her influence was felt by her children only on the rare occasions when she deemed their immortal souls in danger. But she could then be very effective.

Turning from the family to the collections, it did not take my trained eye long to make out that, if Alonzo Hawkins had confined his range to academic painting and sculpture, he had nonetheless selected the better examples. While not entirely avoiding tavern scenes, cardinals playing chess and wide-eyed little girls hugging puppies or kittens, he evidently preferred landscapes, seascapes and portraits.

Sylvester, himself a considerable collector — he had his own gallery on an upper floor — did not seem to appreciate this. He was inclined to be giggly about his father's taste in art, although fulsomely flattering in the paternal presence, and his lip would curl at the mere mention of such names as Bougereau, Gérôme or Meissonier. If I ventured to point out that a Gérôme lion, at least if painted in the African veldt and not in a Roman arena, could be highly effective, or that a Meissonier cavalry attack was rich in exquisite detail, down to the last shining button on an officer's coat, he would wink at me as if to signify that he knew a paid hack like myself had occasionally to justify the boss. But I was beginning to make a very different assessment of his father's eye.

Visiting a gallery with Alonzo on our first excursion together into the art market, I observed him making an interesting choice. It was between two of Sylvester's despised Gérômes. One depicted Father Joseph, the *éminence grise,* in humble cassock and sandals, slowly descending a marble stairway in Richelieu's sumptuous palace, his eyes gravely fixed on the open missal in his hand, seemingly unaware of the obsequiously bowing, glittering nobles on the stairs as he passed. The other, chosen by Alonzo, was of a contemporary Arab market somewhere in the Middle East, full of bluster and life. To draw him out I commented on the more vivid drama of the historical scene.

"Too vivid," he muttered. "Of course, it's very accurately painted. Gérôme had his models dressed up in exact costumes. But those pictures look like stagesets. You can see the people are acting."

Of course, that was just it. *Father Joseph* was like one of Sir Henry Irving's fabulous theatre designs; indeed, Irving may have used it for just that. This was also true, though Sylvester would never have admitted it, of his adored Alma-Tadema's Roman scenes. But I wished to push Alonzo further. Why, I wanted to know, was his criticism not just as true of his own great Meissonier, *The Retreat from Moscow*?

"But that's entirely different!" he exclaimed. "Meissonier was born in the year of Waterloo. He grew up in the Napoleonic tradition. That terrible retreat in the snow and ice was part of *him*. It was in his soul!"

In his soul! So Alonzo Hawkins conceived that man had one. I began to study with a new respect that round balding head, those huge muttonchop whiskers, that bulging brow, those small glinting eyes that I had thought were the hallmarks of Yankee middle-class opportunism and self-satisfaction. Now I bethought me of the rows of busts of Roman senators in the Louvre. Didn't I perceive under Alonzo's relaxed air of amiable hospitality and geniality the hint of a temper consistent with world rule? I even wondered whether a bit of this didn't emerge in his short reply to my next remark.

"Your son Sylvester won't allow any difference between Meissonier and Gérôme. He has little use for either."

"There are too many things for which Sylvester has little use."

Perhaps I read too much into this rather banal paternal comment, but it seemed to me that I detected in it a distancing of the utterer, not from Sylvester alone, but from all his descendants. Was he warning me that I had better start addressing myself to the solitary question of Alonzo Hawkins? At any rate, I did so.

It was not hard to get him talking about his earlier days. I

drew his attention one afternoon to the rather heroic portrait of his much handsomer father by Eastman Johnson,
standing formidably tall and straight in a frock coat with
leonine white hair and big glaring eyes. It seemed more the
portrait of some great angry musician, a Beethoven, say,
than a railroad pioneer.

"It can't have been easy to have been the only son of a
man like that," I suggested.

"It wasn't," he readily agreed. "Father was something of a
tyrant. And very much a disciplinarian. I think I was all of
thirty before he offered me my first compliment, and that
was only a 'not bad, son,' when I got him out of a raw deal
that would have cost him millions. He wouldn't hear of
my going to college — he said that business was education
enough. He worked me twelve hours a day and didn't give
me a share of stock in the company until I was forty. And
when he changed his mind about the benefits of education
and decided my sons should go to Harvard, it was *he* who
paid their tuition so they'd owe everything to him."

"What sort of education did he have himself?"

"Not much. He went to work when he was fifteen. But he
read a good deal. He wasn't nearly as naturally tough and
cussin' as he liked to make out. He despised the new rich for
aping the manners of gentlemen and liked to pretend he was
lower born than he actually was. This used to furiously
embarrass my children, particularly my daughters."

"They didn't approve of their grandfather?"

"Oh, they hated him," he conceded cheerfully. "But they
knew enough to keep it to themselves. I taught them early
which side *their* bread was buttered on."

"But you, I take it, admired your father."

Alonzo glanced up for a moment as if it were going to be
difficult to explain to me all the emotions aroused by that

image. "We ended up understanding each other pretty well, I think. Oh, yes, I reckon we did."

"And he left you everything, didn't he?" This might have seemed bold, but I hoped he would talk about the famous lawsuit in which his three sisters had sought unsuccessfully to invalidate Amos Hawkins's will.

"Well, not quite. He left each of his daughters what any British oldest son would have considered an unnecessary deprivation of the heir. But they wanted more, an even split, I guess, and they had to go to court and they had to get licked. I would have doubled their legacies had they not. As it was, we haven't spoken since. Father wanted to keep his rails in one hand, and he did. So that was that."

It was evident that Alonzo liked to talk about his father. He enjoyed elaborating even on the early days of his own constant humiliation: how his father had insisted that he should perform the most menial tasks involved in the running of a railroad. At age twenty he had been obliged to spend weeks cleaning out the spittoons and washrooms of a Philadelphia station! In such a case — and there were more of them — the paternal aim seemed more to debase than to educate him. The father was always contrasting the son's plain looks and dullness with his own more sparkling personality; he made no secret of his affliction that his subdued and brow-beaten spouse had not borne him a handsomer heir. And even after Alonzo's own marriage to the minister's daughter and the early arrival of numerous offspring, the old man had kept him on a tight financial leash, making him beg for what were almost necessities for the front he was obliged to keep up as an officer of the company.

But gradually, very gradually, as I made out from the unfolding tale, things had changed. Power began to ooze from the older epidermis into the pores of the younger. I

could now even visualize the son, that impassive, humor-
less, temperless man, as a kind of lethal vine twisting itself
ineluctably around the stout trunk of a venerable oak, or
even, more horribly, as a giant anaconda around the body
of a strangled steer. For Amos, it appeared, as early as his
late sixties, had begun to suffer from memory lapses and
delusions of grandeur; he consulted soothsayers and medi-
ums about his investments and entertained all sorts of dubious characters and quacks at his receptions. Yet the one
man whose veto in these later years was slowly becoming
final, the one person to whom the old boy listened with
what was ultimately an almost obsequious respect, and to
whom he deferred at the end as to an all-knowing doctor or
grim dose-bearing nurse, was the once despised only son
and heir.

But if the vision of this process gave me something of a
shiver, there was no recognition of this from my host. He
described it as the simplest and most natural of evolutions,
the only sensible and sane way that the passage of control of
a great business from the hands of its creator genius to those
of its capable caretaker could have been effected.

I had, anyway now, sufficient notice that my client was a
much stronger force in the world of early-twentieth-century
New York than I had had any earlier notion of. It remained
for me to find out what he really wanted to do about his
house and collection. Did he just want a bigger palace than
the one Richard Morris Hunt had raised for the Astors? And
fill it with wild animals and battle scenes?

A surprising experience led me to a different view. He
had asked me up to his dressing room one day to view
a supposed Roman bust of a handsome youth, allegedly
Hadrian's favorite, the Bithynian lad Antinous. I saw that it
was obviously trying to be an Antinous, but hardly contem-

porary, much later, probably a fourth-century Greek copy. I forgot all about the bust, however, when my eye, through the open bathroom door, fell on what actually looked like an El Greco!

I hurried in. It *was* an El Greco, and hung, too, where steam from the tub could reach it! I snatched it from the wall, without even asking permission, and took it to a window in the dressing room to examine it. It was a small replica (Greco did these of several of his masterpieces) of *The Laocoön.* Under a stormy, flickering sky the doomed city of Troy awaited the arrival of the wooden horse, while in the foreground the naked old priest and his two sons hideously expired in the toils of the serpents sent by the partisan gods. I happened to be a pioneer in the revivalist army applauding the Cretan-Spanish painter, but it was almost unheard of to find him at this period in an American collection.

"No, I didn't buy it; it was given to me," Alonzo replied in response to my breathless question. "By a young Spanish grandee who was grateful for my buying a damaged Murillo altarpiece in his family chapel. I had admired *The Laocoön,* and he said I could have it, as his fiancée hated snakes, and he was going to have to take it down anyway. My wife felt just the same way, which is why it's in my bathroom."

"But where it will be no longer," I said firmly. "We must keep it away from steam. It's a perfect beauty! Would you mind telling me, sir, what you first admired about it?"

"Not at all. I was struck by the terror in the faces of the old man and his sons. Because to them there's no rhyme or reason in what's happening. You know the legend. They were trying to warn the Trojans about the wooden horse. They had no way of knowing that the gods had already doomed the city and wanted to stop their mouths. So they were being killed for nothing! As Troy would be destroyed for nothing. Oh, yes, one Trojan may have run off with a Greek whore, but is that a reason to burn a whole town? Well, it was enough reason for the gods. That's justice for you. Divine justice."

I didn't know quite what to make of this. It certainly didn't seem to fit with the pew-sharing husband of Alfreda Hawkins.

"You are not implying, are you, that El Greco found any parallel between the denizens of Olympus and the Catholic deity?"

"Well, not articulately, of course. He wouldn't have lasted long in Toledo had that been the case. But I've read up on his life. When he arrived in Spain, a foreigner who had especially to mind his *p*'s and *q*'s, the Counterreformation was in full swing. Poor wretches were being burned alive right and left. He saw it all. He *had* to have seen it. He even painted a portrait of the grand inquisitor! And I'm sure he was horrified. I don't exactly know why I'm sure, but I am. Yet he kept his mouth shut. That was the price of survival. That's what I learned under my father's tuition, as I've told you. But El Greco found something that I've never found. The light in men's eyes when they've seen something greater than what is burning them or killing them."

I looked again at *The Laocoön*. "I don't find it here."

"No, it's not there. There's only horror there. But you find it in his saints, in his martyrs. As in the Saint Maurice in the Escurial. The saint and the Roman officers are discussing how and when he and his legion are to be executed as calmly as if they were selecting a good spot to bivouac."

"It's perfectly true," I agreed, recalling the picture. "And in the background, which reflects the immediate future, you see all those heads being sliced off as if it were some ordinary abattoir."

"Yes! Because what's true, what matters, is what's going on in the sky! All those soaring, excited angels. El Greco finds his thrills only in the mystic. He doesn't seem to care what the death is inflicted *for*. It's death, the spiritual world that you see in the eyes and faces of his shepherds and saints and magi. And that is the only thing that counts!"

"And what is it that so appeals to you in all that?"

He threw up his hands as if he could never explain. "It's hard to say. But let me put it this way. I bowed my head to the world as I found it — as we survivors must do — but instead of finding the solace that may be reflected by that spark in the eye, I found . . . well, I found that I had simply become one . . . yes, one of those to whom others have to bow *their* heads."

I was fascinated. "You mean an inquisitor?"

"Well, not quite that bad. Let us say a Roman soldier. Like one of those officers talking to Saint Maurice. They didn't *want* to cut his head off. They wanted to talk him out of it. But they were there to obey orders, and if he didn't come around, that was that. Like them, I have no spark."

"No spark?" The discussion was too important for me not to nail him down. "And just what *is* that spark?"

"Look, my friend. I have everything. Everything, that is, that the world can offer. I was too young for our Civil War; I never had *that* to go through. I have a big healthy family and one of the larger fortunes in town. I am respected and even looked up to, however hypocritically. I can sail on the blue sea in my steam yacht and watch my trotters win at the races. And I give enough to my church to widen that needle's eye into a golden gate!"

His sudden laugh was a bray. There was a long pause.

"But you have no spark," I finished for him.

"Exactly. Look in my eye when I die, and you'll see only the panic of Laocoön. I haven't really lived."

"How many of us have?"

"Damn few. I'm not saying I see much spark in the eyes around me. But that doesn't keep me from wanting it. Can you buy it for me, Mr. Lovat?"

"I wonder if I can't." If he was being ironic, I was not. "We might start with El Greco. I think I know where there's another small replica of the *El Espolio* in the cathedral of Toledo to be had."

❀   ❀   ❀

Thus Alonzo and I started on the great collection. It took exactly twenty years to put it all together from our first meeting, in 1909, to his death, in 1930, in the depth of the Great Depression. Of course, there were interruptions: I went home to serve in British Intelligence during the first war, and there were gaps due to family interference which I shall touch on, and even periods when my never too faithful client harkened to the song of other Loreleis in the shape of rival dealers, but the great purchases — at least the ones that I so regarded — were made by Alonzo and myself as partners in enterprise. And it was a real partnership, too. Alonzo developed the eye of a superior connoisseur. Some people find that strange, in the case of burghers untrained in artistic taste, because they underestimate the efficacy in art education of a few bad purchases. The man who discovers that he has thrown away a fortune on a fake learns more than he would have gained in a season of lectures by Bernard Berenson.

Alonzo might have lingered too long in religious paintings, both pre- and post-Raphaelite — always seeking that ecstasy in the eye of saint or martyr — had I not gently prodded him on to Zurbarán and Velázquez and even Goya. But my real breakthrough came when I introduced him to the French impressionists by the unexpected back alley of Watteau. The *Déjeuner sur l'herbe* of the latter master, which I almost forced him to buy, with its rich, dark green forest, almost but not quite — oh, never quite — extinguishing the magically gold and silver glittering tiny figures of the picnickers, served as an introduction to Gainsborough and then to Renoir. And after that the whole world was open; Alonzo even developed a crush on Gauguin. Where could he go, he demanded, after Tahiti? Was that not the ultimate in living? Or in the dream of living?

We were now ready for my master plan. Why should my client not put together a collection that would serve as an illustrated history of Western art? And house it in a fitting structure that, after his demise, could be converted to a museum? I showed him the rough sketch of a Palladian palace that I had whimsically designed, with two interior courts for fountained gardens, which would cover a whole city block.

"Even the greatest American tycoons get cold feet at the idea of building what any Russian grand duke or English marquess would have taken for granted," I urged him. "Here's your chance to break new ground in urban design."

Alonzo loved my idea, but then he, too, got cold feet, and the rather banal Roman palazzo that Horace Trumbauer ultimately reared for him occupied only the same space as his old brownstone. It is, however, now the Hawkins Gallery.

It was the purchase of the great Titian in 1921, the splendid panorama of Pharaoh's daughter discovering the infant Moses, rivaling Mrs. Gardner's *Rape of Europa,* that at last aroused the alarm of the assembled Hawkins tribe. But I was ready for them.

Amos II I saw in his office. It was as spare and grim as Amos himself. Only two pictures adorned the walls: a steel engraving of the Eastman Johnson portrait of his grand-father and a huge brown photograph of a massive locomo-tive, like a prize bull. I seated myself on an uncushioned straight-backed chair to face his solemn perusal.

"I resolved to say nothing, Mr. Lovat, until my father made his first purchase at more than $100,000. Now that has occurred. Will you be good enough to inform me what is your ultimate goal?"

I could have asked Amos whether he had his father's sanction to discuss the matter with me, but I was pretty sure he hadn't. On the other hand, if I antagonized him by a defiant silence, he might have been able to make such a scene with his father as to throw a monkey wrench into the machinery of my master plan.

"I think, sir, that my goal — or rather your father's, for I have none besides his — is the same as your own: namely, to increase the value of his estate."

"You astound me, Mr. Lovat. I had thought you cared only for objects of a rare beauty."

"And what, pray, is more valuable than such?"

Of course, I was ready for him. I showed him an appraisal that I had just had made by Sotheby's of Alonzo's collection, together with a list of the purchase prices. In the past three years the collection had more than doubled in value, a rise considerably greater than that enjoyed by my client's securi-ties. Amos made no effort to conceal that he was impressed. For him a profit was a profit, whether made in paintings or sculptures, or in stocks or bonds, or, I suspected, despite all his church affiliations, in slums or brothels.

"I must see that the pictures are properly insured," he announced gravely. "And I trust that whatever securities may have to be liquidated to enhance the collection, they will not include the controlling shares of Mohawk."

"Oh, never." I had already considered this. It was hardly a stumbling block. The Mohawk shares represented only a third of Alonzo's portfolio.

The other children were even easier to deal with. Miss Dorothy was soon persuaded that a great gallery of art was her father's surest ticket to immortality. Lady Florham was cajoled with the prospect that the great halls of Flinby Castle, to be inherited one day by her eldest son, would glow with portraits by Romney and Lawrence. Sylvester was won over with the easily created illusion that he was my "co-curator"; it was a simple matter to convince him that anything I purchased had been with his guidance. And Mrs. Dorr, the sensible soul, knowing that her father anyway intended to leave the lion's share of his estate to Amos and having already received a good part of her daughter's share, was indifferent to my activities. Only Mrs. Hawkins remained an enigma: she sniffed at all European art as Catholic tainted, but seemed to regard her husband's craze as an essentially harmless eccentricity.

Until! Until it became known to the family, only two years before Alonzo's death, that he was planning to incorporate a museum to which he intended to bequeath the entire collection! I knew this, of course, for he and I had spent hours with his lawyers working it out, but he had not seen fit to take his family into his confidence, and I suspected that one of his legal team had betrayed the secret to Amos II.

The matter was brought up for discussion at a very solemn family dinner that Amos had particularly asked me to attend. He announced in the middle of the meal that his father's art collection was now valued at more than half of his whole estate. Alonzo, caught by surprise and red-faced, demanded suddenly that I be excused from the table if his will were to be discussed.

"But I have every reason to believe, sir," Amos replied in a cold tone, "that Mr. Lovat is party to what I can only call a conspiracy to sacrifice your family and your company to the interests of a museum of his own creation. You may do, of course, sir, what you wish with your own. Nobody here disputes that. We only want to be sure that you know exactly what you are doing and what the consequences may be to those whom you love."

"But still. I shall not discuss the matter before Mr. Lovat."

And now, at last, Mrs. Hawkins asserted herself. She taught me what must have been the faith of the early Christian martyrs. When it came to a matter of dogma, courage was no longer necessary: the meekest of them laid down their lives as unquestioningly as Hindu women cast themselves on their husbands' funeral pyres. Mrs. Hawkins had no need to raise her voice; her tone was calm and clear.

"No, Alonzo, I wish Mr. Lovat to remain. We have nothing to conceal from him or from anyone else. Though let me say at once that I do not agree with Amos that you are entirely free to do as you wish with what is legally yours. There are moral as well as legal rules in the ownership of property. I do not believe that you are morally entitled to leave what came to you from your father away from your descendants. I am not speaking, of course, of decent legacies to friends and charities. I am speaking of the bulk of your estate. You have raised the children in the expectation that they will receive shares that will make them inde-

pendent for life and that your residuary estate will go to
Amos to carry on the Hawkins name and tradition. You
cannot in all conscience depart from this plan now."

The little smile that Alonzo cast down the table at his wife
might have been one of reluctant admiration. "So the great
Hawkins Gallery is not to be?"

"There can be a gallery, yes. How great it will be should be
left to Amos. If your collection passes to him with the residuary estate, he will know just what to sell and what to
keep and what to put in any museum he sees fit to establish.
You have always trusted Amos. What need have you now to
change?"

"So you *do* allow the possibility of a museum?"

"It's not what *I* allow, Alonzo. It's what is right and proper.
It's what a Christian gentleman like yourself should be glad
to do."

And that, surprisingly enough, was all that was said on
the subject. Alonzo appeared to accept the verdict of his
wife as of some august tribunal of last resort. We finished
our meal almost in silence, after which I went home. I never
returned to the house, for I was never asked again. Alonzo
had apparently ceased collecting, and with his usual casual-
ness and impassivity in treating human beings, he had no
occasion to take leave of me. My role in his life was over.

❧   ❧   ❧

But not in his afterlife. In 1931 everything began again.
Alonzo left a time bomb of a will prepared without family
consultation by a firm other than the one he must have
suspected of having betrayed his confidence. In this new
testament he devised and bequeathed his Horace Trumbauer mansion, together with the entire art collection and a
large endowment, to a museum incorporated by the same

counsel who drew the will. To a board of fifteen trustees he named me and, perhaps as a sop to the family, his five children.

The low state of the stock market at the time had sad results for the Hawkinses. To raise the needed funds for debts and taxes, the executors had to sell much of the Mohawk stock and lost control of the company. The family vigorously attacked the will and spurned an offered settlement, with the result that the will was probated as drafted. Mrs. Hawkins and the four younger children received legacies of a million dollars apiece, a big sum in 1931 but considered penury by them. Amos, as residuary legatee, did considerably better, but he was no longer a power in the family company, which had been his whole life. The museum was triumphantly established and remains one of the "crown jewels" of New York City to this day.

The will was widely excoriated, and I was denounced by the gutter press as a foreign Svengali stripping a fine American family of its rights. But time and the popularity of the new museum rapidly covered these sore points, and I became a respected, even a revered elderly figure in the artistic hierarchy of Manhattan. The unhappy fate of some of the Hawkinses was no longer ascribed to the famous will, but I never allowed this to cloud *my* vision. The will was fatal to them.

Sylvester soon went through his million and would have died a pauper had not Amos cared for him. Drink accelerated his end. The earl of Florham, disgusted at the shrinkage of his wife's dower, divorced her to marry a twenty-year-old French girl. Dorothy made such a pest of herself on the board of the museum, protesting shrilly that its policy, even in acquisitions, be a continuing memorial to her father, that she had to be eliminated as a trustee. Even her siblings

THE ATONEMENT

voted against her. And Amos, more and more wrapped in a
gloom to which no one now paid any attention, was heard of
only in his angry letters to the *New York Times* condemning
the outrages of the New Deal. When these ceased, it was
because his memory had failed. Only Mrs. Dorr, the great
bourgeoise, seemed to flourish. Her husband invested her
million with acumen and increased it fivefold.

But I never had even the smallest regrets. I would have
happily done again everything that I had done. I did not
even bother to point out to my occasional detractors that I
had been in no way responsible for Alonzo's testamentary
dispositions. On the contrary, I was pleased to think that
people should give me any credit for so beneficent a public
plan. I would have taken not only the money of the Hawkins
heirs to create such a monument to beauty. I would have
taken, if necessary, their silly lives.

The Last Great Divorce

I DECIDED to write this memoir — or *apologia* (if New-man's shade could ever forgive me) *pro vita sua* — after a long talk this week with my daughter Monica. Monica is thirty-eight and getting her first (and I hope her last) divorce at the same age I was when her father and I split up. It was to be expected that a mother and daughter as close as we are (an intimacy, I might add, that developed only after Monica had grown up and married) should compare notes on two such parallel yet utterly disparate experiences.

Monica's marital troubles belong more to her era than mine. In this year 1961, at the beginning of what her genera-tion are dubbing, in my opinion a bit recklessly, the "Came-lot" administration down in Washington, it is not uncom-mon for a smart, well-educated and better-dressed New York woman of the "silk stocking" district to shed the stoutening and garrulous stockbroker whom she married too young for his broad shoulders and stout thighs to acquire a sleeker, slenderer, more articulate but not necessarily nicer venture capitalist. Needless to say, for all our vaunted close-ness, that is not the way I put it to Monica, who subscribes to all the fetishes of her set and is convinced of the moder-nity and with-it-ness and essential morality of every step in her own self-aggrandizement. There! No one can say I am dewy-eyed about my only surviving child. But what is the point of going through life dewy-eyed? Unless you take the position that it's the *only* way. Anyway, Monica and I get on very well. She knows she amuses me, but she doesn't know how much.

"What I can never understand, Ma, is the scandal that your divorce caused. After all, it wasn't *that* long ago. Nineteen thirty-eight? Plenty of people we know got divorces then and long before then. Look at the Roaring Twenties, for God's sake! But as I recall it, all New York seemed to be ablaze about you and Howard Eberling. Why did everyone take Daddy's side? They did, didn't they? Even your own family? Weren't there even letters to the *Times* quoting the morals in Howard's book and contrasting them to his own morals? What was the big deal? Nowadays the only rows occur over money and custody of children. No one minds the divorce itself."

"That's not quite so, my dear. Your mother-in-law has raised quite a stink."

"Oh, yes. Over her poor darling abandoned Tommy. Who is consoling himself quite happily for his abandonment, if she only knew! And behaving disgustingly about the kids."

"Let him have the visitation he asks for," I counseled her. "As soon as he marries his floozy, she'll be begging you to take the children off her hands. That's what Maisie knew in *What Maisie Knew.* Henry James may have been an old maid, but he kept his eyes open."

"But, Ma, it looks so unmaternal if I give Tommy more than the usual weekends and a part of summer. Nobody knows or cares what happens *afterwards.*"

"You mean, like everything else, it's just a game the lawyers play? Well, I got no alimony and only the right to see you and Alistair on Christmas and Easter."

"But Daddy let us come to you whenever we wanted."

"True. But he had to be the one who determined it."

"I suppose you can't really blame him."

You see? Monica unconsciously reflects the high feeling that existed over my divorce even when she is asking me to explain it. Her deep sense of an injured father is still there. Indeed, I suspect she treasures it.

"I am certainly not blaming anyone. You want to know why people condemned me and Howard. Well, one thing to consider is that in those days divorce was apt to be sought by wives on the ground of adultery. It was usually a case of middle-aged husbands looking for a fresher piece of meat. This might have been deplored, but it was too common not to be generally accepted. What people really minded, in my case, was that I sought a divorce *without* the accepted ground of adultery."

Monica ventured a dry laugh. I say "ventured," for she was never quite sure how far she could go with me, and I liked to keep it that way. "You mean you sought it on the ground of *your* adultery."

"Well, not legally, of course. Your father was the plaintiff. But you're essentially quite right. I put him in a position where he almost had to sue. That a woman should seek her freedom to marry her lover was not so accepted then. Hollywood did not yet set the moral standards of the nation. And there was also the nasty little fact that your father and Howard were closest friends."

"Damon and Pythias, as the gossip columns put it."

"So you've looked them up?"

"Mother, do you forget your scrapbooks? Of course I've been through them. What daughter wouldn't have?"

"That's what I get for being a magpie."

But there was something else about my divorce that was

mentioned in no newspaper column nor probably even in the idlest chatter of the gossips, something that people may have sensed without fully realizing it, something that was in the air only because of its absence. And that was passion. There was *no* passion involved in my divorce. People will ultimately forgive, or at least tolerate, anything that is done at the instigation of an emotion that transcends — or is believed to transcend — the will of man. That is because of their faith that passion redeems them from the animal state. Passion is supposed to be at the core of great art and great historical events. It is the myth by which we live: that if we are not passionate ourselves, at least others, heroes, are. I have met a few passionate persons in my life. Very few. I am not one of them. How about you?

But that, I believe, was the true cause of the scandal: that a woman should coolly rearrange her domestic life to correct an early error. That a sacred oath should be vitiated without the excuse of a great, an overwhelming mutual passion. That a wife and mother should have recognized that common sense might dictate the severance of two marriages!

I have now got out the scrapbooks to which Monica referred. Here is one of those letters, not to the *Times,* actually, but to the *Herald Tribune.*

"Those readers who thought to have been edified by Howard Eberling's mellifluous prose in *Law and Morals* may be jarred by learning that their guiding light has abandoned a faultless spouse to wed Clarinda Eliot, the wife of his closest friend and law partner, with whom, it appears, he has been conducting an amorous intrigue. But perhaps we should not be too surprised. Perhaps Eberling has simply shown himself as practical as a New Deal brain truster feels he must be. He adapts his ethics to his personal needs. In a day when, as he claims, man is ruled by law and not by God, are we not fools to consider any happiness but our own?"

As I look back now on my six plus decades of life, it strikes me unpleasantly that my divorce was indeed the only event in it that stands out sharply from the rather routine existences of my friends and contemporaries. Is it indeed *all* that I shall be remembered for? And if that be the case, is it not incumbent upon me to present my side of the matter? Of course, I take the risk that I may emerge from a truthful relation (and what other kind is worth the trouble?) in a light as unfavorable as shone at the time, and not, as I obviously hope and intend, as a priestess at the altar of reason. But that is the chance I must take. After all, I can always destroy this manuscript. What I have to admit, however ruefully, is that my divorce from Joseph Eliot and my remarriage to Howard Eberling is the "thing" about me.

❦   ❦   ❦

My scrapbooks go back to my childhood and earlier, with pictures of my parents' wedding. Most of the portrait photographs are stamped "rough proof," showing they had been sent on approval and retained by my frugal mother, who rarely ordered the originals. My two sisters and I, in big hats and many frills, tend to look smug or bored; it was before the day of candid shots. In front of a camera one either posed or made a silly face. What was going on behind our placid fronts? I recall the memoirs of a French eighteenth-century statesman that began: "My childhood and youth were played out like everyone else's." Saying which, he skipped to his maturity! Could anything more emphasize the difference between the ante- and post-Freudian eras? Think of the plight of modern biographers deprived of the

· 63 ·

rich soil of infantile resentments that we nourish so tenderly in our aging hearts!

My father, rather untypically in America — though we must never forget the looming image of TR — was the heart and soul of our family, a thunderous presence in the home and a notable one in the intellectual and legal circles of Manhattan. Ellery Tillinghast was the god of Columbia Law School; when asked once by a reporter who was the nation's foremost authority on the law of contracts, he retorted: "I believe Professor Williston at Harvard is deemed the second." He was often retained as an expert witness on legal questions in litigations, but he enjoyed a greater renown as the author of a series of popular books on the law. He loved to entertain, to lecture, to hold forth, particularly to eager, bright young men; no doubt he saw himself as a kind of Socrates, though I fancy he would have crammed the hemlock down his accusers' throats rather than have taken it himself. He used to live so boisterously in the presence of others, as if his energy were somehow sparked by their being there, that I imagined he might have ceased to exist when the door of his study closed on his rare solitude. Yet this was certainly not because Father's corporeal side was diaphanous. He was big and square and chesty and grey, always tweedy and knickerbockered, as if ready to depart for the country. He was kind enough to his daughters, though a bit on the gruff and distant side; it was always perfectly evident that he would have much preferred sons.

Mother, unlike her daughters, was a beautiful woman, tall, fair, poised, with a noble profile and the quiet grace of a muse in a Frederick Leighton academy painting. She appeared to bow to her husband in everything, but actually she ruled the home, regulating every detail of the household and the daily routine with a rigorous and efficient hand. She had

had the intelligence to see that her greatest social opportunity lay in her husband's forte for popularizing law, and had wisely established a salon for writers, lawyers, judges, politicians and professors in the big double brownstone they had bought for a song on the unfashionable West Side of Central Park and in the shingle pile they rented for the summers in Westhampton. Money was always something of a problem, despite Father's considerable royalties and fees as a consultant and expert witness, for he loved to live well, always boasting that he had forfeited the chance to make a fortune on Wall Street in order to live "for the mind"; but Mother knew how to get a hundred cents' worth out of a dollar, and where she had to pick up the slack it was the women of the family, rarely the man, who paid. Never, I believe, has a woman existed with so mean an opinion of the sex she was nonetheless determined to make justify its title of "stronger."

She never bothered to conceal from her daughters any of the crude machinery of maintenance so carefully hidden from her lord and master, nor did she make any secret of her disappointment with our looks. Flora married a dull but esteemed German professor at Columbia, and Elsie, to Mother's frank dismay, a plain but good-hearted dentist, but for me, the youngest, whom she dubbed, with a semi-disdainful snort, the "beauty of the family," she had slightly higher hopes. She speculated that my dark eyes and darker hair might be "made something of" and that if I could only learn to hold myself straight and not "fade off into corners where I could sneer at people," I might be lucky enough to snare a passable mate. How did we daughters react to Mother's toughness? Why, we adored her, of course! I have frequently observed this phenomenon. Mothers, take note.

Mother thought I might have a chance with Howard Eberling. He and Joe Eliot came constantly to the family soirées, all centered, of course, around Father, whose devoted students they had been. They had been classmates at Yale and Columbia Law, editors of the Law Review and were both aspiring clerks in the great downtown firm of Gould & Herrick, which would one day be Gould & Eberling. Joe never made it as a "name" partner. Howard was one of those brilliant young men in whose star everyone at once, and quite correctly, believed. He was a bit on the short side, stocky and well built (he had been on the football team at Yale) with a square set countenance, long brown hair (which he never lost) and strange, opaque, slanty, almost Oriental eyes that seemed to take you in and judge you without yielding the faintest hint of his reaction. Howard's handsome but rigid face was always a mask; his voice alone betrayed his moods. He had been brought up by one of those poor gallant ministers' widows who almost guarantee an attractive son's success in the society which they have penetrated without ever seeming to climb. Howard at the time we met was already being talked of as a "comer" — thanks to Father, he had spent a year as clerk to a U.S. Supreme Court justice before starting in his firm.

"He likes you," Mother observed, more than once.

"He likes me for his friend Joe," I would retort.

"Well, I suppose you could do worse than Joe."

That was true enough. Joe Eliot was pale and skinny, with large brown eyes and rumpled hair; he was often awkward and ill at ease, yet there were angles from which his long, bony, cerebral countenance seemed almost noble, and when he hit upon a subject he really cared about, he could be actually eloquent. And his roots were the kind of old Knickerbocker Manhattan that Mother most admired, far deeper than Howard's. But I was not in love with Joe. Was I in love with Howard? I certainly played with the idea, even though I knew I hadn't a chance. I had never, I was sure, had a chance with any of the men who really attracted me. Despite the grudging praise Mother accorded my appearance, I knew that my nose was too long, my chin too pointed, my figure not rounded enough to appeal to the manly and athletic types that I favored.

It was also true that I had a rather loose temper and was too prone to express my candid opinions. But I did not repine too much over my state. I was sufficiently resigned to what I regarded as simply the way of the world. Certain types mated with certain other types. Certain types of girls got the "dream boats"; the rest got the others. "Others" was all I could expect. Look what my sisters got!

Yet Joe Eliot was better than that. Even I admitted it. He had — as I have had good reason to know — the kindest heart in the world, a nature of singular innocence and a brain as keen as his inhibitions were naïve. He observed far more than he acted on or even reacted to. I used to think of him as gazing wistfully out from behind the bars of his self-imposed limitations. But I never really loved him. Loved him, that is, as I might have loved Howard, had Howard responded to me. Ah, that might have been passion! Had it happened in time. But it didn't, not even a decade and a half later when Howard *did* respond to me. Something happened, oh, yes, but not passion. And what about Joe? Did he love me? Certainly, as a dog loves a querulous and unpredictable master. Never as he loved Howard. I got the flesh, so to speak, and Howard the soul.

Let me go into that. Was their friendship homosexual? To a degree, I suppose. Most friendships have some aspect of that. But I am convinced there was no physical amorous-ness or even the desire for it. Certainly not on Howard's part. And if ever on Joe's, it was sublimated out of all ken. Howard was always Joe's ideal, and Joe gave Howard a devotion and loyalty he had never had, even from his devoted old ma, but which he had always craved and perhaps subconsciously believed was his due. There are homosexuals today who would scoff at such a relationship and call it a hollow simulacrum of love, devoid of the "realities" of oral or anal sex. They are too crude to understand how beautiful such a bond can be. It is true that I broke up that friendship, for I married both men. But I never envied or resented it. Believe it or not.

As I have said, Joe and Howard were regulars at my parents' big Sunday night "do's," where some dozens of punch-drinking guests would gather in the big back parlor until midnight, occasionally ceasing their raucous chatter to hear a piano piece or violin solo. The two young men had been favorites of Father's at law school and knew well their job of drawing him out with the right questions. But in time Joe began to leave this more to Howard and to seek me in the outskirts of the party, where I was usually to be found. He liked my being there. He was naturally an "outskirts" person himself.

Father was an inveterate ham actor; like an old vaudeville star, he needed a straight man to field him his cues. I can hear Howard with him now.

"Professor, I met an old law school classmate of yours downtown the other day. He spoke of you as the inspiration of his career. He said your life was the life he had dreamed as a young man of having."

Father's eyes would now be fixed in a waiting, a half-ominous stare. "Indeed, sir! And who pray was this disciple of mine in the murky fen of law?"

Howard might then name some giant of corporation law fame.

"Ezra Stern?" Father would echo wondrously. "Old Ezra Stern said that? And where did this singular interview take place? In his great office where you sink knee deep in carpet? Under walls hung with his Titians and Raphaels?" No answer was vouchsafed by Howard, for none was expected. Father paused before bursting into his main aria. The humble professor was now Lear on the heath. "Well, return, young man, to that old scalawag, Ezra Stern, and tell him that I'd give up all the books I've written, all the small reputation I may have acquired, for just *one* of his millions! Life for life — I'll take his!"

This, of course, was the kind of shock he loved to administer to his admiring circle, on a par with his claim that a good memory for the tricks taken in a bridge game was a greater solace in old age than all the philosophy of Plato. Anyone who took him seriously was not apt to be reinvited.

I remember the night when Joe Eliot first expressed to me his *real* attitude towards Father. "Your revered sire, when he's alone with a group of men, is inclined to sneer at the idea that women can ever equal men at the bar. He claims their minds are too imitative. But I've underlined in his last book all the phrases he's borrowed from Holmes and Cardozo."

"I wouldn't advise you to show them to him."

"I'm tempted to. He even downgrades his own daughters!"

"Oh, he always thinks women are fair game."

"Maybe that's because he secretly resents how much your mother runs him."

I scanned his pale serious face with a new curiosity. "You see that?"

"Isn't it obvious?"

"Only to the astute. Women have to be subtle to get their own way."

"Not anymore. The world is changing."

"Oh, I guess we'll be depending on you men a while yet."

Joe interrupted me, almost impatiently. "But you're better than that, Clarinda. You don't need a man to do things through."

Well, of course, he was right. It must have been evident to him, even then, how deeply I envied my mother's beauty and sought in my fantasies the way to dazzle men with other means. I talked to Joe quite uninhibitedly about my desire to teach art history, in part because he was such a sympathetic listener (none of my family was ever that) and in part, too, I guess, because I did not yet visualize him, despite Mother's eye, as even potentially a mate.

Joe had quite other ideas. He wanted to marry me. He had been in love with me almost from our first meeting, convinced that I was exactly the right girl for him. Nothing, it appeared, even a total failure of response on my part, could make any difference. He was so modest in his first bashful avowal of his affections that he did not have the presumption to accompany it with a proposal. He simply wanted me to know what was the permanent condition of his heart: that it was not a question of his "waiting for me," that there was nothing else that he could possibly do.

I soon realized, of course, that I had better take him seriously. How much would I ever earn as an art teacher? And how much could I expect to inherit from my freely disbursing parents? I was twenty-two, older in those days for an unmarried woman than it is today, and I had no intention of becoming a dreary old maid. For that is how we still thought of unwed females. Joe Eliot had good character and good family, and he was bound to succeed as a lawyer. I would have been a fool not to weigh his candidacy. It might be said today, I suppose, that I was a fool to be so sure that I would never meet a man who fulfilled my romantic requirements, but I never have. Even Howard.

It was several months after Joe's revelation of his feelings for me that he made his first proposal. He always showed a keen sense of what my reactions might be; he seemed to have sensed the exact moment when my mind was turning towards the possibility of accepting him. The wonder of it was that, knowing me so well, he still wanted to marry me. It was true, though, that I was trying to feel for him something like love.

It was at dinner at a German restaurant, not far from my family's house, that he put the question to me, and then, before I could even respond, proceeded to make it even more questionable.

"If a man asks a girl to take him 'as is,' he should offer her a list of his liabilities as well as his assets. We know that with animals the mating male struts and spreads his wings or whatever he has to spread and tries to show himself in the best possible light. But what's the point of being more than an animal if we don't show ourselves more than that? Isn't it only fair that I warn you that my Grandmother Eliot went bald before she was fifty? What a prospect for any daughter of mine!" But after a smile, he continued in a graver tone. "There *is* a darker spot. It may be over and done with, but it's only fair to let you know. I have had periods of bad depression. The worst one was at Yale in my junior year. Some of my friends supposed it was because I didn't get tapped for Skull and Bones, as Howard did, but that was nonsense."

I felt a twinge of impatience. "But you haven't had one of these 'attacks' since, I take it?"

"No. But one may still lurk. I thought it only fair to tell you."

"And only important if I decide you'll do. Well, we'll have to wait and see."

I had by no means decided I would take him, and I certainly didn't like his method of proposing. It seemed to me that a bit of strutting and crowing and beating of wings might have been preferable to this public confession, even if it did violence to his quiet and reserved gentleman's demeanor. I suggested this to Howard Eberling when he took me aside at my parents' next Sunday evening to promote his friend's suit.

"I can see that talking about a fit of depression is not precisely what a girl expects from an ardent swain," he conceded. "But that's just what's so outstandingly honest about Joe. He's not morbid. He's not even melancholy. He doesn't like to revel in his own misery. I'm willing to bet he'll never mention the subject again. It's simply that you have in Joe a nature that is, well . . . I'm going to sound corny, but what the hell . . . a nature that is actually beautiful in its simplicity and goodness."

"Heavens! With that endorsement I guess I'll have to take him!"

❀   ❀   ❀

Joe was patience and gentleness personified on our wedding night. My mother had been "above" giving me any sexual instruction, and I was a virgin with a somewhat nebulous idea of just what went on. I knew the basic facts, of course, but nothing of pleasure or how to give or obtain it. In fact, I anticipated a mildly distasteful experience that every woman was expected to go through. Joe was not only persuasive but very careful not to hurry me. We did not achieve a full relationship for at least a week, but when we did I moderately enjoyed myself. But I must say, in my own defense, after all that has happened, Joe was never a great lover. His trouble, as I now see it, was that he could never quite convince himself that I really liked it. And for "I," read any woman to his way of thinking — or at least any woman, or lady perhaps I should say, of proper delicacy. He thought that men were made of grosser material and that a gentleman, realizing this, should get his crude business over with as expeditiously as possible and let his gracious consort retire to her slumber and (no doubt) more edifying dreams. I made some efforts to cure Joe of this delusion, but it was too deeply embedded. He really preferred his woman on a pedestal.

Our next sixteen years were good enough ones. Joe maintained they were wonderful. "To be matched with a backer like you," he liked to say, "and to watch the kids" — we had two, Monica and Alistair — "growing up so well and strong and to be forging ahead at the office" . . . and then I'm afraid he would quote Wordsworth about it being bliss in that dawn to be alive. As for myself, I took courses in art and sat on a hospital board; I used to think of doing more, but children were still considered a full-time job, even with a nurse and schools, and none of the wives of Joe's and Howard's law partners worked. And then I had a book class and a bridge group and a country villa as well as a brownstone to maintain; my days were not idle. I read a great deal and wondered whether something more interesting and exciting might still await me in life.

It seemed to me that it could come, if ever, only through Joe's law firm. The senior partner, Nicholas Herrick, a former United States attorney and lieutenant governor of New York, was close to many of the brain trust behind the administration of the New Deal. He let it be known among the partnership that he would favor one of them serving in Washington in the creation of our "new society." I promptly indulged in dreams of government office for Joe; I imagined myself as a political hostess in the capital. But what could I do with Joe?

When I suggested to him that it might be his duty to take a leave of absence from his firm and offer his services to the nation, he heartily approved of the idea — in principle.

"You're quite right, my dear. In times like these, our firm should contribute something. Nick Herrick's thinking of sending Howard's name to the President as a possible member of the Securities and Exchange Commission. But mum's still the word for that."

"Howard? Well, of course, Howard would be fine. But what about you?"

"Oh, we couldn't both go. Someone has to mind the shop. And, as you know, I'm now in charge of the office administration. That's the kind of daily nitty-gritty it's almost impossible to turn over to another partner. But someone has to do it."

"But that's a janitor's job, Joe!"

"Not quite, my dear. I keep the train on the tracks. Unwatched overhead could bust us in a year's time."

"You know they always stick the partner with it who can't say no! You know Howard would never touch it!"

"Oh, you're right there. Howard can't even keep his blotter entries up to date. I have to get his secretary to keep track of his hourly charges. But don't worry. All my partners know the value of my work. They see to it that I get my fair share of the net."

"But none of the glory," I protested bitterly. "It's always

been that way with you. You polish the steps on which Howard rises!"

"It takes all kinds to make a world. Howard couldn't afford to go to Washington if he didn't have a well-run firm to back him up."

"And they also serve who only stand and wait. I should have known that when I married a waiter."

Poor Joe winced, but he offered no reproach. This time, however, I didn't apologize, as had so far been my wont when I lost my temper.

Howard was now second only to Herrick in the firm. He was primarily a corporation lawyer, but it was always his predominant characteristic to reject labels, and he insisted on arguing the appeals in cases of his clients that went to higher courts, where he proved himself something of a star. It had always been like him to refuse to be specialized, both in the office and out of it. If he pulled off an impressively complicated corporate reorganization, he at once wanted you to know that in college he had seen his future as a teacher of philosophy, and if he bested you in an argument about Plato, he would shrug and say it was a simple lawyer's trick. And yet what was the common denominator of his varying moods? An obsessional dwelling on the many-sided genius of Howard Eberling. He was always solicitous about others, but others, like Joe, were always doing things for him.

Except Felicity. And she was a big exception. She was Howard's one major mistake. Yet when he married her, we all thought he had chosen the perfect wife — just the one we all knew he had been looking for. He had wanted a woman with the proper regalia to share his throne. Felicity came of a fine old Richmond family that had found its way north to greater prosperity; she was pretty and bright and affectionate — in short, utterly charming. She appeared to love Howard and, a bit like Browning's last duchess, to love everybody around him. But she drank. It took us all, as it presumably took Howard, some time to become aware of this, but eventually it was only too painfully apparent. And when she drank, she was inclined to be amorous. In time it was rumored that she had occasional — not affairs — but "one-night stands" with men, among whom, alas, were numbered some of Howard's friends. Felicity was later to claim that these had meant nothing to her — that Howard alone was her lover — and I can actually believe her, but what must they have meant to Howard? Fortunately, they had no children.

Yet everyone, even at the office, was devoted to Felicity. Her kindness and charm evoked only pity for her failings, even among the stern. But I always hated her. She had taken something that *I* had wanted, as freely as Eve had taken the fruit from the tree of knowledge and had been too soused even to notice her expulsion from Eden. And when Howard was at last made senior partner of the firm, she simply confided in me with a little wail: "Oh, Clarinda, darling, I won't have to give those terrible tea parties for the wives, will I? I couldn't! I don't suppose you'd be an angel and do it for me? Oh, you would! You *are* a sweetheart!"

What really put me beside myself was that, when Howard took his seat on the Securities and Exchange Commission and rented a beautiful house in Georgetown, Felicity, terrified by the prospect of having to be his hostess in official Washington, spent half her time in New York on the pretext of looking after her garrulous, name-dropping, planter-proud old mother, who winked at her daughter's bibulousness because she tippled herself. To be offered a front-row seat, nay, a veritable box, at the dazzling show of the creation of a new world and prefer what *she* preferred . . . well, didn't such a woman deserve just about any correction that I could mete out?

I carefully assessed my own advantages. I was thirty-eight but much more attractive, in relation to my contemporaries, than I had been when I married. I hadn't developed a grey hair or an extra pound; daily exercises had preserved my figure; my breasts were firm and my skin lineless. Both children were already in their teens, beyond the age, I calculated, when divorce can inflict grave psychological damage. And as for Joe . . . well, he would have Ann Carmichael.

Let me say a word about that. It was *not* an affair. No amount of wishful thinking could have convinced me of that. And I recognize that the love was all on Ann's side. She was one of those brisk, efficient, optimistic, plain but very pleasant old maids who had got stuck looking after invalid, prematurely senile parents until the marriage market was bare. She and a sister of Joe's had always been best friends, and it had been a rather tiresome family joke that she had been in love with Joe since their childhood. But her opportunity — that is, if *I* chose to allow it — came when Joe at last suffered one of those depressions about which he had long ago warned me. I believe it was brought about by a crisis in the office bookkeeping which necessitated the firing of the whole accounting department and horrid charges of fraud, a situation peculiarly agonizing to the sensitive Joe, and aggravated by the sudden death of his father, leaving an unsuspected load of debt. Joe was unable to work for some months and stayed bleakly at home, doing picture puzzles and playing backgammon with Ann, his constant visitor. Think of the contrast *now* between his life and Howard's! I did think of it, all the time. Wouldn't he be actually *better* off married to Ann?

So, anyway, I tried to convince myself. And then came a summons from the blue that seemed to be my ultimate challenge. Like that old hymn: "Once to every man and nation comes the moment to decide." Of course, mine was a very different choice. Howard was giving a dinner party for the chief justice; Felicity had begged off in terror; would I go down and be his hostess? I most certainly would.

The party went off very well; I succeeded in amusing the chief justice; indeed, I think I amused all of the dozen guests. Never had I felt greater elation; I was living at last the life I might have been destined to live. And when it was over, Howard and I sat on the sofa before the fire, nightcap in hand, for a comfortable postmortem. But I had every intention of making it something much more than that.

"You were great, Clarinda. And do you know something? You and I might have been a great team!"

Ah, he had asked for it! Already. And I was ready to answer him as clearly as if responding to a demand bid at the bridge table. "We still could be."

"You mean you'll come down again if I send you another SOS?"

"I mean that I'll not only come down, but that I'll come down and stay."

He permitted the slightest pucker to crease his smooth brow. "And what about old Joe? Do we ask him too?"

I was sure that directness was the way with Howard. "No, we leave him to his antidepressant pills and the tender minstrations of Ann Carmichael." I made my tone dry and matter-of-fact. "Joe has little need of me, Howard. In fact, he hasn't really needed me for years. I've faced that."

"I can't believe that! Are you sure?"

"Oh, I'm sure. My real function was to ward off the depressions he's always been fighting. And I did so for years. But now they're back. Ann is just what the doctor ordered for them. I could ward them off, but she can cure them. And what is more, she loves doing it. As for me, I hate everything connected with mental illness. And if you hate something, you're not going to be very good in dealing with it. You and I are basically free, Howard. Felicity is never going to rid herself of her problems until she has to face them alone. You're just an excuse for her going on and on in the same old way."

Howard looked steadily into the fire now for what seemed an endless minute. "What are you really trying to tell me, Clarinda?"

"Nothing you didn't already know. You've always been the only man I wanted. I took Joe because you urged me to. I knew you'd never have done *that* if there'd been any chance for me."

"And you think now there is?"

"I *hope* now there is. You need a woman who will try to make up for all the things Felicity has done to you. Or hasn't done to you. Why shouldn't I be utterly frank? I don't think you or I owe her a damn thing. I want to sleep with you tonight, yes, but if you feel otherwise, just say so and I'll understand. But I yearn for a little straight talking after all the hot air. I think Joe's a self-absorbed neurotic and Felicity's a bitch. And I'd love a little happiness. Take it or leave it. We can still be friends."

He sighed deeply, as if there would never be an end to the complications of life. "You're a very attractive woman, Clarinda."

"Only because one man makes me so."

He looked me up and down now, with an appraising stare. I wondered if this was the way men sized up girls in brothels. I hoped so.

"Well, there's only one thing we need decide tonight, isn't there?" he asked with a small smile. "Shall we go upstairs?"

It was very satisfactory. Howard made love to me twice. The kind of frenzy that he exhibited, so in contrast to his usually sober demeanor, convinced me that he had been deeply humiliated by his wife's infidelity and that the doubts which it had engendered in him as to his own potency were the cause of his supposed failure to take revenge with infidelities of his own. I was confirmed in my belief that the way to hold him would be to convince him that he was the greatest of lovers and that Felicity's promiscuity was simply the inevitable product of her nymphomania. My course was mapped out. Nobody could stop me now.

❀   ❀   ❀

My course, however, was not to be an easy one. Howard was only too willing to let things continue just as they had started: as a clandestine love affair. It not only saved his sexual pride; it solved his sexual problem. His government work involved many trips to New York, and he rented a floor in a West Side brownstone, where we could discreetly and comfortably meet on given afternoons. He shied away from any discussion of how we should regulate our future, insisting (how like a man!) that so long as we had the present, we had everything. As I had suspected, his biggest problem — and mine too, of course — was Joe and not Felicity. Howard obviously dreaded hurting his old friend and scandalizing his law firm. It was natural enough.

But I was convinced that he would be a happier and more successful man married to me. I believed that I could concentrate his disparate ambitions on a higher political goal and lend him material assistance in obtaining it. An affair was all very well, but I knew my own nature well enough to be sure that it would never be satisfied by the senses alone. Howard was my last chance for the full, the real life, and I could not afford to let it pass in the cul-de-sac of love.

The only way that I could think of to shock Howard into action was to appeal to the old-fashioned gentleman in him. I had learned a good deal about this endangered, if not vanishing, species from Joe, a stalwart survivor of the class, and I suspected that there was some of it left, if considerably less, in his friend. If Howard could be once convinced that my domestic life and reputation had been ruined by our affair, he might feel obliged to do the "right thing" by me. And if Joe were the one who left me, or, better yet, divorced me, the problem of keeping our adultery secret from him would vanish, and we would be left with the much simpler one of disposing of the once unfaithful Felicity. I brooded long on how to accomplish this. If I bared myself to Joe — which would have been my preference — or allowed him to discover my adultery by some seeming carelessness, Howard might feel released from any duty towards me. I had no friend who would serve the purpose, so I finally resorted to the horrid device of the anonymous letter.

I hated to do it, but how else? In my doctor's office I borrowed his nurse's typewriter to "dash off a note" and wrote a sentence warning Joe of our rendez-vous and suggesting that he have it watched on certain afternoons. I then posted it to his office.

How he immediately guessed I was the perpetrator of the little plot I have never known and never, I suppose, shall. Had the nurse looked over my shoulder? It is most unlikely, though Joe *did* use the same doctor. No, I must assume he divined the whole thing from his bitter reading of my character.

At any rate, he came home the following day, brushed by me in the corridor without speaking and went up directly to his room. When I followed him and stood in the doorway, he was already packing a bag.

"What's all this? A sudden business trip?"

He replied gruffly without turning to me. "I'm moving out. In books the man goes to his club. Mine has no rooms available, so I'm going to the Gotham." He straightened up now and faced me. It was a Joe I had never seen before: firm, decided, judgmental, oddly cold. "Shouldn't a man move out when his wife is planning to marry her lover?"

"What on earth makes you think I have a lover? Much less planning to marry him?"

"Do you deny it?"

I hesitated. This was not in the script. "No."

"Very well, then." He turned back to his packing. "We can communicate through our lawyers. I assume you will use Dorr and Graham." This was the firm in which my father was "of counsel." "I will let you know whom I shall use. Obviously, I can't use my firm."

"Why obviously?"

"Because I shall be naming Howard as co-respondent."

My heart gave a little bound of hope. But who would have thought Joe could be so hard and clear? "Then you know about me and Howard."

"I have known about you and Howard for some time. Felicity put me on to it. She and I agreed to let you both have your little fling and perhaps get it out of your systems. But what I did *not* know until today was that you had made up your mind to acquire Howard as a husband at whatever

cost to friendship, loyalty, family, children or anything else
. . . coldly, calculatingly, cruelly . . ."

"Joe, what are you saying!" I cried.

"It was you who sent that letter, wasn't it?"

"No!"

Joe's little laugh was sour. "If you hadn't, you'd have
asked: what letter? I take it, anyway, that you want your
freedom. And I'm willing to give it to you. On certain condi-
tions. I want a valid divorce, no fancy Reno business. I've
already given you more than half of all I've made; that
should do you financially, even if Howard eludes you at the
last moment. I shall want custody of the children, but I'll
give you my word that you can see them whenever you like,
and you know that *my* word, anyway, is good. Finally, I shall
sue you for divorce on grounds of adultery, and you will not
contest. You'll suffer some slight disgrace, even in this day of
tolerance, but it may have the advantage on which you've
been counting of bringing Howard to the altar, or to whatever place such unions are sanctified. Of course, I could tell
him how you've engineered this whole business, but my
failure to do so will be my sole revenge for what he's done
to me."

I shuddered. Almost involuntarily I raised my hands to
my eyes. "Oh, Joe, I could never have imagined I'd bring you
to such bitterness!"

"That's because you never thought of me at all. And now,
if you don't mind, I'd like to get on with my packing."

❀   ❀   ❀

Things worked out exactly as Joe had predicted. When
Howard was unexpectedly (to him) served with process in
Joe's suit, he told me grimly that same night that it was now

his duty to leave Felicity to be free to marry me. I didn't like his putting it so squarely in the line of duty, but I had embarked on my course of action, and I was not going to rock my boat — already in swirling white water — for any weak scruples. Felicity raised the roof with her wails; she proclaimed to the world that she had been a terrible spouse but that for two years now she had led a life of spotless virtue and no alcohol and that Howard had seemed to have totally forgiven her until *I* came along. It may have even been true. She did, however, agree at last to a Reno divorce and a large settlement, and both marriages were sundered in a matter of weeks.

The outcry was quite as horrendous as Monica has indicated. My father led the hue and cry by loudly proclaiming his support of Joe and forbidding me his house. The entire partnership of Joe and Howard's firm, plus many of the clients, bewailed the betrayal of friendship and the fouling of a partner's nest. Relatives and friends were unanimous in their denunciations. It looked as if Howard and I would start our new life without an ally in the world.

Yet it died down almost as quickly as it had exploded. Those things do. Howard felt he had to resign from the firm, which I encouraged him to do, particularly when I learned that he might be offered an assistant secretaryship of state. I told him we would turn our backs forever on New York and find new worlds to conquer in the federal sphere.

Which we did. The four years of the war were the happiest — the only really happy — ones of my life. As some well-paid workers in defense factories were supposed to have said: "This war is too good to last." Howard, trusted and valued by the President and Harry Hopkins, was included in conferences with Churchill, Stalin and Chiang Kai-shek; he became as big a man as even I could have hoped, and my parties in the capital, glittering with high brass and braid, were those of my youthful fantasies. It was all quite unbelievable, and the crush of work and pace of travel kept my husband from brooding too often on the origins of our connubial existence.

But at the end of the war Howard had a shock in store for me that had all the force, in *my* life anyway, of the explosion that had brought about the Japanese surrender. He calmly announced that he had accepted a teaching post at Cornell Law School, which would give him the time to write a book he had long had in mind. My frantic arguments against isolating ourselves on the shores of Lake Cayuga in a confined academic atmosphere were like so many wavelets against a hard wet rock. He was going; I could come or stay as I wished. Of course, I came.

I resigned myself as best I could to life in Ithaca. For two years I hoped against hope that he would feel the urge to return to the center of things. He never did. He loved his classes; he loved his writing. He was agreeable enough to me, but our relationship had changed. We were more like two potluck college roommates making the best of a small congeniality than a wedded couple. I sometimes suspected that Howard was making up for something, that this new life was a kind of atonement. He followed the fortunes of his old law firm with the greatest interest, maintaining a correspondence with some of his former partners, though not, of course, with Joe. "We'll never see or hear from *him* again," he would murmur ruefully, half to himself. I began to understand how much he had once depended on Joe's constant backing and approval. It had taken the strenuous demands of the war effort to compensate for it.

We did, however, meet Joe again, a year before my husband's sudden death of a stroke. It was at a book party given by Howard's publishers for his last title: *Morality and Crime*. He had put Joe and Ann's names (they had long been married) on the invitation list in what he deemed the vain hope that they might, after so many years, relent and attend, and indeed, to everyone's surprise, they did.

"One can't hold grudges forever," Joe told me, after taking the hand that I had hesitantly held out to him. "The human body changes its cells every seven years, and it's been more than that. You and I are new people, Clarinda. Or at least we can hope so."

"Funny that we feel the same, isn't it? But perhaps *you* don't. Can we sit for a minute and talk?" I saw Ann eye us jealously across the room. If she only knew how little she had to worry about! Joe and I seated ourselves on a divan. "If you ever wanted me to be punished, Joe, let me assure you I have been."

"You're not happy in Ithaca?" He might have been asking me about a vacation spoiled by bad weather.

"I have no particular friends there. No real outlet. Nothing basically to do. Howard has his classes and his books. He seems absorbed. Or do I mean detached? Detached, of course, from me."

"But you rub along together well enough, don't you?"

"Oh, we rub along. But I can't help wondering at times if he isn't basically trying to get back at me."

"For what?"

"For pushing him into the limelight. For caring too much about his being a great man. It sometimes seems to me it's as if we had been in a repertory theatre and I was the director and he the star, and instead of casting him as Tamburlane one night and Romeo the next, I made him play Hamlet all through the season."

Joe seemed mildly interested at last. "But Howard always wanted to be a big somebody."

"He wanted to be several big somebodies. He conceived that to be his genius. And *you* were the director who saw that. *You* were the director he wanted and has always missed. Oh, Joe, you could help me so much!"

He was dry again. "And why should I want to do that? What is it, Clarinda, that you need?"

"To have you tell me that things haven't worked out so badly for us, after all. You've been happy with Ann, haven't you? And Felicity's been on the wagon for years now and is supposed to be quite content with that sanatorium doctor she married. And I had those wonderful Washington years, where Howard, for all his reservations, *did* help make some history."

Joe gave me a long look in which I read all the superficiality of his offered truce. "You forget Alistair," he said at last.

Of course, he would have to have the last word. Our son, Alistair, always a shy and withdrawn youth, who had shown a subdued but touching sympathy for both parents at the time of our divorce, had subsequently faded out of the educational process and drifted from job to lesser job in the grip of drugs. I had blamed his failure on the times. It was obvious that Joe held a different theory.

I think it is honest of me, anyway, to end this account with the one piece that won't quite fit into my puzzle.

The Maenads

E RASTUS THORN would smile deprecatingly whenever he heard himself described as the *arbiter elegantiarum* of Southampton's summer colony, but his heart received it as a fitting tribute. When he made his midmorning appearance at the Beach Club with all his tall slender dignity, arrayed in what a man of less than his sixty years might have deemed a slightly excessive coloration, but "rich not gaudy" — the newly pressed pants a soft pink, the jacket a glowing yellow, the beautiful panama, which he doffed to greet ladies, exposing his distinguished grey locks over an eagle's beak nose — he might have been an admiral coming on deck to survey a far-spread flotilla rather than the gaudy umbrella tables and bronzed bodies under a July sun.

The ladies returned his salutes. Some approached with questions. Mrs. J. Borden Ijams wanted to know whether it was true that a young male employee had joined the club members in a giddy snake dance that had ended the Saturday night revelry. Erastus gravely admitted the fact and its impropriety; it would not be repeated. He, of course, had been head of the house committee for twenty years. He would only murmur in extenuation that a certain debutante might have issued the unwarranted invitation. Another lady protested that it had not been *her* son who had circulated a

smutty story about the President of the United States at a
dinner dance where a son of the chief executive had been
present. It was the summer of 1937. Erastus assured her that
he knew perfectly well who the guilty party was; apologies
had been made to the hostess. He then lowered one eye in a
grave chicken wink to indicate the colony's unspoken sympathy with the indiscreet raconteur.

Erastus had been so long divorced that he qualified as a
bachelor. From the first day of June to the last of December
he occupied the same suite at the Hampton Inn, spending
his mornings at the beach, his afternoons on the green and
his evenings at dinner parties. He was the accepted authority on all matters of dress, precedence and decorum; his
function, as the ladies of the dunes and inlets enthusiastically put it, was "to keep us up to snuff." His winters were
spent in a tiny brownstone in Manhattan and in an even
tinier office on Wall Street, where he transacted the odd bits
of brokerage in securities, insurance and real estate with
which he had accumulated his small but adequate fortune.
But his winters, he maintained, were essentially for "hiber-
nation"; the hot months were those for which he really lived.

Since his divorce, so long back, from Gabriella, who now
lived, with her irritating airs of superiority, in what she
deemed the more intellectual and less frivolous neighboring
Westhampton, Erastus had not been associated with her sex
in any romantic way, except, of course, for an occasional
"flirt" with a flattered dowager, accompanied by sent corsages, deep sighs and the exchange of *vers de société*. There
was even a legend that he had been heard to murmur,
leaning forward as an amply endowed lady had tucked her
eyepiece under her bodice, "Happy lorgnette!" These were
games, after all, played by known rules. But this summer
something much more jostling had happened to him. He

had fallen in love, and he did not know what it would do to him.

Certainly his attentions to Ilona Loring had been too marked to escape the notice of the summer colony. Nor had he tried to conceal them. Indeed, hadn't he taken an odd little boasting pride in them? But how his old friends, particularly his lady friends, were going to react to this new development in his life was still very much a question. Did all the world really love a lover? Or would he be derided as an infatuated old peacock? There was already the horrid danger that Ilona, twenty years his junior, was seeing him in that light. *If* that was what her merry laughter meant. Or did it mean — God grant it! — that he amused her? She had not had to befriend him, but she had.

There she was now, waiting for him at her usual back-gammon table, far too sure of herself to mind in the least being seen waiting for a man. She waved a vigorous arm to summon him to her side. He hurried over and took his seat. With hardly a word of greeting, they rolled the dice to see who started, and commenced their game.

Ilona Loring (she took back her maiden name after each divorce, the circumstances of separation having left her with no taste for the least reminder of the broken union) was — or until recently had been — the premier beauty of the colony. She had raven hair and long Latin eyelashes, ivory skin and glinting, sportive black eyes, and she dressed like a glorious summer day, though always a bit formally, with very high heels and bold costume jewelry. Her figure, at forty, was voluptuous if just a trifle plump; no doubt it was for that reason that she never appeared in a bathing suit. She would have looked well enough, but there were younger bodies about, and she eschewed competition.

Erastus watched her, enraptured. Was there anything

lovelier than the speedy competence of those white hands with the scarlet nails as they shook the cup or scooped up the dice? All of Ilona's movements, so brisk, so definite, so finely adapted to her every purpose, the way she clicked her purse shut or tapped her high heels down a varnished floor, seemed to predict how, in quite another mood, she might be seductive, languorous, still.

He paused to assess the game and smiled. "I double."

She accepted his double; it was reckless, but she *was* reckless. He rolled two fives, picked up two of her men and closed her home board. She could only watch him now as he rolled and threw.

"I see Emden Coal and Coke is down another five points," she observed. "That's ten this week. What do you think?"

It was like her to waste no time in what they both recognized, without a word exchanged, as a compact. He could always beat her at backgammon; for the hundreds of dollars lost she expected some market tips. Though supported by the carefully doled-out allowance of a rich but exasperated mother, Ilona was usually as broke as she had left each husband and was always in search of a windfall. Mrs. Loring allowed her to winter abroad, but stipulated that she pass her summers at the maternal abode.

Erastus did not answer her question at once. He was rapidly throwing off his men now. At the point where no throws could bring her victory, he put down his cup and lit a cigarette.

"What about Emden?" she repeated.

"I'm not selling. There's talk of a new patent."

She nodded. Business bored her; she afforded it the minimum of time. But she made no move to reset the board. They would talk now for a bit, which was what he wanted.

"How are your lovely girls?" he asked.

"My lovely girls, thank you very much, have gone to church with Grandma. Under bitter protest, as usual. They wanted to come here with me. But Mamma insists that, as members of her household, which they are, poor things, three hundred and sixty-five days of the year, they must do as she tells them *except* when I'm under her roof, and that I'm not under her roof when I'm at the Beach Club gambling with that old satyr Erastus Thorn."

Erastus was enchanted with the epithet. "And you back Mrs. Loring in that?"

"My dear man, what else can I do? I have the utter selfishness to spend two thirds of the year in France and think it far better for my daughters to lead a regular life at Mother's and attend Miss Chapin's School in town than be exposed to my crowd in Paris and Nice. Don't you agree? I'm sure you've heard Mamma on the subject of my friends."

"But I doubt very much that I'd see them through her eyes. They must be charming, your friends."

"Oh, they're long on charm, I agree. My mother sets a low value on charm, though she professes to see it in some of her group here, where it quite escapes me. Still, I live and let live. That's one thing I learned in France."

"And you bring some of that older and subtler culture to the sandy beaches of this barren island." Here he allowed himself the mild affectation of a courtly bow. "Seriously, my dear Ilona, I suggest you are giving your daughters the best of two worlds. They have the necessary discipline and schooling with your exacting parent, and they learn the nuances and delights of gracious living in the summers with you."

"What crap you talk, Rastus."

But he wondered if she didn't like it. Old satyr! Wasn't

that hopeful? Satyrs were not wholly mockable; they could be dangerous, couldn't they? And did she really get many compliments such as his in Southampton? Everyone there knew Ilona, had always known her, and nobody was wholly exempt from her charm, but her way of bringing up her two daughters, sixteen and fourteen, the fruit of the first two of her four disastrous marriages, was generally regarded as irresponsible.

He decided to reaffirm his flattery. "You may call it crap, but you know there's truth in it."

"I know just what there's in it, my friend," she replied with unexpected firmness. "And I don't need you to tell me. I've sacrificed those girls to my own need of fresh air. I knew I'd stifle if I lived over here the year round. I prevailed on my mother to do my job. What is unfair is that the girls, who naturally admire and emulate an absent parent, do so at the expense of my poor old mamma! They transfer all the resentment that I richly deserve to the grandmother who does *everything* for them! Of course, it's horridly unfair, but when has life not been unfair?" Here Ilona threw back her beautiful head and laughed. "Oh, if there's a purgatory, I shall be well pricked by those little imps with pitchforks!"

"You may find me there to ward them off."

"Oh, you. You'll be in an even lower place."

"Me? But my life has been exemplary, Ilona."

"Far from it."

"You see into my heart, then? A man is not always responsible for what rocks it." He debated leaning forward to take or at least touch her hand.

"Oh, of course I know you're an outrageous old flirt. But that's not why Gabriella divorced you. She told my mother the whole story."

Erastus's arms fell to his sides. He was dumbfounded. It

took him some seconds to compose himself. "And what, may I ask, is the tale that my embittered and highly imaginative former consort unfolded?"

"You really want to hear it?" She shrugged. "She told Mother that you did Sid Larkin out of his brokerage commission when you sold the old Mitchell place to Elise Fearing."

Erastus was simply appalled. He stared out at the glittering sea as if he expected a tornado. Ilona was speaking of a deal that had taken place two decades before! Sid Larkin had been everyone's favorite real estate broker in Southampton, and Erastus, who had gambled in a small way in local properties, had indeed listed the Mitchell house with him, but had later taken the position, as many sellers do, that Mrs. Fearing had really purchased it directly from himself. He tried to explain this to Ilona, who was already bored with the subject.

"That's not how I heard it," she retorted. "Mrs. Fearing told everyone you'd gypped poor Larkin, and she paid him his commission herself. She told your ex that when you had amusing friends like Erastus Thorn you either gave them up or put up with their slickness."

"And you mean to tell me, Ilona Loring, that *that* was the reason my wife divorced me? You actually entertain so preposterous an idea!"

"No. For Gabriella it was simply the last straw. What the hell, Rastus. Everyone knows what a puritan she is. And you know you're a sharp one. I even rather like you for it. We're two of a kind, in a way." Here she held out a hand. "Shake on it? I didn't mean to upset you so. You know I always say the first thing that pops into my head, and Mamma was telling me that story only last night."

"You were discussing me?"

"We were. And not only your sins. Your virtues, too. Mother is far from being your enemy, Erastus. She was merely looking at all sides of a question."

"And what was the question?"

"You can ask *her*. But we're still pals. Is that right?"

He took her hand, not to shake it but to kiss it. "Yours in the ranks of death!" he exclaimed solemnly.

"Well, let's hope we don't have to go *that* far. You'll be at Margaret Schecter's tonight?"

"Of course."

"Why of course?"

"Because you'll be there."

"And how do you know that?"

"I asked Margaret. I find I can hardly go out anymore without the anticipation of seeing you there."

"Really, Erastus, you *are* a fool." But she laughed, and quite pleasantly. "You'll compromise me!" And she laughed again, more loudly.

How he would have loved to! And how little chance he had! He gazed out over the sea again as she turned to chat with a friend who approached their table. He imagined a love affair with Ilona; he reveled in the sudden picture of himself sacrificing all his occupations for her amusement, all his money for her pleasures. He luxuriated in the spectacle of a wasted life, for she would never really care for him, never — it would be Swann and Odette in Proust, and at the end he would shake his head sadly and consider all he had given up for a woman who was not even his "style."

The chatty lady moved off, and Ilona picked up her dice cup. "Another game?"

"I'd rather talk for a minute."

"Heavens! What can I tell *you*? Is there anything in this busy little colony that you don't know?"

"I know very little about you, my dear."

"You know too damn much! My life, alas, is an open book. And it's on the Index."

"Oh, but that's just the superficial part. What mysteries must lie beneath the glittering enamel of that lovely surface!"

"If they only were mysteries!"

"And if I could only be included in one!"

"How would you wish to be included, Erastus?"

"How would any man?"

"Good gracious me, is this a proposition?"

His silence and gravity were meant to convey his reproach of her levity. When he spoke, he hoped it was with a quiet meaningfulness. "It's a simple declaration of my abounding love and admiration for you."

"Very well. Then let me answer it with a simple declaration of my abounding determination to keep you as a good friend and backgammon partner. I've told you, Erastus, in Southampton with Mother I'm on *vacation*. From the middle of June to the middle of September I'm a respectable daughter and mother. Oh, I allow myself backgammon and bridge. But that's *all*."

"It seems I must follow you to Paris."

"Follow me where you will, old dear. I'm always glad to see you. But of course I'm apt to see you in the light of my summer abstinances. There'll always be a distinct Southampton air to you."

"Then there's no hope?"

She burst into another of her ribald laughs. "Oh, there's always hope when the lady is skipping through her forties and some delicious young rotter has just walked out on her. But watch out for my mamma, Erastus! I think she may be rummaging around the hall closet in search of her shotgun. Seriously!" There was another terrible laugh. "Shall we have another game? No, let's have a drink. Isn't the sun over the yardarm?"

She rose and moved to the bar, where she was at once joined by members of her usual crowd. Erastus, fleeing the contrast of their ages to his, resumed the perambulation among the umbrella tables that his backgammon game had interrupted. But although his greetings of friends were as courtly and mock-stately as ever, his mind was in a spin, and only habit produced the mellifluous phrases.

Had Ilona meant what she had said about hope? That if he followed her to Paris and waited until she was abandoned by some callow youth, and low on funds and high on alcoholic intake, there might be a chance for an older, more faithful friend, willing to empty the purse of his savings at her pretty feet? A love affair? A real love affair? Such as had happened to him forty years back? It might kill him, but what the hell?

He had long cherished the intriguing fantasy of ending his career on a deeper note. Who has not enjoyed such dreams? His had been to startle a world that had never plumbed his true value with the revelation that he was capable, to the extent of tossing aside all mundane occupations, of giving himself to a great love. And it might be a way, too, of showing the world that this love, being the real *he*, was a far finer thing than the object that had aroused it, that it might even demean that object. Ah, yes, it would be Swann with Odette: the epicure of the arts, the lion of society, the friend of the great, abandoning the *gratin* for a little demimondaine who didn't even have the sense to appreciate him.

But before him now was the massive figure of the colony's premier virgin, his hostess of the coming evening, Miss Margaret Schecter.

"I'm looking so forward to tonight, dear Margaret."

"Eight o'clock sharp, Erastus," was the gruff reply. "My cocktail 'hour' is half of one."

"May I be so bold as to inquire if the *placement* of your guests at table has been irrevocably settled?"

"And if it hasn't?"

"Dare I beg a favor?"

"What has ever stopped you?"

"Would it be too much if I asked you to seat me beside the divine Ilona?"

"It certainly would! What do you think I'm running, Erastus Thorn? A disorderly house? You forget yourself!"

And turning her back on him, she marched off in a way that slammed the door on any appeal or even apology.

Erastus concluded that he had better go back to his rooms at the inn. Decidedly, he was not himself.

❦   ❦   ❦

It had always been his trouble, from his earliest days: the lingering suspicion that no matter how many persons he captivated by his charm, his wit and his competence in practical concerns, no matter what little gains he made (or lost) in gambling and market maneuvers, no matter how smart and natty his appearance, no matter how much his background and general ambience seemed to resemble those of half the snobs at the Beach Club, there was still about him a faint aura of the bogus, the adventurer, the man who was not quite "the thing."

Sometimes he wondered whether it was not simply that society, deeply and irredeemably philistine at heart, distrusted any man who tried to dress it up in robes a little more comely. But that never quite answered the question.

Why, for example, should people hold against him what so many did themselves? That story of the brokerage commission — he could cite half a dozen examples in current real estate transactions where Southamptonites of the most unimpeachable reputation had done the same thing. People simply didn't know the market as he did. And why, a few years back, in the very pit of the Depression, when he had had his two sons on scholarships at a private school, should he have been criticized for driving a newly purchased and conspicuously elegant Hispano-Suiza? It was only because it was foreign that it had been noticed, and nobody knew what a bargain it had been. And why should he have the reputation in gambling games of quitting when he was ahead, when half the dowagers of the summer community notoriously did the same?

It might have been, of course, that his activities were more open to the gaze of his summer neighbors than those of other men. His habit of dealing with real estate in Southampton and his love of gambling at parties, plus his not being identified with any sacred bank or business, might have put him at a moral disadvantage with men who could indulge in any shady deal in downtown offices and still pose as beneficent angels at the beach or on the golf course. Nor had the magnificent grandfather who had reared the early orphaned Erastus much helped. Emmanuel Thorn had made and lost a fortune by running a notorious lottery, since outlawed, and had subsisted thereafter into a too hale and hearty old age on lesser wheelings and dealings, a well-known figure in racing circles and fashionable spas. The old sport, with his glittering gold accoutrements, had known everybody who was anybody — the men, anyway — and his worshipping grandson had learned at his feet the skill of taking quick advantage of every tip, trend and secret. Erastus himself had developed into a dashing enough young blade, dressed to the nines and consuming oysters and martini cocktails with other bloods (usually blue bloods) at stylish bars prior to eight-course formal Fifth Avenue dinner parties, and he had hoped for an ultimate respectability in winning as his bride the demure and beautiful Gabriella Sands, whose staid if impoverished Knickerbocker background boded well to obscure the offensive gleam of the never quite forgotten lottery.

But that again had been just his bad luck. Gabriella, who had originally seen him as a charming brand to be plucked from the burning, a task, as she deemed it, to atone for the unseemly passion that had drawn her to him, had at last given up the hopeless task of weaning him from an existence of watchful opportunism and reducing him to the death-in-life of her father's dim little bank, and had withdrawn with her two prim boys to a disapproving isolation.

And she was still watching him scornfully from her cottage in Westhampton!

By evening Erastus had pulled himself together sufficiently to present himself at Miss Schecter's door at eight o'clock.

There had never been an acknowledged conflict between him and his hostess, but that the rivalry between them for the social guidance of the colony was deep and abiding he had never doubted. Would she have felt the same way about a female rival? He doubted it. Did she hate men? Huge, wide-hipped, square-faced, with carefully set dyed red hair and imperious manners, the stalwart mistress of the biggest shingle pile on the dunes had never, so far as anyone knew, been associated with either sex romantically, and didn't there have to be resentment swept away somewhere under the thick carpet of her gruff self-satisfaction? Did she suspect that Erastus, her contemporary and partner in the single state, was revealing a hitherto hidden weapon in his sudden brandishing of a more than gallant interest in a beautiful younger woman?

Surely it was possible. Her greeting of him was barely a nod. He turned to the other guests and waited impatiently for Ilona. She arrived, late as usual, with her mother (without whose pushing she might not have appeared until halfway through dinner) and actually blew him a kiss as Miss Schecter hurried her into the dining room.

At table he found himself neighbored with Mrs. Loring. Ilona's mother was very thin, very elegant, very rouged and powdered, with high cheekbones, deep facial wrinkles and neatly waved blue hair. She spoke in the high bell tones of New York society of the nineties. It was difficult to tell her pose from her sincerity — if indeed there was any difference.

"I have all the luck tonight," he began, with a little bow.

"It is not luck, Erastus. I asked Margaret to put me next to you."

"She responded to my wish."

"Not at all. You asked her to place you by Ilona. And that is just what I wish to discuss with you."

"You see it perhaps as a case of *mater pulchra, filia pulchrior?*"

She ignored this. "You know me of old, Erastus. I come straight to the point. You have let it be seen by everyone how much you admire Ilona. How would you feel about becoming more than an admirer?"

"My dear lady, you cannot possibly mean . . ."

No. She could not. The flicker in those serene blue eyes, the tiny widening of that fixed smile, reminded the trespasser of the moat and the raised drawbridge.

"I am suggesting, Erastus, that you might propose marriage to Ilona."

So *that* was what Ilona had been hinting at! And he thought he knew the summer colony! That Mrs. Loring should find him eligible and willing to qualify as her fifth son-in-law was a riddle that he needed more time to work out.

"And what, may I ask, makes you suppose that your daughter would be amenable to any such proposition?"

"Well, darling Ilona is not exactly in a position to turn her back on anything that I seriously suggest. She is completely dependent on me financially, and she has made such inroads upon my resources, I don't mind telling you, that her future is by no means assured unless we start putting her life in some sort of order. The time has come when she needs the protection of a more stable union than she has had in the past. An older man who will advise her and help keep her extravagance in check. A man of good will and affable temper who knows the world and its ways and will not fly off the handle at every folly and impetuosity, but will use patience and common sense in dealing with what is basically a woman of great spirit and character."

"And that is how you see me? But, dear Mrs. Loring, even if all that were true, how . . .?

"How could you afford it? I'm coming to that. Oh, Ilona and I were very practical when we discussed this. I assume that your means are adequate for yourself alone, but that you might not wish to be liable for Ilona's debts. I would undertake to take care of these and pay to *you* — not to her — an allowance covering the extra expenses of the married state. It would be my hope that you and I could work out a schedule that would eventually make sense of Ilona's presently disordered life."

"Well!" She certainly *had* thought it all out. "And would it be the idea of the future Mrs. Erastus Thorn to continue her residence abroad? And would that be with or without Mr. Thorn?"

"Well, of course, you know that Ilona would never part with an inch of her precious liberty. That's what her husbands could never understand. But she and I thought that a gentleman of your years and discretion, with your wide knowledge of men and women and your benign wisdom and tolerance, might be inclined to take a broader view of matrimonial mores. That's a compliment, really, Erastus, if you take it in the right spirit."

He nodded, as if thoughtfully. "Ah, is that what it is? I was wondering. I should not be too possessive, in other words. Indeed, I should eschew jealousy altogether."

"Well, doesn't age bring moderation? Or shouldn't it? Is there any particular glory in the raw passions of youth?"

"Except that your sex *does* seem to like those passions."

"Well, there you are, anyway, my dear Erastus. You can think it over. The table is turning, and I must condole with Pinky Thayer about his arthritis. It *is* arthritis, isn't it?"

She might have been telling him that their little bit of business had taken quite enough time. How many minutes, after all, should one waste on the purchase of a *mari complaisant*? But he took his revenge. "Not arthritis. Hemorrhoids!"

She turned swiftly from him without a smile. He had

gone too far. He *was* beginning to go too far. What was happening to him?

At the bridge table after dinner he found that Ilona was his partner. Had that, too, been arranged? She flashed a smile at him across the table as if they shared a joke at the expense of their neighbors. Did she regard him as already sewn up, delivered? The useful man who would buy the tickets, handle the customs, escort her to larger parties, make out insurance forms and tax returns, take care of bill collectors, explain cancelled trips to travel agents? And then he marveled at the beautiful quick gesture with which she spread the pack on the table to draw for deal. He pulled a card. The jack of hearts! She smiled again. If she would sleep with others, surely she would not deny her husband! And, oh, dear Venus, what rapture even if he had to share her!

They played three rubbers, and he and Ilona won nine hundred dollars. Erastus, according to his wont, pulled out his watch.

"Bedtime for this old codger."

Ilona demurred. "How about one more rubber?"

There was a sudden ominous presence behind Erastus's chair. "Could I have a word with you, Mr. Thorn?"

He followed Miss Schecter to a corner, where she addressed him in a low, firm tone. "There's got to be a stop to this ducking out when you're ahead. If you leave now, you won't get another rubber in Southampton this season. I can promise you that!"

He nodded without a word and returned to his seat. They played two more rubbers, and his take for the evening was seventy-five dollars.

He offered to drive Ilona home, but she left with her mother in the latter's limousine.

"See you at the club" was all she offered him by way of a good night.

❀   ❀   ❀

He called on Gabriella the next day at noon and was received rather somberly on the porch of her beachside cottage at Westhampton. On the wicker table between them was a bottle of ginger ale and two glasses. His ex-wife was attentive, not wholly unsympathetic, but very cool.

"If you're really sincere, Erastus, in seeking my advice, you must be prepared for some very plain talk on my part."

"Since when, my dear, has *that* not been true?"

"And you can't attribute any home truths that I may impart to some aspect of lingering jealousy."

"Alas, no," he murmured, unable, even with her, altogether to suppress his habit of gallantry.

"Then prepare yourself."

In the preparatory pause that followed, Erastus stared at that pale round countenance surmounted by the halo of unwaved grey-brown hair and those unrelenting opal eyes. Why had she ever married him? Was her life one long penitence for having given in, however briefly, to Eros? Would she have preferred, like an erring vestal, to have been buried alive for her betrayal of virgin vows? And why, for that matter, had he married her? Had it really been for respectability, or a response to the ancient urge of the bedazzled barbarian to debauch the high Roman priestess?

"It is humiliating for me and the boys to see a man of your age prancing about the skirts of a whore."

"Really, Gabriella! Your tone! You might be a presence from the Massachusetts Bay Colony."

"Maybe I am. Maybe that's just what you need. Isn't it what you married me for? What are you going to marry *this* woman for? To share her with half the men at the Beach Club? Except you won't even share her! You'll be the only one who *doesn't* have her. Ilona Loring has told all her friends that if she has to do what her old mother demands it will be her first *mariage blanc!*"

"You heard *that?*"

"Don't think we don't have ears just because we live in Westhampton."

He leaned forward over the table as if he were going to be sick. "Can I get myself something stronger than ginger ale?" he pleaded.

Without a word she rose, disappeared and returned with a bottle of cognac and a small glass. Gratefully, he poured and drank.

"Gabriella, what has happened to me?"

"You've tried to change your type, my poor old friend. And the women won't allow it. You have been accepted as the old king of the Beach Club and even crowned. Everyone has been amused by your courtly manners and pseudo-gallantry. They have not even objected to your slickness. For you *are* slick, Erastus. But so long as that was in character, it was allowed. 'Watch out for old Thorn; he's a sly one!' was even said with affection. But when you start slobbering over a woman young enough to be your daughter, watch out. They have scented blood, and they'll tear you to bits! You can be an old boulevardier, or a misogynist, or an inconsolable widower, or even a fairy, or a real man. But you must choose your part and stick to it!"

"Gabriella, do you know you're the only person who's ever taken me seriously!"

"But I've cared about you, Erastus."

"Could I move over here? You have a spare room, don't you?"

At last she smiled. "What would people say?"

"I'd marry you!"

And now she laughed. "A second *mariage blanc*?"

"Why not?"

"For that's what it would have to be."

He took another sip of the cognac and sighed. At least people would know it had not always been that.

The Foursome

<hr>

THE GLENVILLE Golf & Tennis Club, a modest red-brick Georgian affair with long, rambling white wings, sprawled atop a hillock in Westchester County from which, on a clear day, which was rarely Saturday, one could spy, across the gently rolling, mildly wooded countryside, on the horizon, two tiny grey nobs, the twin towers of the World Trade Center. It was as if, as Harry Hartley liked to put it, they were the probing eyes, projected insectlike, of the relentless city, reminding its larval commuters that they would be due at their station on Monday morning to catch the 8:05.

Harry, with the other three of his regular golf foursome — they played every weekend — sat on the porch, after their eighteen holes, drinking the first of the two drinks that long custom allowed them before going home to lunch with their wives and mostly teenage offspring. Harry's thick curly hair and rather boyish looks seemed faintly to contradict his neat grey flannels and sober blue sport coat and the restlessness of his wandering eyes: Harry was not a boy at all; he was forty-seven, and a worried forty-seven. The other three were about the same age: Alexander "Sancho" Stone, the "success" of the quartet — he managed a flourishing fund-raising company — sleek, trim and dark; Bertie Post, an insurance salesman, who was losing hair and gaining weight, probably because his wife had moved to Buffalo to take a better job in her dress-making business; and Don Grayburn, the handsomest, still blond and straight and thin, an expert trader in odd lots.

Usually they talked business and politics; at times they swapped stories; at others they discussed their families and domestic problems. They rarely indulged in local gossip; they got enough of that at home. But what their weekly sessions — after the game — were really dedicated to, though this was rarely articulated, was the relaxation of the tensions of daily life, the letting down of the guard, the frank indulgence in the politically incorrect, the shrugging recognition that the world was a cornucopia of disillusionments. The bond between the four was supposed to be as tight as that between priest and confessor, though, of course, there were leaks. Don was known to talk a bit too freely to his adoring Amelia, and Sancho's Alva was clever enough to get anything out of him she really wanted to know. But what the hell? Most of what they said, God knew — if God ever came to the Glenville Golf & Tennis — was innocent enough. And nothing that the wives didn't basically know already.

Harry was waiting until they had their first round of drinks before saying what he knew he had to say. He had long suspected that the time had come, and his discussion that morning at breakfast with Joanne and their fifteen-year-old, Amy, had precipitated it. Joanne had had a bad night; her usually lovely blond hair had looked scruffy and strangely grey.

"Well, I hope you have a *lovely* game this morning. I'll be showing the old Winters' place by the seventh hole to a client, so don't send a ball through the window." Joanne was a real estate broker, and weekends were her busiest time. "And lay off that second drink, will you please? I hate to have lunch in a Sweet Adeline atmosphere."

Harry said nothing. He knew that she knew he always came home perfectly sober.

"Mummie, I don't see why you're always so down on Daddy's golf games. Can't he have a little fun?"

"What I mind is that it's his *only* fun."

Harry looked up from his paper. That was going further than she usually did. "What do you mean by that, dear?"

"Oh, you know perfectly well what I mean! It's the only thing your foursome really lives for. To get together and tell each other how much you hate everything. Everything and everyone!"

"Every*one?*"

"Oh, forget it! I've just had a bad night, because I lost a big sale yesterday. And I know these people aren't going to like the Winters' place. And it's a beautiful day, and I'd rather be doing something with you and Amy. Oh, never mind me!"

And, almost in tears, she quit the table. Harry did not follow her; he knew just when and when not to intervene. And this scene had been coming on for weeks, if not months. He would have to tell the boys about it. If it had happened to him, it had happened to them. Or something not too different.

Sancho was beckoning the waiter for their second round when Harry announced gravely that he had a speech to make. There was an immediate attentive silence. They were tolerant of speeches.

"It's about our foursome. Or really not so much about our foursome as about our wives. And what it does to them. Let me go back in time and tell you a couple of things about me and Joanne that maybe even you three don't know. When we married, she was going gung-ho in the advertising business. Oh, she was well down the ladder, of course, but she had a couple of good accounts of her own, and there was an atmosphere about her of up-and-at-it. We had a two-year wait before the first baby, and the doctor thought there might be something slightly wrong gynecologically, so we were a bit careless about precautions, and then, bango, the second baby was upon us!"

"Irish twins!" exclaimed Don.

"Irish twins, exactly. And then Joanne decided she couldn't handle the demands of her job and be a good mother as well. So she resigned her position, but in doing this, as she made entirely clear, she was relying on *me*. My salary as an associate in my law firm was twice hers, and if I made partner, which then seemed probable, it would be three times. Obviously, it would have been ludicrous for *me* to have stayed home with the babies while she worked . . ."

"I don't know," said Bertie, perhaps thinking of his wife in Buffalo. "Today it might have seemed heroic."

"Anyway, Joanne and I agreed on the course to take," Harry continued. "And for some years it worked out well enough. We had our third child, and the nursery was preoccupying. And then Joanne became active in local affairs; you all know the great job she's done with the bird sanctuary and the historical society. But things changed with the crisis of whether I'd become a partner in my firm. I'm afraid I kind of lost my nerve there. I made frantic charts and graphs showing the ages of the partners, where they'd been brought up, what their private means were — I even peeked at night into some of their private files — to see if I could make out what associates might expect to make the grade with them. I finally decided my chances were only fifty-fifty. So when Hudson River Trust offered me a job in their estate department, I panicked and grabbed it. I thought it was security for life — a good compromise."

"And Joanne agreed?" Don asked.

"No, Joanne didn't agree at all! That's just what I'm coming to! Joanne was very insistent that I should wait. 'Stop all your fussing about what motivates whom,' she told me, 'and keep your mind on your work.' She even claimed that she was entitled to a voice in my decision because she had given up her own career in reliance on my doing the right thing."

"But that's preposterous!" Bertie exclaimed. "How could she have known your situation better than you?"

"Very easily," Sancho answered, shaking his head wisely. "She could have had more objectivity. Wasn't that so, Harry?"

"Alas, yes. And she certainly had more guts. 'You've got to take *some* chances in life,' she kept telling me. 'And this is an educated gamble. If we lose, we lose. What the hell? There are other law firms.' She was most likely right. And Hudson hasn't worked out too well. As all of you know. Their trust department didn't grow as expected, and the raises I'd counted on didn't materialize. And now we're even threatened with this merger with Union Savings."

"I hate to say it, Harry," Sancho intervened, "but these mergers are always followed by the elimination of nonprofitable or duplicating areas."

Don and Bertie eyed Sancho with disapproval. It was like the most prosperous to utter the most dismal prognostications.

"Don't even say it!" Harry exclaimed with a shudder. "But the reason I'm telling you all this is to get to what I owe Joanne. When it became apparent that mounting costs of college education were not going to be covered by my salary at Hudson, she decided to go back to work. I had to agree.

She got only menial offers in the advertising business — her friends had gone way beyond her and were now rather snotty tycoons — so, like so many Westchester girls, she fell back on real estate. Well, I don't need to tell any of you that, despite her occasional discouragement, she's done pretty damn well."

There was immediate agreement around the table.

"I heard she handled that Packard estate sale."

"That commission alone should pay for a year at Harvard."

"And everyone says she really tries to give the customer the house he needs. Doesn't waste your time, like the other girls, showing you palaces you can't afford."

"It's all true," Harry agreed. "She works her tail off. At night she's so exhausted she can only watch a little news on TV before turning in. And it's taken a terrible toll on her temper. I can't blame her, but she does take it out on me. She's always after me to change my thinking or my habits."

"How?"

"What's wrong with them?"

"We thought you were the model husband and father!"

"That's not how she sees it at all. She doesn't quite put it this way, but what it boils down to is that she thinks that to the extent I've failed as a breadwinner, I should compensate as a family man. That I should spend more time with the children. That I should try harder to understand them."

Don and Bertie at this exchanged serious glances. When the former spoke it was as if by agreement between them.

"None of us can see how you could be more understanding than you've been about Freddy, Harry."

Harry sighed. "Well, obviously none of you would be exactly pleased to have a gay son. And it's true that I've tried to be sympathetic with Freddy. But Joanne keeps hammering away at the fact that I haven't really *accepted* his homosexuality. She points out that I still want him to go to a psychiatrist, that I can't face up to the fact that he's *made* that way and that it may be just as good a way to be as ours. And that's true! In my heart I regard Freddy as a tragic freak. I *do*! Though I never say it. Except, of course, here. And Joanne *knows* that I talk about it here."

"Well, why not?"

"What are a man's friends for?"

"Harry, you've been a saint with that airy-fairy friend of Freddy's who's always at your house, falsettoing about Proust or Henry James. I couldn't have put up with him no matter what Alva had asked of me. God help me, I'd have kicked his ass down the drive!"

Don and Bertie laughed. This last was from Sancho, who, as the others well knew, had never defied his wife.

"And then there's Nelly and her Hispanic lover," Harry continued, regaining his momentum. "He's in her class at NYU. He's really more black than Hispanic. He comes on weekends and Joanne lets him sleep in Nelly's bedroom. He's a decent enough fellow, I suppose, but his father runs a laundry in Brooklyn, and, as far as I'm concerned, we might as well be from different planets. I try — I really do try — but I feel, with all of them — not my Amy, not my roly-poly fifteen-year-old who's still young enough to look up to her pa, but the others — Joanne and Freddy and Nelly — I feel their eye is always on me to catch me in some slip of the tongue that will reveal what a philistine and homophobe and racist and male chauvinist I really am! It's enough to make a man all those things!"

"But what is it that Joanne really wants of you?" Bertie demanded.

"What she really wants she won't say, because it wouldn't

sound right, to a proper liberal. But of course I know what it is. She wants me to give up our Saturday foursome."

"Is she really that unreasonable?"

"She does not want to *sound* that unreasonable. But that's what it comes down to. She's always taking potshots at us. 'What would the boys in the backroom think of *this*?' or 'I suppose your little club really howled at *that*?' She says that every time she prods me an inch into the modern world, you all are ready to yank me back a foot. Well, come on, fellows. You're not going to maintain none of you has gone through something like this. Sancho, why don't you tell us just what Alva thinks of our Saturday morning sessions."

He had picked Sancho to start because Sancho liked to talk about himself, even if proved embarrassing.

"Well, we hear a lot about wives' careers today," Sancho began, in the voice with which he presumably opened one of his "fight talks" at a premier session with a new client to be indoctrinated in the mysteries of fund-raising. "And it's always about what the wife's career should be, not the husband's." He was very clear, very definite, ready to smile, but intent on the goal of education. "But let me confront you with the curious instance of a spouse who wants, not her own career, but her husband's; in my own case a wife who wants *my* career. For that is what Alva aims at; make no mistake."

"She wants to oust you?"

"Take over your job?"

"Oh, come off it, Sancho. We all know Alva."

"You think you do. But wait. No, Alva doesn't want to oust me. She wants to *be* me. She wants to run Stone Enterprises with me. She says we're the perfect team: I provide the ideas; she goes after the clients. As you know, our daughter Jill is already in the business, and she backs up her ma a hundred percent. I sometimes think they could carry on well enough without me. Because the ideas are all there; they're working. All we need is more buyers."

"Well, is that anything to complain about?" Harry wanted to know. "It sounds to me as if Alva's right; she's just what you need."

"I have no complaint about Alva's taking an interest in the business. That would be fine. But she wants to quadruple it. She looks to the day when we'll be in charge of great university drives for a hundred million dollars or more! And that's going to involve a drastic change in our life style. Alva regards Glenville as a social backwater. We should move to New York, she's always telling me; get a penthouse on Park Avenue. To hell with the cost. We can borrow. She says none of you boys is any real help in getting business. When I point out that I got the Glenville Hospital drive from Harry and the Peterson School campaign from Don, she says that was all in the past and peanuts, anyway, to where we're headed!"

"Well!"

"The awful thing is she may have a point!"

"Then suppose you move to town. You could still drive out for a Saturday's golf game."

"Can you see Alva letting me go? To Glenville? Dream on, boys. Once she had me settled in the city, we'd only leave it for the Creek Club or the Piping Rock on Long Island or maybe the sacred Hamptons!"

There was a bitter silence as the other three contemplated the undoubted truth of Alva's contempt for them. Harry turned to Bertie.

"Perhaps Lily is too far away in Buffalo to be much concerned with how you spend your Saturday mornings."

"Lily is very much concerned with them," Bertie replied

promptly. "In fact, she blames you boys for keeping me from moving to Buffalo."

"*Is* it we who keep you?" Don demanded.

"Well, you're certainly a factor. Our foursome is a big thing in my life; I'm frank to admit that. My insurance business hasn't been doing very much lately, and it was always a living to me, never a passion. You all have known that. And having a retarded child — now, happily, institutionalized — and a daughter married and living in Australia, there hasn't been much comfort in home life. So, damn it all, I *have* cared about our Saturdays. I know it's true that Lily's promotion was contingent on her moving to Buffalo, but she *could* have stayed in New York. It's asking a lot of a man to pull up all his stakes at my age and move to a strange city."

There was a sympathetic silence. But the group was not really in the end on Bertie's side. They all knew how meagre his insurance sales had become.

"Joanne talks to Lily on the telephone every week, Bertie," Harry said. "She says she wants you desperately to come. She says that with what she's making now, you can retire from insurance altogether. And there's a fine golf club right near the house she wants to buy."

"You'll find another foursome up there, Bertie," Sancho suggested.

"A better one, too," Don interjected. "It shouldn't be hard."

Bertie looked as if he might weep. But he knew when he was beaten. Harry turned to Don for relief.

"Can we hear from the one man whose wife has *no* career?"

Don was quite ready, even impatient, to tell his story. "You guys probably don't think I have any of your problems because Amelia's the old-fashioned type of wife. She's never wanted a career, been perfectly happy at home with the children, and now that they're older, she gives most of her time to the Garden Club of America, where she's carved a nice little niche for herself. So that side of our lives has run smoothly enough. But that's not all of it. Not by half. These modern ideas have a way of infiltrating the lives of even the most conservative women. The sexual revolution has even hit the home!"

"You don't mean that Amelia is looking beyond your own stout hips and broad shoulders, Don!" exclaimed Sancho, with a crude laugh.

"No, I don't," Don replied, quite serious. "But she's expecting more of them. She's perfectly clear in her mind that a woman who elects marriage as a career is just as good as the woman who wants to be a doctor or lawyer. She takes no back seat on that issue. But she holds that professional women have upped the ante for the nonprofessionals. Marriage must offer satisfactions as great as those offered by law or medicine. And that means that a marriage must be kept in constant repair, as she puts it. One must never take one's partner for granted. That is something, I gather, that husbands are particularly prone to do."

"But you're a most punctilious spouse, Don," Bertie pointed out. "Only the other day you were showing me that little book where you had all those birthdays and anniversaries carefully listed."

"And who do you think bought me that little book? Amelia makes me tell her every night at cocktails just what I've done in the office that day, and then she goes through hers. We must *share* everything. And, this is a bit embarrassing, but what the hell — we all know how women are — she's even made me read one of those manuals about improving one's sex life in middle age. Men get lazy about that, she claims."

"Did you get any good ideas?"

"We might all use a few tips."

"Yes, Don, share the wealth. But I thought you were looking a little tired when you showed up this morning."

"Ha, ha. Very funny, fellows. But I bet I'm not the only one whose wife has fantasies about better performance. What Amelia is getting at is that a husband must help fill in the gap when the children leave home. I see her point. I happen to get an enormous kick out of the stock market and my odd lots. What does she have that's quite that good? I have to make up for it. In some part, anyway. After all, she stayed home all those years with the children. And she did a damn good job of it, too. I'm very proud of our kids."

"And just how do you 'make up,' Don?" Sancho asked roguishly. "I mean in the daytime. I shouldn't dream of penetrating the world of your nocturnal emissions."

"I suppose every foursome has one vulgarian. But maybe that's not always a good thing. I'll tell you what, Sancho. When you move to the wicked city, maybe Amelia can take your place here on Saturday mornings. *That's* what she really wants!"

"But I know Amelia's never broken a hundred!" Bertie groaned.

"The foursome is doomed!" Sancho cried.

"That was already clear." Harry looked at his watch. It was more than time to go. "Of course, you will move as Alva wishes, Sancho. And Bertie will go to Buffalo. And Don will train Amelia until she breaks a hundred. I'll bet he succeeds, too. And I will tell Joanne that in the future we may do things together on Saturdays. Perhaps I'll help her show her houses. But not quite yet. We needn't say farewell. We'll have a few more Saturdays. And in the years to come, perhaps anniversaries. Who knows?"

Saying which, he left the table without another word.

At home he found Joanne preparing a salad dish.

"Did you sell the Winters' place?"

"Of course not. And I think those bastards are going to another broker." She turned to him with an unexpected smile. "The things we do so Freddy and Nelly can read Kerouac and Burroughs in a great classics course! I feel like a poor swallow that has to build two nests in a single summer. Why are we so keen to reproduce the species?"

"So we may overpopulate the globe."

She came over to give him an even more unexpected kiss. She was making up, presumably, for the little morning scene. "How was your game?"

"Terrible. A ninety-six. But it may be one of the last. With our old foursome, I mean."

"What are you telling me!"

"It's breaking up. Sancho and Bertie are leaving Glenville. And all of us agreed that we were taking too much time away from our families."

"Oh, Harry, just because I was tired and cross this morning!" She sank into a chair in an attitude of utter despondency. "It's good for you boys to blow off a little steam every now and then. And what man your age wouldn't sometimes dream of something fresher and younger and more admiring to come home to than a tired old real estate broker?"

"Now, darling, you are *not* a tired old . . ."

"Of course I am! But don't you ever think I have some of the feelings you have? Even where the children are concerned? Do you think I never dream of Freddy as a brawny, grinning football player with his arm around a pretty girl, and Nelly as the belle of the ball waltzing with Sir Galahad?"

"*Do* you?"

"Of course I do! Do you think I never get sick of all the cant I have to take from the young, day in and day out? Sometimes I find myself almost hoping that the dreaded merger with your bank will go through and that they'll close down your department and we can move to Mexico and live on Social Security and a handful of municipal bonds!"

Harry burst out laughing. "Except you'd never do that. You'd work your ass off until you were head of your agency and could support us all!"

"And then you'd really have something to complain about to the boys!"

"But I wouldn't be able to afford the club dues."

"Oh, I'd pay them." She rose to put her arms around him. "I think the club might be the last thing I'd let go."

Lear's Shadow

———— ❧ ————

LETTER FROM LADY GAYLEY, DORMY HOUSE, RYGATE,
KENT, MAY I, 1905, TO THE BARONESS BURNHAM-COATS,
14 IVY TERRACE, LONDON.

Dear Baroness:

You have once or twice asked me why I have never added
Cordelia to my little collection of autobiographical essays on
the Shakespearean heroines I have been privileged to play,
and I have decided at last, in view of the wonderful encour-
agement you have given me in composing my little series,
that I owe you a full and candid answer.

You must not think that this response has been extracted
from me against my will. I am really happy to share even my
less happy memories with you. No one has done more for
my acting career. It was you who stood by me in those early
days when my loving but disapproving parents warned me
that a career before the footlights and a lost character were
practically synonymous. It was you who induced my father
to step for a moment, so to speak, out of his naval uniform
and made him see that a proper interpretation of the shining
heroines of Britain's greatest dramatist might contribute to
our nation's glory even as a victory on the high seas! I well
remember how you impressed him by pointing out that the

Virgin Queen, a kind of dramatic actress herself, had taken the sceptre of her warlike predecessors and raised it to the heights of which the poets sing!

And you have continued your help, even after my retirement, by inducing me to write my essays on the heroines I have sought to bring to life on the stage: Juliet, Beatrice, Helena, Imogene, Portia, Ophelia, Constance, Viola. And even after you had had my poor efforts printed in those splendid private editions, you went further and sponsored their presentation to the public. An actress's life was once written on water; you have given me a printed permanence!

Of course, it was only to be expected that my modest efforts to express to other Shakespeare lovers my appreciation of his most wonderful creations — and I impenitently claim that his heroines were these — would expose me to the jibes of the smart young critics of today, to whom nothing is sacred. You know, dear Baroness, my romantic habit of speculating, at the close of each essay, as to what might have happened — if any survived — to the characters after the fall of the final curtain. I remember how touched you were by my sorrowful prediction that Imogene, struck to the heart at discovering her husband's vile suspicions and plot to kill her, and then again by the sight of what she wrongly deems to be his headless corpse, might, despite the joy of her reunion with him, have wasted away to an early demise. And I recall gratefully your satisfaction at my suggestion that Portia might have looked after the ruined Shylock in his desolate old age and even reconciled him to Jessica.

And don't you think that a critic who found such harmless speculations out of order might have had the decency to pass them by without comment? Was it really necessary for the *Times* man to say he was looking forward to a sequel to

The Taming of the Shrew called *Kate's Turn,* and one to *Romeo and Juliet* entitled *Our Two First Families: At It Again!*

But like many a retired actress missing the boards, I am waxing garrulous. I must return to Cordelia.

You wonder why I played her only once, in Manchester, some sixteen years ago. We were supposed to go on to London and didn't.

No, indeed we didn't.

My company had decided to do *King Lear* and had hired young Edmund Strother-Jones to direct it. He was then considered very much the coming thing in forward-looking theatrical productions. He was full of new ideas and admired by all the smart young things of London. And he certainly had charm. Indeed, you might say he was riddled with it.

He was small but very lively, with curly blond hair and laughing blue eyes, always nattily and tweedily dressed, always amusing, impertinent, even brilliant, inclined to play the clown but also capable of pulling himself up and exercising something like what my dear father used to call "command presence." He had a fortune of his own, left him by some dim colonial forebear and extracted, as he used to put it, from the sweat of slaves; it was his boasted penitence that he would blow it all on the arts. He seemed to know everyone of colorful reputation in the great world, from the rakish circle of the Prince of Wales to that of Oscar Wilde. But although I never knew his name to be linked romantically with that of any member of our sex, he was in no way implicated in the terrible scandals that later destroyed the career of the talented but devil-driven author of *Lady Windermere's Fan.* Indeed, Strother-Jones had the courage to sign a public petition calling for the mitigation of Wilde's sentence.

But that was like him. For all his habit of making mock of our most sacred traditions, for all his jokes about the government, the peerage, the royal family and even the Church of England, he was in his conduct a perfect citizen. He broke no laws, and he was afraid of nothing. Nothing, it seemed, could touch him. Or so he thought.

He professed a great admiration for my acting and had particularly admired my Imogene. Indeed, he found me at my best in those roles where the heroine, at one point or another, adopts male attire: Julia, Rosalind, Viola and Portia, as well as the daughter of Cymbeline.

And then, after one of the conferences in which he expounded to the cast his ideas for the production, he took me aside for a private talk. He was suddenly more serious than as yet I had seen him.

"Agnes, my dear — I'm sorry, but in the theatre both the first name and the endearment are *de rigueur* — I do not know how expert you are in theatrical history, so stop me if I'm telling you what you already know. We believe that the fool was played by Robert Arnim in the original production in 1608. You have already noted, I am sure, that I have not yet cast anyone in that role."

This was followed by a pause and a critical stare. He wanted to be sure he had my total attention. He certainly had. I even began to suspect what he had in mind.

"As you know, the fool disappears from the play in Act Three, Scene Two, with the line: 'And I'll go to bed at noon.' No explanation is offered to us for his dismissal. The only other possible reference to him is at the very end of the play, when Lear informs us that 'my poor fool is hanged.'"

"But isn't he referring to Cordelia there?"

"So most scholars affirm. Though why a lamenting father should refer to his beloved daughter and the queen of

France as a 'poor fool' escapes me. At any rate, the obvious reason for the elimination of the fool from the play is the demands of casting. Cordelia had to be played by a boy or at least a young man, and if Arnim was tied up in the part of the fool, who was there? Answer: no one. So Master Will was told to edit his play so that Cordelia and the fool were never onstage at the same time. Arnim could easily have taken both roles. And I have little doubt that Arnim did."

"Which is what you want *me* to do."

"Agnes, darling, you've hit it!"

I must admit I was intrigued. The fool in *Lear* has always struck me as one of the richest roles in the canon. His wit, his devastating clear-sightedness, his touching timorousness punctuated by sudden strokes of daring, and, above all, his absolute devotion to his misguided and temperamental master make him wonderfully lovable. And what a scene stealer! An actor playing the fool properly will know that every eye out front is on him. To play the fool *and* Cordelia! If I could pull that off, my name would ring down through the annals of theatre.

But Strother-Jones had an even greater surprise for me.

"Can you imagine, Agnes, what must have gone through our bard's mind as he watched the first rehearsals of his play? Arnim no doubt was wonderful in both roles, but no matter how skillfully he altered his style to be first the clown and then the princess, wasn't there something derogatory to the appreciation of great drama in the audience's amusement at watching the trick? It was almost an exercise in prestidigitation. And then there is the gender confusion. It is one thing for a man to play two men or two women, but when you mix it up . . ."

"Well?" I waited tensely for him to go on.

"Well, wouldn't it suddenly have dawned on our great

genius how to solve the problem? Cordelia *is* the fool! We are told that the fool 'pined away' when our lady went to France. Hearing this — for we know that Cordelia had her spies in England — she secretly returns, persuades the ailing fool to let her don his clothes, packs him off to France or some safe spot, and takes his place in her father's entourage. She wants to see for herself just how her sisters treat him."

I gaped. "Are you telling me that Shakespeare actually intended us to believe that?"

"Of course!"

"Then why isn't it in the text?"

"It almost is. The scene showing Cordelia in the sick room of the fool trying on his fool's cap would have been in dumb show and left out of the first quarto, where there were no stage directions. There couldn't have been any dialogue, obviously, as Arnim played both parts. The fool would have been represented by someone in the bed with his face turned to the wall."

I was almost hypnotized. Surely it would be the greatest and most challenging role ever attempted by a Shakespearean actress!

"Think of it!" our director went enthusiastically on. The mad old king on the heath, howling at the storm, feeling utterly deserted, not knowing that his three companions, Kent-Caius, Cordelia-fool and Edgar-Tom, all in disguise, are his most loyal friends!

Well, it took him some time to persuade me. We had two long sessions, in which I put to him every objection I could think of.

What reason had he to suppose that Cordelia, so bluntly honest, so almost crudely plainspoken in the division of the kingdom scene, could so easily adopt the sly, insinuating archness of the fool?

Because both are dominated by the compulsion to tell Lear the *truth*. Both are grimly resolved to penetrate the mist of illusion in which the old man has encased himself. Cordelia has had ample opportunity to observe the fool at close range; she knows all his jokes and ditties and mannerisms.

Why does Cordelia not tell the loyal Kent who she really is? Because she doesn't recognize him in his disguise as Caius, nor does he her in the fool. Nobody recognizes Edgar in Tom, either, not even his father. It was not a very observant court.

Why should Cordelia-fool disappear just when Lear leaves Gloucester's castle to make his way to Dover? Because she has not learned of the blinding of Gloucester and has every reason to believe that the escort which he has promised will get her father safely to his destination. She has to get back to her army; she has an invasion on her hands.

Why does Lear, bearing onstage the corpse of Cordelia, assert that "my poor fool is hanged"? Because Cordelia has told him in prison of the disguise she adopted. Wouldn't she have been bound to do that?

I ended by agreeing to do both parts and going along with his crazy theory. It would certainly have won us some interesting reviews had we ever opened in London. Sarah Bernhardt as Hamlet and the Cushman sisters as Romeo and Juliet would have been put in the shade. But Manchester was destined to be our only audience and that for a single performance.

We London professionals tend to be a trifle condescending when we open in "the provinces," but this kind of snobbery sometimes has the advantage of loosening our nerves, reducing our tension. I know that in taking on two such disparate roles in the same play I was glad initially not to be under the glare of the London critics. The opening scene of the division of the kingdom went very well. My Cordelia was very grave, very restrained and proudly bitter. When I rang out my reply to Lear's "So young and so untender?" — "So young, my lord, and *true!*" — I could almost feel the throb of the audience's reaction.

I cannot resist adding here, dear Baroness, a comment on the impact with which our divine poet could endow a single word. You will remember how Polonius's banal list of do's and don't's is suddenly electrified by his "To thine own self be *true!*"

But when in my dressing room I had made my hasty change of apparel into that of the fool, it seemed to me that I was acquiring something more than a suit. It was a very curious feeling indeed. It was not exactly elation; it was rather a kind of suppressed excitement, as if I were preparing myself for a difficult task, not devoid of danger, but which was absolutely called for by a sense of duty.

Approaching the wings for my entrance, I postured myself for the mincing steps with which I should approach the king. Instead of this, however, I found myself darting onto the stage as if propelled by a blast of air, falling to my knees and hurling my cap at Kent, who had just taken service with Lear. And in a high, falsetto tone, ringing in my own ears, I heard my cry: "Let me hire him, too. Here's my coxcomb."

Then I found myself dancing around Kent in an unpremeditated and totally unrehearsed little jig, all the while chanting the lines about what an idiot the king had been to give all to his daughters. It was as if I had been seized with a kind of fit, yet I had the oddest sense that it was a divine fit, that I was playing the fool with a zest, a bite, that was tingling the nerves of my audience. But where had it come

from? What was it? I saw the quick surprise, quickly con-
cealed, in the eyes of my fellow actors. Obviously, they
thought this was a trick, a surprise that I had kept from
them.

When the frowning Goneril swept onstage to reprimand
her father, I did a somersault, as if in panic, to get away from
her — totally unplanned again — and shrieked: "Yes, for-
sooth, I will hold my tongue!"

And then pointing to Lear, I threw my head back and
uttered a pealing laugh. "There's a shelled peascod!"

I was so upset that, once offstage, I hurried to my dressing room and locked myself in. I ignored the knock that I
knew would be Strother-Jones. I even had a sip of the
cognac I kept for the moments of worst tension. I could not
think. I would not think. I had to go on too soon, in the
scene where Lear sets out for Gloucester Castle.

The same new spirit invested me again the moment I was
back onstage, and again I noted the muffled consternation
of the cast. But the scene went well until my exit line,
delivered after Lear is already offstage, as an aside to the
audience with a wink:

"She that's a maid now and laughs at my departure,
Shall not be a maid long unless things be cut shorter."

At which point, dear Baroness, I not only winked — and
very lewdly too — but (I can only write this because I know
it is for your eyes alone) I clapped both my hands in a vulgar
gesture of protection over that part of a man's anatomy
whose "cutting short" would incapacitate him from imple-
menting the fool's prediction.

Now you *know* it was not your friend Agnes Gayley who
did that! The proof of it was that I pronounced the words

"departure" and "shorter" vulgarly as "departer" and "sharter," which would never have occurred to me.

Of course there were shouts of ribald laughter from the coarser men in the pit, though I have no doubt the ladies were horrified. Some probably even left the theatre, feeling they had been falsely lured to a burlesque.

Offstage I rushed again to my dressing room, but this time I was followed too closely by Strother-Jones, who slipped in behind me and shut the door.

"Agnes, darling, why didn't you tell me you had all this up your sleeve? You're sensational! You'll be the rage of London!"

"Edmund, something has happened to me, and I don't know what it is! It may be something hellish! I can't go on!"

The director stared at me intensely as if seeking to discover something or somebody in me or behind me.

"Do you suppose the spirit of Robert Arnim has entered into you? Oh, Agnes, what a glorious, fantastical idea! Could this be the proof that our version of the play actually *is* what they played?"

"Our version? *Your* version, thank you very much! I have nothing to do with it. And that final gesture of mine! You *know* that wasn't me!"

Strother-Jones made no reply to this, and I wondered if he, like so many cynics of his sex, did not assume that my stage career had begun with experiences remote, to say the least, from the protected girlhoods of my class. I remember a "friend" (There is always one such) who brought to my attention a gossip column in a yellow journal that insinuated that it was only my mother's stern guard over my dressing room that had finally caused the "frustrated" Sir Lucas Gayley to propose. I needn't tell *you* what a foul libel that was.

Strother-Jones's attitude, plus my humiliating subjection

to the dark spirit of whatever it was that had possessed me, brought on a flood of tears, and I told the director that I could not go on. Appalled, he proceeded to lecture me about my duty, which of course is the effective way to treat anyone brought up in the tradition of the Royal Navy, and when he pointed out that the fool's part was almost over anyway, and that there were no further offensive lines, I pulled myself together and prepared for my next entrance.

Nothing awful happened in my remaining appearance in that part, and when I uttered the fool's final line — "I'll go to bed at noon" — I breathed a sigh of relief and hoped that he would never awaken.

Reverting to Cordelia in the great scene of her reconciliation with her father, I felt that I was putting on the best performance of my career. When Lear tells me sadly that I have indeed some cause not to love him, my gently repeated "no cause, no cause" rang out with a sweetness that surpassed anything I had done. But an accident — if it *was* that — awaited me that was to end the run of our play on its opening night.

My spoken part was over, but it remained for me, as a hanged corpse, to be borne onstage by my stricken and dying father. Strother-Jones had insisted that I be clad in the fool's garb! There would be no fool's cap, however, on my head, so that my long blond hair would clearly reveal to the audience that I was indeed Cordelia.

Now what was our director's point? That Cordelia in prison had redonned the fool's garb to *amuse* her father? Or to convince him finally that it really was she who had accompanied him to Gloucester's castle and witnessed his raging on the heath? Strother-Jones refused to explain this bit of stage folly except in almost mystical terms. "It will be one of the great moments of theatre! The mad old monarch is to be spared nothing. He must lug in the murdered body of the daughter-fool, who represented the ultimate in loyalty and love. It is civilization itself, incarnate in the divine wisdom of the fool and in the deep heart of Cordelia, that has been strangled by the evil in man."

Unhappily, our Lear stumbled as he crossed the boards, and I was thrown down, with severe damage to my kneecap that took a good year to heal. The rest of our tour was cancelled.

And that is why I never undertook Cordelia again. Call it superstition if you like. I didn't dare. Tom Belter, who enacted Lear that night, always maintained that he had received a rough push which had caused him to stumble, though no one onstage had been near enough to have done that.

I took it anyway as a warning. We had been playing games with a great work of art. I sometimes dream that it was the spirit of the bard himself who was reproving us. Of course, nothing ever happened to Strother-Jones himself. Nothing ever happens to Puck.

The Hidden Muse

IN THE WINTER of 1947 the long corridors of the Wall
Street law firm Grimes & Duncan, lined with law reports
and hung with prints of old New York and the solemn photographed likenesses of deceased partners, punctured by the
always open doors into the cubbyholes of clerks and the
occasionally closed ones of their seniors' paneled dens, con-
stituted for David Hallowell, a twenty-eight-year-old naval
veteran, the first reality in his life with which he could
enthusiastically cope. The balance of his existence had con-
sisted of his preparation for the legal life to which he had
always seemed committed: six years at a private boys' academy in the city, another six at Pulver, a boarding school in
Massachusetts, and seven at Columbia, for college and law,
all under the aegis of a devoted widowed mother, bravely
determined, despite economic odds, to train him to follow
in the footsteps of a father, brilliant in promise in law, who
had been felled by heart failure in his early thirties.

Doris Hallowell had been a loving parent to her small,
plain, only child, whose early years had been smitten by
rheumatic fever, not fully cured till he was fourteen, but
David had sensed in her a premonition, almost a longing,
that once she had qualified her son to be what his father had
been prevented from becoming, she could quietly chant her

Nunc Dimittis. So if those years had not really existed for her, did they have to have so much reality for him?

Reality had largely existed for him as a boy in his secret scribbling, his making-up of wonderful tales; and the rest of life, at school, at college, he had kept at a kind of arm's length, avoiding the too critical notice of teachers and peers by doing a few simple things well and scrupulously minding his own business.

But education had hardly ended before its preoccupying place was taken by war, a war that seemed to eclipse not only the past but the whole future for which he had been so carefully tutored. It was not so much that he had imagined that he would be killed in combat as that he would somehow fail to survive the whole experience. It was all so fantastic to his reclusive nature, so discombobulating, so like a fretful dream, that any existence that might or might not ensue would be so different as not to be the existence of David Hallowell at all. He could never quite believe, for example, that it had been *he,* on the bridge of an amphibious vessel approaching a beachhead, who had shouted the command to let go the stern anchor and open the bow doors, or that it had been he, David, on a stormy night in the harbor of an English channel port, waiting in a line of ships for his turn to disembark the wounded at a crowded pier, who had had to order the bridge gang to remove a doctor hysterically screaming that his patients were dying on the lurching tank deck below.

No, he had never quite believed in any of it. He had not once been hurt or even rendered acutely uncomfortable. He had managed to shave and shower almost every day of his four years of active service. He could attribute his strange immunity only to the curious fact that he seemed not to have been there.

Was it, he sometimes wondered, because he had abandoned his secret muse? After all she had done for him at school and college, he had peremptorily abandoned her in order to devote all his energies to her sister of law. Ah, but that writing at Pulver, how he had loved it! For all the academy's dark New England winters, for all the grey Episcopal gloom of its dreary boxlike dormitories huddled around a grim Gothic chapel dedicated to an unimaginable god, for all the false cheer of its school spirit and the relentless siege of its sports, David looked back on his years there as a bridegroom might look back on his honeymoon. For there had been born his only love. On long dark freezing afternoons, after the season of organized athletics, when only daily sheets had had to be filled out showing the hours spent on such required individual exercises as calisthenics or running or handball, he had unhesitatingly put in false versions and hidden away in empty classrooms or warm cellars to write his stories. One of these, a historical romance, had actually found its way into the school's periodical, but in harsh print it had seemed to its author so pathetically below what he had intended that he had felt as if it had been purloined from his desk and published to humiliate him. And then, too, at Pulver "success" had little to do with literary success. There was never any doubt about *that*.

In the greater, the even intoxicating freedom of Columbia, where one could be as alone as one desired, David had learned to live more freely with his dangerous muse. In sophomore year he had written a whole novel, short but whole, and in a fatal moment, in a sudden, passionate need for a judge, he had shown it to his mother. She had not for a moment made the mistake of underestimating what its production meant, nor been fooled by his airy statement that it was only an exercise of the imagination, a flight of fantasy, almost an indulgence. She had instantly and correctly detected in his work of fiction an enemy as fatal to her purpose as the most alluring siren or the most addictive drug.

"Let us find out right away what sort of a talent you have, my child. If it is your wish to become a professional writer, let us be sure that your ability is worth any career that you sacrifice to it!"

Oh, she had been fair, damnably fair! She had persuaded him to let him take his poor book to an old friend and classmate of her late husband, whose name had become one of the great ones in publishing and who had edited the work of a famous novelist whom David passionately admired. And the great man had been kindness itself.

"Your writing shows a certain grace, my dear young friend, and a nice intuition about people. Keep it up, by all means. But your mother tells me that you want my serious advice about adopting it as a full-time career. I have to say that I should not advise you to let it be the one arrow in your quiver. Fiction as good as yours is not infrequently found in an editor's mail. Competent writing is more common than it used to be. It may be that yours is a talent that will grow, but who can tell? I should not give up a profession like law or medicine for it, if that be the question."

David was shattered. He resolved in a fit of despair to give up writing forever, and thereafter applied himself conscientiously to courses that would be of use to him in law school. His mother was dismayed by his violence and depression, but she was nonetheless convinced that he had adopted the wiser course. He did well in law school and, on graduation, received an offer from the famous firm of Grimes & Duncan, an even more prestigious organization than his father's old one. Doris Hallowell could now have sung her Nunc Dimittis, had she not enjoyed perfect health.

But the surprise that awaited her son, after the war had receded, was his discovery that he had found at last a world in which he could belong. He wasn't getting ready for anything; he didn't have to fight anything; he was simply *there,* with people who were also *there,* and perfectly content to be *there.* Much of his natural shyness and reclusiveness fell away before the easy congeniality of men who had so much in common. There were twenty partners, formal but usually friendly presences, and some fifty associates, industrious, keen and sometimes tense; there were cheerful and attractive stenographers and smiling office boys. There was competition, of course, for only one of every five clerks could expect to "make partner," but those passed over could expect to be absorbed by clients or other firms. Indeed, those who left were sometimes supposed to do even better than those who stayed, but such a possibility would never have induced any clerk to leave voluntarily. A partnership in Grimes & Duncan was the Valhalla to which all aspired.

David's first and most prolonged study was of his office roommate and immediate superior, Larry Grau. Grau was the perfect subject, for if the firm was already beginning to take shape in his mind as the topic for a novel, Grau was just the right hero. He was older than David, if only by a couple of years — though that marked a definite superiority in the steep ladder of legal ascent. He had a handsomely square face and jaw, with thick short hair and an expression of sober intensity, occasionally lightened by a surprisingly charming smile. He was, as might have been expected, assigned to the corporate department — he was already deemed an expert in the exchange of securities — and he was notorious for his long hours of work, even in a firm that was dubbed a sweatshop by some of its rivals. But he took off a generous amount of time to guide and counsel David, who was only too glad to be taken under his wing.

Once he and Larry had started a registration statement for the Securities and Exchange Commission for a corporate client's proposed stock issue, their days and nights became enmeshed in the grey canopy of unremitting toil. Larry was a perfectionist; there seemed no end to the number of drafts to which each document was relentlessly subjected. Weekends were noticed only because there were fewer staff to assist them in the office; clean shirts and underwear and toilet articles were kept in the drawers of their desks. But David enjoyed the sense of keeping up with his tireless but always good-tempered leader. He felt his nerves calmed and his senses almost anaesthetized by the gradual intoxication of his own total involvement in the task. And when the job was done, and he was presented with his copy of the black-bound volumes containing the handsomely printed pages of their work, he would feel the thrill of creation and revel in the seeming vacation of a brief period of mere eight-hour days. He was closer to Larry than he had ever been to another human. He loved Larry.

Their friendship extended beyond the office. David on weekends visited Larry and his wife, Shelby, and their two small children in the housing development in lower Manhattan where many of the meagerly salaried clerks of the office dwelt. Shelby Grau was amiable, disorganized and lovable; she was the perfect spouse for so industrious a husband, for no matter how late he came home, she was barely ready for him. And David noted that it was probably just as well that Larry worked as hard as he did, for anything he was doing he found hard to stop. If he bicycled for exercise, it would be until he dropped; if he drank at parties on Saturday nights, he would continue till morning. And when he took an interest in David and his work, it was a great interest. David was utterly happy with the Graus. He needed no other social life.

But the most curious thing about his new life was not the Graus, or even his enthusiasm for registration statements; it was something more amazing, and that was his return to writing. How could it be, given the pressure of his office work? It might have been because he had learned the trick at Pulver of making use of odd snatches of free time, of having always a small notepad in his pocket in which to jot down an idea or a sentence or even a whole paragraph. He had taught himself how to pick up a sequence of thoughts exactly where he had left it, like an opera singer at a rehearsal picking up a note in the middle of an aria at a wave of the conductor's baton. So for the composition of the novel that was shaping in his mind about the law firm that employed him, he could use spare moments waiting in a government office for an appointment, or the quarter of an hour in the early morning before opening his mail, or a solitary lunch at a cafeteria, or, most heavenly of all, a whole rare weekend at home when his mother, assuming him involved in legal work, never dared interrupt him except for a meal.

Although he suspected that Larry would have regarded any such subsidiary interest as defecting from the law a portion of a loyalty that should be total, he felt that, with himself, law and literature were almost the same pursuit. After all, he cared for what the other clerks cared for, and he could do whatever they did. He shared with them that brief glow of the postwar spirit when things seemed to be worthwhile simply because they were civilian things. The pace of work and the low salaries meant that the firm occupied most of the clerks' lives — even socially they depended on each other for late night weekend drinking parties — but David was entirely content with such. He did not want any life outside Grimes & Duncan. His new friends and their highly communicative wives provided him with all the congeniality and excitement and material that he needed.

Even the endless firm gossip never tired him. He was continually interested in who had dared to say what to each partner, who had made a fatal gaffe at a closing, who had dared to tell off the arrogant old head of the stenographic pool, even what handsome bachelor associate was supposed to be having an affair with the younger wife of a partner. There was a good deal of bitterness over raises and partnerships, but David noted that there was a fairly general consensus that the firm was essentially a meritocracy and that aptitude was the key to success.

Yet, for all his intense interest in what went on around him, he began to suffer from an uneasy sense that he was living, so to speak, on his capital and that time was running out on him. On a Saturday night, at a fellow associate's party, after several drinks, perched on a window seat by the ever congenial Shelby Grau, David felt a sudden, anguished misgiving. Had he not totally misconceived what the firm meant to him as opposed to what it meant to his fellow guests? They cared only for what it could do for *them,* and he only for what he could do with *it.*

"Do you know, Shelby, I've just realized something? Every man in this room is clutching a secret fear that he won't be made a partner in Grimes and Duncan. And I'm clutching one that I will be!"

"Really, David, I never heard anything so conceited. Not that I don't think you won't make the grade, but at least not before my Larry."

"Oh, he's a shoo-in — everyone knows that. But it isn't a matter of conceit with me. It's a neurotic terror. Help me, Shelby!" There was a note of actual anxiety in his forced smile, and her eyes widened.

"Don't you *want* to be a partner?"

"No!"

"Why in God's name not?"

"Because I'm Peter Pan. I want to be young forever!"

Shelby shrugged, as if reassured. "Peter Panic, I'd call it. Grow up, David. And don't go around telling people what you've just told me. Even Larry. Or maybe I should say, particularly Larry. And if you really mean it, get the hell out of the firm while you're still unmarried and free, and do something where you don't have to be afraid of getting ahead."

It might have been a pail of cold water dumped ruthlessly over his fuzzy head, but he certainly knew that she was doing him a favor.

❀   ❀   ❀

On the rare nights when Larry Grau was not working late, he and David would sometimes stop for a drink at a downtown bar before taking the subway home. It was not always a good idea, for Larry's reluctance to quit after the first round might imperil his getting home for supper. But on a night after Larry had closed a long and difficult deal — one in which David had not been involved — there was no denying his friend a congratulatory quaff. And then, suddenly, at the bar, as he took in the peculiar glow on Larry's countenance as the latter slowly raised his glass to his lips, he realized with an absolute conviction that there was more to congratulate his old office roommate about than the mere signing of closing papers.

"Oh, Larry," he breathed, "You've made it, haven't you? You're a partner!"

"As of the first of the year. Mr. Duncan just told me. I haven't even told Shelby yet."

David saw his friend now as a kind of shining legal Galahad. He was awed by his own awe. Yet at the same time he knew — oh, even positively! — that it was not for the likes of him.

"Go home to Shelby!" he exclaimed. "Go home at once and tell her! Don't even finish that drink!"

And for once Larry obeyed him.

David, sitting alone at the bar, had two more drinks, but they served only to clarify his thinking. The bell had rung for him as sharply as for his friend. On that next New Year's Day there would be two fewer associates at Grimes & Duncan. He faced a future that had no assurances, and he felt no exhilaration. But he would be coming to terms with himself, knowing that it would be with himself that he would be coping. And that, after all, was something.

He dined alone at the little café by the bar and drank a bottle of wine, slowly, for he did not want to be drunk and he did not want to see things too clearly. Not just yet. There would be plenty of time for that. Indeed, there would be nothing but time. He thought of all the things he could do with the firm in his novel now. He could turn the senior partner into a monster on the scale of Balzac or a figure as cheery as Mr. Pickwick; he could make all the lawyers as dull and banal as if they lived in Emma Bovary's Yonville or as shrewd as barristers in Trollope; he could render his friend Larry as brave as a Conrad hero or . . . but he would no longer be a warm and living part of it. Maybe it would be better to be a Larry, after all. But that was no longer his choice.

Realist in Babylon

THE SPRING of 1980 would mark the seventy-fifth anniversary of the founding of Chelton, originally an Episcopal preparatory boarding school for boys in Dublin, New Hampshire, but now, like most of its New England counterparts, a coeducational, nondenominational academy, and the headmaster had consulted me, as one of his trustees, about who the principal speaker should be. His real purpose was to ask me to sound out the candidate he favored, Hugh Orrick, also a school trustee, to see whether he would not only speak but accept the school's quadrennial award to the graduate making the greatest current contribution to the welfare of his city, state or nation. Orrick was my friend and exact contemporary; we were each now fifty-five and had been formmates at Chelton.

"It's all very well to startle the alumni every now and then," I pointed out dryly. "They have to learn they mustn't take their old alma mater too much for granted. But have you considered the effect on future awardees of your giving the prize to Orrick? How are you going to clean it up enough to make it acceptable to honorable men once you've given it to the likes of him? Of course, you can say it'll be four years away and that memories are short, but still . . ."

"Oh, come now, Ben. Hugh Orrick's not *that* bad. His fortune has been legally made. It isn't as if he's ever been threatened with an indictment or involved in a public scandal."

"I'd say his whole life was a public scandal!"

"And you call him your friend!"

"I do. But I've never left him under the smallest illusion that I approve of him. I've always given him the benefit of my undiluted opinion as to what I think of his rags of newspapers and his methods of acquiring them."

"But think of the good he's done with his money, Ben. Think of his contributions to schools and museums!"

"You mean think of his contributions to Chelton."

"Well, why not?"

Ed Herrick was round, sleek and idealistic, with a rather baby face and a terrible earnestness in seeking to adapt himself to new ideas. The worst thing, according to his creed, that could happen to the head of a preparatory school was to be caught behind the times. He came of a family well known in banking circles, but having known nothing of capitalism but its profits, he was perfectly willing to be as cynical as any radical about its legends and motives.

"When you're in the fund-raising business, Ben, as every headmaster or college president is today, you soon make the discovery that most of the dollars people give you are dirty dollars, or at least have some taint on them. Trace my own revered ancestors far enough back, and what do you get to? The opium trade in China. Look behind that expensive shirt you're wearing, and what do you find? Some Californian sweatshop where illegal immigrants toil fourteen hours a day. The point is that the world has become so unified that nobody can operate in a moral vacuum. College kids protest their universities' investing in South African stocks, but if they knew what they were about, they'd be nixing every security on the big board!"

"Tell me, Ed. Just how much has Hugh given the school? What's the grand total to date?"

"Five full scholarships. A chair of English. The new squash courts and the hockey rink."

"The rest is silence."

Of course I put the question to Hugh, and of course he very graciously accepted. But, as always, there was something in his tone that implied that *he* was the one conferring the favor. And of course, again, I agreed to introduce him at the commencement proceedings and composed as complimentary a summary of his "brilliant" business career as I could square with my conscience. I had to keep reminding myself that, after all, very few of any graduating class pay much attention to the hot air from the dais on the day they receive their diplomas. And I amused myself after writing my address by writing the one I should *like* to have delivered, which is the one that follows.

❀   ❀   ❀

Hugh and I, as school chums, were drawn to each other by the very opposition of our temperaments. He had some qualities of leadership, but lacked popularity; I was no leader at all, but was sociable and easy to get along with. He despised what he called "the mob"; I was inclined to find sympathy and cheer in a crowd. But we shared a tendency, not characteristic of our peers at least until their last year at Chelton, to be always looking beyond the borders of school life to what we fancied was the "real world."

Hugh's sophistication, which made him seem maturer than the rest of the class, might have made him a target of their jealousy and resentment, obsessed as they were with sports and smut and the obliteration of any show of independent thought, had it not been for his size and blond good looks and the fact that he was a good football player. He was also quick to take offense and handy with his fists. He did me the dubious honor of crediting me with the same scorn of school values that he felt. He dazzled me with his vision of the college life to come, when smart clothes, polished manners and a quick wit would be assets hardly dreamed of in the rough-and-tumble of schoolboy life. Chelton to Hugh was simply a necessary stage to be got through; the alternative, some dreary boys' day academy in New York, was unthinkable. The New England "prep" school, philistine as it might be, was as necessary for an American gentleman as Eton or Harrow for an English one.

He loved to talk about his parents and the smart social life they led. He did me the compliment of assuming that mine led the same, or at lest could have, I suppose because our fathers had been in Chelton together. But my father, an overworked and overconscientious family doctor, and my mother, a dedicated volunteer social worker, led very different lives from the glittering Orricks. And to tell the truth, they were not much impressed by the latter. But I felt no need even to hint at this when Hugh would show me a newspaper photograph of his parents splendidly costumed as Louis XVI and Marie-Antoinette at a charity ball. There is nobody, after all, quite so agreeably flattering as a snob who is nice to *you,* and Hugh could be very good company indeed. I reasoned to myself that I could accept his friendship without his values. And I have, haven't I? Yet here I am, a trustee of the institution giving him a prize for good citizenship!

I saw Hugh's parents when they came up to school once a

term to see him. They would never take their meals in the simple private inn that the school ran for such visitors; they would drive for miles, if necessary, to some delicious country restaurant, where Hugh and I would be allowed a school-forbidden glass of wine. I thought it very grown-up and delightful. I could see why the Orricks were so popular in society. They were large and cheerful and emphatic, smartly and tweedily attired; one could imagine that they rode capably to hounds and were first-class shots and that their appearance at a dinner party assured the other guests that the company was first class. He was a bit dry, a trifle abrupt, impatient perhaps of unorthodox views, but she was different. However skillfully she fitted into the world that one felt her husband had chosen, one suspected that she could have fitted just as easily into others, even perhaps better ones.

She was big, as I say, like her son and husband, but she stood up to her bigness, never cowered. Her features were strong and handsome, and her fine, firm figure bore well the dark, rich colors in which she covered it. Her hair, dyed a fashionable auburn, was always carefully set. Her voice was attractively rough, and her laugh infectiously cheerful. She gave the impression of a hearty realism and a sound common sense, much needed in an artificial world, but at the same time one felt sure that she was abreast of every nuance of each new fashion. The world she had to live in, she seemed to confess, had better be dressed up to look as well as it could. For, truly, it did not amount to much. But then what world did?

She understood Hugh well; I was convinced of that from the beginning. And she saw that I might be one to exercise a good influence upon him. But she loved him too much; she idolized him, really. Her three older children, all daughters, all attractive and well married, even by Orrick standards, she loved also, but not in the same intense way. On Hugh she lavished the affection that her loyal but temperate husband did not need.

An example of her close interest even in Hugh's school career occurred in our next-to-last year at Chelton. I was an editor of the school paper, and I tried to enlist Hugh's support in submitting an essay or story. He wrote a piece that was both ingenious and amusing in support of the duel as the only way to uphold the standard of social manners in a world of gentlemen. A man would think twice, he argued, before uttering a vulgar slur or a gross slander if he knew he might have to back it up on the field of honor. Would you carelessly call a man a communist if you could be called out? I liked the piece, but he wouldn't let me print it.

"*Nota bene,* my dear Ben, that one mustn't enter the arena too soon. Why create a a record of juvenilia to be dug up later and thrown in one's face? Wait until your talents — if you're lucky enough to have any — have matured, and then spring like the goddess Athena from the brain of Zeus! Waiting is the key to half the good things in life. And remember, there aren't too many of them. Or perhaps timing is the better word. As Mother pointed out on the Caribbean cruise we took last spring vacation, give yourself a day or so to sort out who's who in first class before chancing any acquaintance. That overfriendly couple who thrust themselves upon you as the ship pulls away from the pier will turn out to be the biggest bores aboard. And you'll never shed them once they've got their paws on you!"

But Mrs. Orrick showed herself in a less exclusive mood on a winter weekend when we had lunched at one of her country inns, and Hugh and his father were absorbed in listening to a football match on a radio in the lounge.

"Hugh showed me his piece on dueling, Ben, and I liked

it, though I think it may be just as well not to print it. The duel's hardly an issue today, thank heavens, even if Hugh does want to revive it. So like him, isn't it, to defend something that contributed to elegant manners — if it really did? You can be sure, if it *was* revived, that Hugh would spend all his afternoons practicing with a sword or pistol. He'd want to be damn sure it wasn't *he* left lying prone on the field of honor. Oh, Hugh's a snob; we can face that. We all are, to one degree or another, and it needn't be altogether a bad thing, so long as we recognize just what we may be doing to the people we have the presumption to look down on. Hugh shouldn't let people see that he sneers at school accomplishments. And the best way for him to do this is to stop sneering at them. On some of them, anyway. Let's start with the school mag. I'll talk to him."

Her talk must have had immediate effect, for only two weeks later he came to me with an excellent and thought-provoking essay on the pros and cons of instituting an honor system at Chelton, at least for the upper forms, which I immediately accepted and which was widely and hotly debated by both boys and masters.

Hugh now took more interest in school affairs, and his last year at Chelton could almost be called a success. He was on the football team and a prefect of the school and attained something like a mild popularity. But his career at Harvard was a distinct disappointment, at least to me and, I think, to his mother. Election to the socially select Porcellian Club seemed the only accomplishment of four years of partying, where he seemed to have spent almost as much time in New York and Palm Beach as he did in Cambridge. I was at Yale, so not on hand to give him any unwelcome advice, but I sent him a sarcastic postcard from time to time when I read his name in the social columns.

On graduation, however, Hugh surprised everybody by not going on to law or business school and by not joining his father's brokerage firm on Wall Street, but by taking a modest job as a fact checker on *The New Yorker* magazine. Our old school friendship, cooled by four years of separation and very different interests, revived now that I was attending Columbia Law.

"The hours are regular," Hugh informed me, in explaining his job preference, "and the atmosphere congenial. If they're not all gentlemen — or ladies — they know precisely what ladies and gentlemen are. One cannot be misunderstood at *The New Yorker*. It is possible indeed to be too well understood, but that is a risk no really intelligent man should be afraid of taking. And the sense of accuracy is exhilarating in a careless world." I was to remember his saying this later when he was the press lord of rumor. If he deviated from the truth, he knew just what he was doing. He went on: "If a story writer speaks of a thunderstorm at a given time and place, I must check the weather reports to see if it actually happened."

The smallness of Hugh's salary was made up for by a trust fund bequeathed him by a grandfather. It enabled him to keep a small but elegant one-story apartment in an East Side brownstone, a horse at the Piping Rock Club stables on Long Island and to maintain an active night life in Manhattan. If I didn't read his name at least once a week in the social columns of the evening journals, I would call him up to see if he were ill.

Such a man was bound to marry, and to marry, as the Orricks would put it, well, and I soon read that Hugh was seen often in the company of Delphine Simonds, the "dark-haired beauty and heiress" who had attended Vassar and now worked on *Vogue*. We were now in 1950, when it was still not necessary for girls like Delphine to have careers, but it was thought right that they should at least start one. I knew that the matter was serious when Hugh asked me to dine with him and Delphine on a Saturday night — just the three of us.

"I don't want your opinion," he warned me blandly. "Just your applause. I know you'd never cross swords with my mother, so I tell you Delphine is *her* candidate."

Well, he certainly had my applause. I liked Delphine very much. But I was not sure she was right for Hugh or, to put it more bluntly, that he was right for her. She was not, to begin with, nearly as good-looking as the society columns made out. She made herself up to best advantage — how could she not, with *Vogue* behind her? — but her eyes were too close together and her mouth too small, her cheeks slightly too puffy, and her expression too breathlessly enthusiastic. Was she stupid? But no, she saw things clearly enough; she sensed almost at once that I did not share her frantic admiration of Hugh and, interestingly enough, did not hold this against me. She *knew* that other people did not necessarily see life as the noble adventure that she imagined it to be, and she only prayed — oh, I could feel how desperately she *did* pray — that those others would leave her and her illusions — if illusions they had to be — alone.

She offered me in her lively tones an example of Hugh's work on *The New Yorker*.

"He had to check this story about a naval officer in the war who mistakenly led a convoy over a row of sea buoys, badly damaging their bottoms. Well, it seems the story was based on an actual incident in Norfolk, and the officer was still around and might sue. So Hugh had to change the locale from Norfolk to Pearl Harbor and go down to Washington and spend a whole day in the Hydrographic Office! Isn't that wonderful? How many magazines would do that? And think what great training it is for Hugh! With a mind as razor sharp as his, his only danger might be in jumping to conclusions. Now he'll know how to look for every detail, every angle, in whatever it is he's doing. There's no limit to where he may go! Or am I being silly? Are you looking at me with those bright lawyer's eyes of yours, Ben, and thinking what a damn fool of a girl your friend is mixing himself up with?"

"Don't overpraise me, my dear," Hugh warned her with a smile. "People will start immediately looking for flaws. Ben, as it is, is only too aware of mine."

After the engagement was announced, Mrs. Orrick asked me to lunch with her at her club. Like her son, she sought my approval rather than my judgment.

"Do you see why she's so right for him?" she asked me straight off. "It's because she wants him to be a great man. And the right kind of great man, too. Not just a rich man or a hot-shot tycoon. But a congressman, perhaps an ambassador. Someone who really contributes to the world. Anyway, she's a girl after my own heart."

"She certainly has a heart of her own," I observed, a bit dryly perhaps. "And she's given it all to Hugh."

There was a pause. "Do you imply he needed one?"

"Don't we all?"

"Some more than others. You and I know, Ben, that Hugh has a heart, but we also know that he's not likely to lose it. Now don't look so grave. I don't mean anything bad by that. Lots of people never lose their hearts. They're simply made that way. Hugh's father's like that. And he's been an excellent husband. I can always say that if he hasn't lost his heart to someone as good as I am, he probably won't lose it to others. But we live in a maudlin world, where oodles of silly souls think that losing their heart is the great business of life. Whereas finding it might be the trick for most of them."

I knew that Mrs. Orrick liked to exaggerate her own coolness and sophistication. Perhaps it had been a useful therapy for one united to Mr. Orrick. But I suspected not only that she had a heart to lose, but that she had probably once lost it. But no one would ever hear a word about *that*.

"Let us hope that Delphine will be as happy as you have been."

"Let us *pray*. Very devoutly. But I can only be truly concerned with the happiness of one of that couple, and you know which that is. Parents can be monsters, Ben. You will find that out one day. They kill for their young."

"But you have taken Delphine alive."

"And I intend to keep her that way. Alive and happy."

It was not to be expected that such a man as Hugh would remain long as a mere checker on *The New Yorker,* but as we all expected him to rise on the staff of that distinguished periodical, we were surprised when he switched to *World and Company,* of which popular monthly he became the feature editor in a scant three years' time. *World and Company* had its serious side, but I would not have thought it was quite serious enough for Hugh. It was a glossy, sleek magazine, with splendid colored shots of luxurious villas and their interiors and strikingly posed portrait photographs of such brilliant thinkers as Einstein, Bertrand Russell and Walter Lippmann. It was in witty and stimulating interviews with such as these that Hugh first made his name. *World and Company* rendered intellectuals chic; it matched the cocktail party and the charity ball to the laboratory and the lecture podium. Its logo might have been a smartly gowned

Joan Crawford bent over an open book, her great eyes behind huge glasses taking in the unknown.

Hugh's doubling of the circulation brought him to the notice of Arvis Grantley, the department store heir who had bought control of Supermedia, the publishing syndicate that owned *World and Company*. But Grantley is so important to the rest of Hugh's story that I must pause to describe him.

Like not a few of our latter-day tycoons, Grantley had inherited a fortune of a few millions and turned it into one of dozens. The reckess heir of yesteryear who dissipated the hard-earned gold of his forebears in Monte Carlo or in the fleshpots of Paris has been replaced by the man in the parable who converted his five talents into ten. It is now three generations from shirt sleeves to cutaways. For Arvis Grantley was the best-dressed man in Manhattan; at least there was none better. His father had been a simpler type: the chain-smoking, wise-cracking, foul-mouthed journalist who would have seen nothing in Lincoln's assassination but the story of the year. Arvis, brilliantly expanding the small paternal empire, and acquiring magazines and radio stations as well as newspapers, had made a national name for himself, but he still blushed at the memory of the vulgarity of his father's ways and means and hoped to give his enterprises the gloss of a civilizing, taste-improving influence. Hugh was just the man for him.

One might have thought, in our day and age, that Arvis would not have needed Hugh. He was, after all, a personage in his own right, with a fine, strong physique, thick black shiny hair, and a hearty approach to people. He piloted his own plane and sailed his trophy-winning yacht. He had a keen nose for what the public wanted, and he supplied it vigorously, managing his businesses with the ruthlessness of one who fears above all things to be taken advantage of because of his advantages. But his Achilles' heel was that he could never quite believe he was what Hugh so easily and obviously was: a gentleman of the old school — what old school? — born and bred. Hugh explained all this to me with his usual apparently careless candor.

"You and I, Ben, see our old friends throwing away, right and left, all the so-called privileges of their background. 'It's a new world,' they keep crowing. 'Get on with it!' Poor fools, they don't realize, half of them, that those privileges, or the memory of them — in other people's minds — may be the only assets they have left. A goodly number of our new arrivals on the social scene want nothing better than to duplicate the ostensibly despised lives of yesterday's W A S P. *Plus ça change,* my dear fellow. Of course what they want is never quite the same thing, but a sharp eye can spot the differences and act accordingly. Where, for example, do these new people want to go for the summer? Not to Newport; they think it's stuffy. It's not any stuffier than any other place, but remember: truth is nothing. The image is all. The Hamptons are the Keewaydin for these new Hiawathas. Very well. Buy in the Hamptons. Same old game in a slightly sillier hat. Now, tell me, who would smell out that Arvis Grantley, handsome, rich, well mannered, a decoration, surely, to any social gathering, harbors a secret fear that he's a meatball because he didn't go to Groton or Harvard and because his old man didn't go to college at all? Well, I tell you, Hugh Orrick would smell it out. And that's why Hugh Orrick is going to be his right-hand man!"

Was it really as simple as that? Of course not. Hugh was a bit of a genius himself in divining the image into which the reading public wished to see its notables converted. But certainly his intimacy with Arvis contributed importantly to his ultimate success in Supermedia and eventually in the company that took over Supermedia. And that intimacy was based on Hugh's ability to convince Arvis that he was in every way Hugh's equal: in wit, in charm of manner, in the sizing-up of others, in the winning of friends and admirers, in the whole social game and all its ramifications.

As Hugh rose in influence in Supermedia, first a board member, then secretary and treasurer, his control over *World and Company* became absolute, and the character of the latter changed. There was less emphasis on politics and economics and more on fashion and social news. Hugh himself, though writing less for it, came to specialize in profiles of movie and stage stars and best-selling authors, providing details of their often hectic private lives that on occasion created near national scandals.

I had now an established law practice, and Hugh sometimes retained me on a minor matter, largely as a token of friendship. My small firm was not up to the handling of his big stuff. One day when we were lunching I asked him whether a current article in *World and Company* might not engender a nasty libel suit.

"My dear Ben," he replied, with his usual note of genial condescension, "by the time my trial attorneys, Messrs. Schenk and Schenk, have got through with a plaintiff, he is apt to be very sorry he ever decided to sue. They are very clever indeed at playing the little games you lawyers love to play. Swamping the poor litigant with interrogatories and demands for every file in his attic, probing into his closets and secret life, exposing him to every kind of humiliation in court — don't look at me that way, Ben; it's your profession, not mine. I refuse to dirty my hands in the business. My counsel are rated A–V in Martindale. Do I have to look further? You say that piece was damn near pornographic. Well, isn't that more truthful than dishing out the dirt the way we used to, sandwiched in between articles by Walter Lippmann and John Mason Brown? The function of the media has always been to give the public what it wants. And if you don't do it, you can be sure someone else will. People are going to read what they want, and, increasingly, to *see* what they want — in the movies, on the TV screen. And one day they'll want to make that image real, to reach into the camera and pull it out to play with it. You and I may live to see a movie star President of the United States."

"And will that be a good thing?"

"You don't get it, Ben! It's not a good thing or necessarily a bad thing. It's *the* thing, what's going to happen, something we can't stop. You take it all too seriously. The papers and magazines Supermedia puts out don't really much influence the tide of men's affairs. They're as basically innocuous as the hair restorer that doesn't restore, the halitosis cure that doesn't purify bad breath, the body odor that leaves one's natural stink. They provide a mild anodyne to the misery of living in a world that has never quite made sense since cavemen decided to cover their bare asses with animal skins. I daresay I do as much for humanity as you, *mon semblable, mon frère!*"

I don't know whether I could call Delphine one of Hugh's victims or not. He was the perfect gentleman as a husband, as in everything else, unfailingly courteous and considerate, supportive of her in general conversation, solicitous as to her preferences in theatres, excursions and interior decoration. And he was an affectionate, even an exuberant father to their two little daughters. Not did I ever hear Delphine utter a word of criticism of him. Her earlier dreams of Hugh as a statesman or at least as one enrolled in a noble cause she seemed to have forgotten or tucked away in the depths of her memory. The only evidence that I had that she was bitterly disappointed with the increasingly brilliant social life into which Hugh led her was that she had started to drink.

Alcoholism is a mysterious ailment, because it has such a multiplicity of causes. It is almost impossible to predict which of our nearest and dearest will turn to the sought relief of the bottle. Sometimes, when the habit strikes a seemingly happy and successful individual, one can only surmise a bodily, a somatic cause. I suspected that Delphine blamed only herself for having assumed that her husband was a Christian gentleman as well as a gentleman and that when she perceived that, like the Tin Woodsman in the Oz tales, he had no heart, she concluded that only a fairy princess could give him one. It was certainly not his fault; that, I am sure, was her opinion. He was what he was; he could be no other, and what *she* was, and presumably always would be, was an ass. And asses might as well quietly sip their way to consolation.

Because her father had been active in the conservation of city landmarks, Delphine had been anxious after his death to preserve the family mansion, just west of Washington Square, an attractive red-brick affair with a Greek revival, columnar porch. But as the paternal estate had been much diminished by death taxes and some bad investments by the old man, Hugh, as executor and trustee, had solicited an offer from an apartment house builder, premised, of course, on demolition of the mansion. Delphine's brother, an amiable idler who had hitherto left everything in the hands of his capable brother-in-law, suddenly developed the mettle to oppose the sale, but Hugh and his shrewd counsel easily prevailed. The brother's suit for landmark status was defeated, and the mansion was razed.

Hugh made short work of my protests at one of our luncheons. I had been concerned with the case; one of my partners had even submitted an amicus brief to preserve the old house.

"My dear Ben, the time to save landmarks was when we still had some. Where were all you screamers when Penn Station fell to the wrecking ball? The New York that was glorified by the works of Stanford White, Cass Gilbert and Richard Morris Hunt is gone. Look about you, my friend. The remnants of the old city that you are trying to save are mostly tasteless derelicts. Did you know that Delphine's family mansion didn't even have an architect? Oh, you didn't? Well, learn it from me. It was only one of a row, thrown up by an Irish contractor."

"But the point is, Hugh, that we've reached a level where, to have anything left, we must hang on, even to the second rate!"

"What a confession! To be old, then, is enough. I wish I'd had that in writing before this mansion business started. It might have saved us a lawsuit. But I say to hell with the second rate, which, by the by, is usually the third or even the fourth rate. Let's make a clean sweep of it and present the lords of the glass cubes with a tabula rasa! Who knows? They may make something of it. The Lever Brothers building isn't half bad."

Delphine, so far as I knew, did little to back up her brother in the mansion fight, but her drinking grew noticeably worse. Like many alcoholics, she was strangely unaware of how visible her intoxication could be. She might stare blankly at her partner at a dinner party, obviously not following the thread of his discourse, and then neglect to rise from the table when the others did, until Hugh had glided silently to her chair and helped her to her feet.

In the drawing room afterwards, on such an occasion, he would let her sit quietly on a sofa, but always keeping a wary eye on her, and when it became evident that she was going to get up and address the company with some inane story, he would suddenly appear before her, holding her coat. There would be no chance for her to protest that it was early; there was something too final about his tall figure, erect before her, grasping the mink wrap and unyieldingly smiling. He might have been a kind but inexorable doctor, with orders that both knew could not be gainsaid.

Arvis Grantley, present with me on one of these painful occasions, could hardly contain his admiration of Hugh's way of handling it. Leaving the party, he took my arm for a moment on the street to comment on it.

"Don't you agree he handles her elegantly, Ben? Have you ever seen greater tact? Never a word to anyone. Not so much as a sigh or a glance of reproof. He knows it's his problem and his alone. What would be gained by discussing it? And he knows just when to take her home, so that she never becomes your problem. It's art, man; that's what it is. Great art!"

But a dark thought came to me in the taxi going home. Was it possible that Hugh, adept in finding the most un-likely pluses even in a mire of minuses, was handling his wife's intemperance in just the way to bring the greatest credit on himself? However, I pulled myself up. There was always the danger of being *too* hard on Hugh. After all, he was handling his problem as well as it could be handled. I knew he had tried to take her to Alcoholics Anonymous, and, so far, she had quietly balked.

A sad lunch that I had with Hugh's mother enlightened me on the inevitable solution of Hugh's marriage. Mrs. Orrick, to compensate me for what she quite mistakenly called an intrusion on my time, had taken me to the most expensive French restaurant in town.

"I think Hugh's going to be needing you, Ben, so we might call this a briefing session. Delphine has at last agreed to go to a sanatorium to be dried out. That, I know you will agree, is long overdue. But, even more important, she has agreed to a divorce. The marriage has become a nullity." I could only nod, and after a rather solemn pause she continued. "The lawyers are drawing up the papers. There are no problems. She has enough money of her own, and Hugh will give her more, even though she's not asking for it. There is no dispute about the children; she will have them as much as she likes as soon as a doctor pronounces her capable of looking after them. In the meantime they're quite happy with Hugh. It is not in any of that that you come in."

"Where is it?"

"Hugh will marry again. Too soon, I fear. I hope you will try to keep him from making too worldly a match."

I had to laugh at this. "And just how am I to stop it?"

"With your telling sarcasm, my friend. With your telling jibes."

"And who is better at them than his splendid ma?"

"Well, I didn't do so well with Delphine, did I? Oh, she *seemed* to have everything one could ask of a girl, I admit. But an old hand like myself should have caught the scent of whiskey on her breath. Even the *future* scent of whiskey. But all that's over the dam. The point is, dear Ben, that I may not be around long enough to help. I have a nasty lump — well, I needn't tell you where. No, no!" She held up a hand to arrest the unwelcome flow of my sympathy. "I can't bear people who talk about their own demises. They are things one should keep strictly to oneself. I only tell you to make you see how alone Hugh is going to be. And he's not going to find many true friends in the circles in which he is now circulating. But enough of this. I've given you the word. Now let's talk about you. Is it true that you're going to represent the children in the Willcox will case?"

֍ ֍ ֍

My wonderful friend Mrs. Orrick died six months later, and Hugh was rigidly expressionless in his grief. Her death was the only thing he would never talk to me about; I believe that she was the only person he ever loved. But I had no chance to use my wit to limit his matrimonial choice, for, without a word to me, he married Lally Aldermeyer, the most beautiful woman in Gotham — and she really *was* as lovely as her photographs — and the widow of Clarence Aldermeyer, who had left her, in conjunction with the children of his earlier alliances, the controlling interest in a chain of television stations.

She had charm, great charm, and she made rather a fuss over me as her new husband's "oldest friend," but she had the strange impersonality of some famous beauties: the world seemed to exist as a setting for her looks, her jewels, her gowns, her houses and gardens. She was always playing the lead, the role of the dazzling great lady. One wondered how she would be if things didn't go her way, but then they always did go her way.

When she made the discovery that Hugh was even more

· 163 ·

interested in business than he was in her, it did not bother her a bit. So long as he played his role at her parties and, presumably, in her bed, he was welcome to all the businesses in the world.

"You know, when Hugh was courting me," she told me one night, "he used to make fun of all the men in our world who prated about their hours of work. If they can't get their job done in six or seven hours in a day, he would say, they must be stupid. It's so vulgar, he insisted, this constant touting of one's toil, as if there were any value in sweat! So I assumed, of course, that when we were married, our life would consist of long holidays on tropical islands and exciting excursions to remote and romantic spots. And now what do I find? That we can hardly budge. Because he works like a nigger!"

She laughed; she was not in the least bitter. All she had discovered was that he was just like her first husband. Lally looked down on men, but very tolerantly. She always knew that she had in her own pocket everything she needed to get what she wanted when she wanted it. She had no great yen at that moment to travel to remote and romantic spots. And if the yen took her, why off she could go.

"I guess you can't get where Hugh's got without sweating it out" was my only comment. "It'll probably be worse before it's better."

My words were prophetic. It got a lot worse. The Aldermeyer chain was gearing itself up to acquire Supermedia, and a bitter proxy battle loomed. I am not going to go into the details; several clever and biting articles have already appeared in financial journals. Suffice it to say that the take-over was successful, and that the victorious Aldermeyers provided for Hugh Orrick, secretary, treasurer and first vice president of Supermedia, the most golden parachute that their counsel could conceive and still get away with.

Arvis Grantley, although equally enriched in defeat, was savagely bitter. In an interview with the *Wall Street Journal* he stated:

"There is no question that Hugh Orrick played the role of the Trojan horse in this whole affair. That the merger will cost Supermedia hundreds of jobs and destroy the life work of the man he had the treachery to call his friend is a matter of complete indifference to him. Nothing matters to Orrick but the buck, and the fastest buck is the best one. We are told that the day of the WASP is over. Hugh Orrick makes one wish that were true."

Hugh, in his inimitable fashion, was simply amused by this outburst.

"Observe how people always talk ethics after they've just lost a round," he told me. "Grantley was not always so prone to sermonize. He and his kind are always yammering for a free market, but when they get one, they don't like it. If the price of your stock dips below your book value, people are going to buy it. Isn't that the capitalistic system in a nutshell? Very well. If that makes it too hot for you, stay out of the kitchen. Business has never been ruled by sentiment. What I like about the times we live in is that people, smart people, anyway, are more honest about what they have to do. We've given up the cant which in the old days allowed a Rockefeller or a Daniel Drew to rob you while he shook a Bible under your nose!"

Hugh has now reached what I suppose (or at least hope) will be his zenith. The new media giant that he has put together has filled the newsstands and supermarket checkouts and silver screens with the trash that he claims people want and will always get. And so long as they are bound to get it, he insists, isn't it better that the profit should go to Hugh Orrick, who collects the finest French eighteenth-century art and furniture, which he will ultimately bequeath to the great art institute of which he is a valued trustee, rather than to some untutored barbarian who won't know what to do with his money except cram it into a foundation for some silly cause like the elimination of diseases which are nature's answer to overpopulation?

❀   ❀   ❀

I was wrong about the graduating class not listening to Hugh. They not only listened to him; they warmly applauded. It was 1980; we were in the Reagan era. The national wounds of Viet Nam were somewhat healed; youth was no longer so angry. And Hugh showed all his charm: he told his audience right off that the best way to start in business was to inherit or to marry a controlling interest in one's corporate employer. He then related a series of funny stories about newspaper scoops that had outraged public opinion but that had later turned out to be absolutely true. He proceeded, on thinner ice but still amiably, virtually to identify libel and pornography with the exercise of rights guaranteed by the First Amendment. And he ended on a cozy note about a congenial lunch with the President and First Lady in which they swapped puns.

But his final announcement, which came as a shock to me, for I had missed the last meeting of the board, was that he had persuaded Arvis Grantley to become a trustee of the school.

"I thought Arvis hated your guts," I murmured in Hugh's ear in the cocktail period before the headmaster's lunch following the ceremonies.

"Ben, Ben, will you never learn about the world you live in? There are no permanent quarrels among real business-men. People lose their tempers, of course, but they get them back when it pays them to. After all, whatever was done to them is something that they almost certainly have done to others. And it's been one of the goals of Arvis's life to be on the board of a school like Chelton!"

As I had said earlier to the headmaster, the rest is silence.

The Golden Voice

NEW YORK PUBLIC LIBRARY ORAL HISTORY INTERVIEWS:
SEAMUS Mc LANAHAN, ATTORNEY; RETIRED SENIOR
PARTNER, MCLANAHAN, HAMPDEN & LLOYD; FORMER
DISTRICT ATTORNEY, MANHATTAN; FORMER U.S.
AMBASSADOR TO ITALY. TAPED JAN. 9, 1950.

WELL, I GUESS you're right, Mr. Jonas. If I don't do this
damn thing now that I'm eighty, I'll probably never do it. And
I suppose I should be grateful that you want me to do it at
all. A lawyer's life, however distinguished, like a singer's or
an actor's, is writ on water. How many remember, after a few
years, his passionate briefs, his golden oratory? And what is
this but a pleasant opportunity for me to carve a slightly
deeper niche for myself in legal history? Or a final brief for
Seamus McLanahan to argue that those most remembered
in law, the Maitlands and Blackstones and Marshalls and
Holmeses, are not necessarily the ones who have contributed most to its development. Note that I say development,
not progress. Progress is something I haven't had much
acquaintance with.

And then of course I love to declaim. Even to a recording
machine. I've always been a bit of an old ham; we litigators

have to be. This interview could be like one of Browning's dramatic monologues; I could be Bishop Blougram and you . . . what was his name? Mr. Gigadibs. Which part of my stretched-out life shall we start with? My obscure beginnings as the son of a Tammany judge of a less than fragrant reputation? And my stalwart determination to obliterate the family obloquy with a more reputable career? Or shall I tell of my early struggles at the bar as a negligence and criminal lawyer, capped by my brilliant success as a district attorney who caged the villains and made the streets safe, at least in the evening journals? Or leap at once to my ambassadorship and all the brilliant parties I and my late wife hosted in Rome for the moguls who later backed Mussolini? Or would it be safest to coast gently through the long, happy, sunlit years of my senior partnership on Wall Street, revered, nay even adored, as the grand old man of the bar and the champion of laissez faire economics? That last is what is most expected of me, isn't it?

No, you'd like to hear something of my failures? You don't really believe I *had* any failures? Well, Mr. Gigadibs, there you are wrong. You are terribly wrong. My whole life has been a failure, not a tragic failure, but a pathetic failure. And *that,* my friend, is the only thing worth talking about, and talk about it I shall.

The great and abiding ambition of my life was to be appointed to the United States Supreme Court, and the great and abiding irony of my life is that I was offered by President Harding (you needn't rise) the one thing that more than any other would have placed me in line for that goal. This was a seat on the circuit court of appeals for the second federal district, generally considered the number-two tribunal of our land. And I turned it down!

Why? I had just resigned, with the change of administration, as ambassador to Rome, where I had incurred some heavy debts. My late wife, God rest her soul, had had high standards of what our position there required, and her receptions had been the finest in the Eternal City. I was tremendously proud of her. She was a wonderful woman, Mr. Gigadibs; she had great looks and style; people turned in the street to see her pass. I have a snapshot I always keep on my desk that shows her standing in the center of a garden party group, her tall commanding figure in a sweeping white dress of a style most suited to her — 1912 or thereabouts — gazing down with her mild grave attentiveness at a shorter man addressing her. Looking at it, I can almost hear her responding to him and the tone of her voice: crisp, clear, sensible, to the point and yet humorous, understanding, kind. Nothing in her background had prepared her for diplomacy — she had been the adored and motherless only child of an old scholarly professor of Greek at Columbia — but she assumed the role of ambassadress as easily and naturally as if she had been born and bred in the chancelleries of Europe, and as she would later assume the role of the wife of a large law firm with social obligations in Manhattan and Long Island. She knew that all she needed was a sense of balance, a sense of humor and the application of her own shrewdness and intelligence to the problems of the immediate present.

As neither she nor I had any inherited money to speak of, it was necessary for me to draw up a plan of austere living to be able to pay off my debts on a judicial salary, if I was to accept the President's offer. Kate thought this impracticable. I was already being assailed with tempting offers from Wall Street law firms, and she pointed out with perfect reason that if I took one of these I should be able to clear up my obligations in four or five years' time.

"And what reason is there to suppose that you won't be offered another judgeship then?" she asked. "You'll be even more eligible after a few years of practice."

And so indeed it seemed.

But that was not the way it worked out. My old cousin, Pat Reilly, my closest friend and lifelong critic, told me that once I had accepted the senior partnership of Hampden & Lloyd (which promptly became McLanahan, Hampden & Lloyd) and started to rake in the big bucks, I would never leave the firm. "And if you should ever wish to," he warned me, "that fancy bride of yours will find plenty of airtight reasons to make you stay."

Well, this was not quite fair to Kate. She always made it perfectly clear to me that she was willing to give up the big house we bought in fashionable Westbury, Long Island, and our Park Avenue apartment and content herself with the smaller quarters consistent with judicial pay, or with a faculty cottage on any campus if I wanted to teach. It was true, of course, that she enjoyed the social life that my firm and its clients entailed: the big dinners of the international bankers, the parties at the Creek and Piping Rock clubs, and so forth, but so did I. And it's equally true that I loved running the big firm, which was easy to do, as I could delegate most of the administrative chores and play the benevolent despot, reserving my primary energy for the big cases, which I argued in appellate courts with a team of brilliant young men to do all the research.

It was fun, damn it all, great fun!

And it's delightful, as one ages, to find oneself turning into the grand old man of the organization, even of the downtown bar. Law firms were much smaller then; my own, one of the largest, had only twenty partners and perhaps three times that many associates. It was possible, even advantageous for one man to be in more or less complete control, to make the final decision as to who made partner and what percentage each partner should take. There was a definite esprit de corps to be drawn on, and a largely cheerful acquiescence, so long as the fees rolled in, to the need to run a "tight ship." It was said of me that my charm (yes, I'm bold enough to repeat the word), in addition to my prestige, oiled the rustiest wheels, that I could even tell an older partner that the time had come for his percentage to be reduced without embittering him. I remember a brash young clerk in a skit at the no-holds-barred annual firm dinner assuming the role of one such reduced partner and declaiming: "Mr. McLanahan put his arm around my shoulder and confided to me that the time had come for us old farts to take a cut. But when the smoke cleared I realized that only one old fart had taken a cut." Everyone roared, including myself. There was no bitterness. They all knew that my fees justified my large take, even in my seventies.

The only thing that troubled me was the evanescence of my work. What would remain of all the mellifluous and polished prose of my meticulously structured briefs, of the ringing oratory that I had poured forth to those black-garbed jurists in Albany, New York and Washington? It was all very well for my admirers to dub me the most winning of advocates before the appellate bench, but who in the future but the driest legal scholars or the most indefatigable of researching clerks would ever look up my briefs in the dusty files of the larger bar association libraries? My only hope of anything like a permanent contribution to the law would be if one of my phrases, or even a whole sentence or paragraph, happened to be culled by the young clerk of a justice and inserted in the opinion that he would write for his chief. On such clerks would the latter's fame depend! Is it for this that we litigators toil?

Of course, no other call to any bench came for me, let alone one to the supreme tribunal. In the period of sweeping challenge to the constitutionality of the major New Deal legislation in the 1930s, when the Supreme Court, with its conservative majority of five — made up of the consistent right-wingers McReynolds, Butler, Vandevanter and Sutherland, joined on occasion by Hughes, Stone or Roberts — was eviscerating the prospects of social change, it was my duty, in representing our great corporate clients, to take the side of the eviscerators. Obviously I had to support the proposition that the Fourteenth Amendment offered the same guarantees of liberty and property to a giant company that it did to a street beggar, that any agreement between that same giant and the humblest laborer was protected by freedom of contract, and that the commerce clause should be restricted to cover highways and toll bridges. I had great fun with these arguments and had some astounding successes, but the votaries of the New Deal, smarting no doubt from the latter and imbued with the fire of revolutionaries, labeled me as one of their most dangerous opponents, and my chances of *any* federal appointment were done away with until the election of Eisenhower, when I was too old to be considered.

Well, were they not right? Would I have been a good member of the sacred nine? Of course I would! It was wrongly assumed that my briefs represented my personal opinions. Though it is regrettably true that many attorneys, if they consistently represent a certain type of client, tend to adopt the political and economic creeds of that client, I happen to be that rare creature, a *true* lawyer: an argument is always just an argument to me. I am able to face each new case that comes up with an open mind. I had no bias in favor of the bankers of Wall Street or of the New Deal reformers. Indeed, I can see a great deal wrong with each. Remember, I was not born to wealth.

The question may be asked, How, had I been appointed, would I have decided the issues before me? By precedent? By a literal or broad construction of the phrases of the Constitution? By a sense of the general welfare? Or by mistily gazing into the subjectively imagined future of a noble democracy?

Well, I don't have to decide, because I haven't been appointed. But no one knows better than an old pleader before that court how justice after justice selects the particular role that he wishes to see himself immortalized as playing in the pageant of history and then cuts his opinions to fit that role. For the poor old Constitution can be twisted into any shape you want. The man who thinks it guarantees forever any right he deems himself to have is a dreamer. Have we not seen, only a few years back, a unanimous court allow the imprisonment without trial of thousands of American citizens, innocent even of any alleged crime or misdemeanor? And are there not legislators in this very day arguing that a man may be actually preferred over another because of his race or color? We may live to see torture restored for purposes of military intelligence. The public decides; the words are then construed. So it has always been.

I dare to make this claim for myself. I might have been the first justice of that court to take my seat without a preconceived notion of just what the Constitution should be.

❦   ❦   ❦

NEW YORK PUBLIC LIBRARY ORAL HISTORY INTERVIEWS.
SEAMUS Mc LANAHAN. TAPE 2.

After our first session, Mr. Jonas, you asked me a very troubling question. You asked me if I blamed my wife for not taking that court appointment back in 1922. You suggested that if she hadn't been quite so lavish as a party-giving ambassadress I mightn't have run into debt and could have afforded to take the proffered seat. I see what you're after. Before I agreed to make these tapes I looked you up, and I've even glanced over your little book on women's rights. I am aware of your thesis that brilliant women not only should but *must* have careers, if for no other reason than that, trapped in the home, they may use their creative energies on the wrong things. You give as examples some of the great hostesses of the old days who wasted their husbands' millions on marble palaces in Newport and gaudy entertainments.

But unlike those silly women, my Kate, whatever she did, did for my sake. Mesdames Astor and Vanderbilt were glad enough to let their sulking husbands go off on yachts for long cruises with drinking male friends so long as the money was left for them to spend on their balls and galas. Kate would never have given a party without me; she wanted each entertainment to add a gloss to my reputation as ambassador, or, later, as leader of a great firm. I used to believe that if she always seemed to be on the side of my taking the more lucrative or newsworthy position, it was because she sincerely believed that such was my true destiny, which lay rather before the footlights than in the dusty backstage area of judicial chambers or professorial cubbyholes.

But now, thanks to your impertinent question, I have been, since last week's taping, ruminating over the past, and I have had the humiliation of uncovering at least the possibility that my wife may have been motivated, not by her own vanity, as you have supposed, but by a conscientious effort to spare me a cruel disillusionment.

You look pained and surprised. But personal questions often bring out more than the questioner bargained for.

What has happened is that I've been to see my wife's oldest friend, Arabella Travers. I didn't want to go to see her, and now I wish to hell I hadn't. I've always detested her, and she me. But she knew Kate better than anyone else who's still living, and I had to put a question to her. She told me frankly that had I not come, I should not have learned what I did, that she had given her word to Kate never to reveal it and that only my urgent curiosity had released her from her vow. My curiosity, my hat! She was only too anxious to spill the beans! She positively scrambled to do so at the first excuse I offered her.

But I must first tell you about Arabella. She is one of those frustrated old-maid lesbians who has wanted all her life to put her tongue where the law won't allow it and has tried to make up for her enforced chastity with gluts of art and poetry and rather steamy friendships with handsome normal women who don't understand, or don't wish to understand, what is behind her lavishly offered affection and multiple gifts. For she is rich, Arabella; she can always offer you a seat in her Rolls-Royce, her opera box, her chartered plane. You can picture her, can't you? Big, stocky, with suit-like dresses and low-heeled pumps, hair short and straight, strong as an ox but always fussing about her health, walking with a cane she doesn't need, and forever calling attention to her needs, her whims and what she quite wrongly considers her "lovable" little foibles. A bear playing kitten.

The dream of her life, when Kate's first husband died, was that Kate might move in with her and share her home and wealth, and when I loomed up to frustrate her plan — though Kate would never have complied with it — she came to regard me as her private devil.

Of course, Arabella and I had to appear to get along. Kate made that clear early in our marriage.

"I quite see that you and Arabella are never going to be friends, and I shan't try to make you. We'll ask her to our larger parties, and I shall expect you to be civil. I'll see her in the daytime, for lunches or matinees, when you're working. I know that she can be trying, but you must recognize that she's been a part of my life since we were little girls. It's a kind of congeniality — a shared language if you like — that no new friend can ever quite give. Can you see that?"

Well, actually I could. My cousin Pat Reilly was like that, the one who told me I'd never quit my law firm.

And so it was that at five o'clock yesterday I found myself in Arabella's splendid dark-paneled Jacobean living room, filled with beautiful American colonial furniture (I concede her fine taste) but spoiled by the clutter of memorabilia covering every table and shelf, silver-framed photographs, figurines, cameos, medallions, odd bits of jade and gold, books, magazines, old theatre programs, everything.

"So you're going to 'do' Kate in your oral history?" she asked gruffly. "It's to be more than one of those masculine tributes: 'To the beloved partner of my life, my debt is too great to be put in words.'"

"Yes, that is why I'm here. To do more than that."

"Which is?"

"To express fully my debt to her. To put it in words. Isn't that what we lawyers do?"

"Ah, what you lawyers do!" Her eyes rolled upward. "But tell me. What precisely is it that you think you owe to Kate?"

"Well, my happiness, to begin with."

"*Were* you so happy?"

"I was, Arabella." I was beginning to be irritated.

"With your life or with your career?"

"With both. But in particular with my life. I came here to discuss what I owed in my life to Kate."

"You owed her the happiness of your life?"

"Just so."

"What about the happiness of your career?"

"Well that, presumably, I owed more to my own labors."

"And not to hers?"

"How could I owe her those?"

"How could you not?"

I was angry now and beginning not to care what I hit her with. "Well, since you put it that way, I'll say something that I wasn't planning to say."

"You mean we might really talk?"

"If that's what you want to call it. To put it right on the line, I'm not really sure — in fact, I've never been entirely sure — that Kate wasn't at least partly responsible for my failing to follow the line that might have led me to the court. The Supreme Court, I mean."

Arabella grew thoughtful. "And what did Kate prefer to that?"

"My forensic glory. If that doesn't sound too vain to you.

My reputation as an advocate, as a kind of grand old man of the bar. My position in Wall Street and in society." I knew I was probably making a mistake to go on, but the woman had provoked me. "And of course there was more money in that. Much more."

"And Kate cared about money?"

"She cared about some of the things money could buy. She cared about our position in the world. I don't mean that vulgarly."

"How *do* you mean it?"

"Kate wanted me to be a great man. She wanted people to look up to me. And a great man has to some extent to live like one. He can't bury himself away in a hovel. Kate was not averse to the trappings of high status."

"You mean she liked being an ambassadress? Flashing with diamonds as she received the great at the top of a marble stairway?"

Despite her sarcasm, I was struck by her picture. "Yes, in a way."

"And you didn't? The glory of the bench was enough for you?"

"No, no. I was just as bad. I loved the glitter as well as the gold. But my point is, was *that* the better side of my nature? Was it the side that Kate should have encouraged as she did?"

"But if it was the only side?"

I paused for a moment to regain control of my temper. If we were in for a real fight, I needed to be cool. "What exactly are you trying to tell me, Arabella?"

"Simply this." She looked at me so hard that I turned away. "Kate always knew that you weren't a legal philosopher. That your mind was not essentially a creative one. She saw that your forte was manipulation, that you could juggle with words and make them say anything you wanted. That you could be a great advocate or diplomat. But never a great judge. Never."

I breathed heavily. "You're saying that to put me down," I growled. "You've always hated me."

She didn't bother to deny this. She simply allowed her continued fixed stare to assert its irrelevance. "What Kate thought of you was not uncomplimentary. She didn't believe that you properly estimated your real gifts. She used to liken you to Tennyson. And you know how she admired *him*. Tennyson and Swinburne were her two favorite poets."

"All sweet mellifluousness," I commented bitterly. "And precious little thought content."

"They rated beauty over thought, it is true."

"And that was Kate's opinion of my briefs and oral arguments? That they were beautiful to read? To hear?"

"Well, isn't that enough?"

"Hell, no! They had to be full of thought to *win!* And you know how often I won, Arabella."

"You're not likely to let me forget. But I don't agree that even a winning brief has to be full of thought. Thought, as Kate and I always concurred, true thought, is designed to discover truth. A brief can be ingenious, subtle, imaginative, brilliant, but how often does it seek to discover truth? Indeed, its very function is more often the reverse."

And with that I abruptly quit the chamber and her abode. And I shall now take this occasion to end our taping session. I shall have to do a lot more thinking about what that wretched woman has told me. For if it be true — and I am still far from making that concession — perhaps my "Tennysonian" career had best, after all, be left to the dusty corners of bar association libraries.

Unless — oh, yes unless, and now it strikes me that I may have hit upon a saving grace — oh, yes indeed! — I decide to write a book on *how* to write a brief. A beautiful exposition, clear as crystal and studded with ample quotes from my finest arguments! Why not? Arabella may have shown me the very way to outwit her own spiteful evaluation!

Honoria and Attila

=========== ∽ ===========

WHEN I HAD RETIRED, at age seventy, in 1987 as editor of *Style,* the fashion magazine to which I had devoted the best years of my life and most if not all of my creative energy, I had thought I could rest, so to speak, on my laurels and wait until my husband, Dan, a few years my senior, should give up his status as "of counsel" to his law firm and join me in the cruise circuit. But I found it was generally expected that I should write my memoirs, and I even had two very tempting offers from distinguished publishers. I was put off, however, by the interest they showed in how I had converted what they saw as a privileged or elitist background into the basis for a practical success in the world of the fifties and sixties. It seemed to me that to these editors I was of interest only as the specimen of an endangered species surviving in a zoo, or to use an ugly modern neologism, a wildlife conservation society.

"What does this term WASP really mean?" I asked Dan irritably. "I know it used to stand for White Anglo-Saxon Protestant. But now it seems to be expanded to cover Scots, Germans, Scandinavians, and even, since the Kennedys, Irish Catholics. Why do people keep harping on these archaic distinctions?"

It gave Dan the chance to embroider on his favorite

theme: ethnicity. He liked to maintain that ideologies and religion were obsolete, that the only imperatives left in our moral code were: Be proud of your racial origin, and don't knock other people's.

"People dread being lost in a common mould. Which is what is happening, all over the planet. So they cling to their fast-disappearing ethnic characteristics. You can't beat it, Alix. It's not *what* you are, it's *who* you are. Write your story as the last of the w a s p s. Yours and Kitty's. Wasn't that what you made of *her,* and of your magazine; the last glorious sunset of an era?"

"No!"

"Then *say* it was! And you'll have a bestseller."

Well, I wasn't going to do *that,* but it did occur to me that I might write down, perhaps for the ultimate edification of her children, the story of my beautiful and glamorous sister, now twenty years gone, the victim of a ravaging disease that destroyed her looks, her spirit and even in the end her courage. That destroyed everything, indeed, but my enduring love for her.

   ❧   ❧   ❧

My maiden name, Alexandra Schuyler Whelan, has certainly a w a s p ish ring. The Whelans may have come over from Ireland in the eighteenth century, but it was from northern Ireland, then essentially a Scottish community. In 1917, the year of my birth, all the traceable members of the clan lived in or around New York, and all were not only listed in the Social Register but had been since its inception. My paternal grandfather, a banker, had committed suicide when he was ruined in the Panic of 1907, but this was considered a respectable finale, particularly if others were involved in his ruin. My father was a fashionable portrait painter who "did" the people who couldn't afford Sargent or who couldn't persuade Sargent to paint them, even if they travelled to London to do so. Oh, yes, we were what the French called *bien*, very *bien*.

Some of us think of a particular period in our lives as the "real" or "true" time, though it was not necessarily the happiest or the most eventful, and for me this was the year 1937. It might have been because it was my debutante year, or it might have been because it hovered, a last bit of seeming peacefulness, between our emergence from the Great Depression and the outbreak of war in Europe. Anyway, when I think of Mother, a then paramount influence in our lives, I see her as she was in that year: in her middle fifties, tall, strong in bone and muscle, but very thin, very pale, with a swishing, high-heeled stride, raven-haired (not dyed), with black darting eyes and large handsome features. She was an arresting figure and took full advantage of it, always ready to pit herself against another person, male or female, her equal or her inferior (she would admit to none higher), and ready to play the game according to the rules or with brass knuckles, as one chose.

Born of an ancient but impoverished Hudson River family, Mother had used her striking looks and dominant personality to capture Calvin Tracy, heir to a vast western mining fortune, and had been a great hostess in the second decade of our century, entertaining famously in her great Stanford White mansions in New York and Long Island. But Mr. Tracy, whose natural pomposity and self-importance were swelled by the illusion, common to the sons of tycoons, that his money was the mark of his own genius, eventually bored her to frenzy, and she deserted him without a scruple for the charming Howard Whelan.

In taking this step, Mother magnificently scorned the mores of "Old New York," abandoning her claim not only to the Tracy millions but to her Tracy children, clasped to the bosom of their outraged sire. It is true that Mr. Tracy had settled something on her at their marriage, and with this and Father's commissions for portraits, she did well enough for a while, but the Depression and Father's leaving her for a young woman of twenty (Mother was as irate as if she herself had never broken a marriage vow) and the rearing of myself and Kitty put a heavy strain on her resources. Somehow or other, however, she always managed to keep up a brave show, and by 1937 she had rehabilitated herself socially so well that only a handful of old dowagers still refused to receive her, and their disapproval was more a source of ridicule than of any real concern. Mother acted as if time had to be on her side, which may have been the reason it so often was.

If it was not equally on the side of the more structured society in which she had been raised, that never bothered her. She knew how to use to good advantage the bits and patches that were left of it, and any deluge that might follow her own demise was of no more interest to her than it had been to Louis the Well Beloved. She scorned people who did not know how to use every honor card in their hand to maximum advantage. "We're nothing but patchwork quilts," she used to tell Kitty and me. "A bit of looks, if we're lucky, a bit of style, of lineage, of nerves and gall, of useful connections — or at least connections that can be made to look useful — of a nose for survival, of an eye to look the world in the face and damn its impudence. I cannot stand people who are always bowing their sheepish heads to what they call the wave of the future. They're like the idiots who blubber about wanting to be loved for themselves and not for some rag of an asset they're lucky enough to have purloined from the past."

She always treated us girls as adults. If we said anything that offended her, she would make no allowance for our tender years, but strike back as if she had been attacked by a contemporary. Yet I think we both knew that she was basically on our side in the rough game of life; it was certainly she who convinced us that it would be rough. My size and awkwardness discouraged her, though she enjoyed my toughness in argument; she maintained that she could "make" something of my personality, even in a ballroom, by establishing me as a "character." But Kitty, of course, was her ace of trumps.

❀   ❀   ❀

The portrait photograph of myself and Kitty, taken by the fashionable camera artist Ira Hill and published by the *Herald Tribune* in the account of our joint coming-out party at the Park Lane Hotel, expresses for me nostalgically our shared hopes for the future, already tinged with a dim distrust, a vague apprehension. I am shown seated (because of my height), in profile, my hands clasped in my lap, looking straight ahead with an air of seemingly passive resignation. Kitty, the beauty, is standing over me, looking down at my head, one hand resting on my shoulder. We are both in white, with corsages of white chrysanthemums, our thick dark hair perfectly waved. We are debutantes — that is obvious enough — and we accept the business of being debutantes — oh, yes. There is no rebellion in the picture, only a subdued atmosphere of acquiescence. We might be members of the chorus of a Greek tragedy.

That Kitty is standing, so that she dominates the picture,

was surely the intent of the photographer. As I say, she was the beauty, the *real* debutante, with those clear, gazing grey eyes, those perfectly oval cheeks, that high, pale "priestess's" brow giving her an air of noble impassivity. In contrast, I am too big, too heavy, with features that might have been handsome enough if more delicately sculpted. My debutante year had been postponed until Kitty's in the following, as Mother maintained that she couldn't afford two big dances. And I was willing to have it so, entirely content to be a shadow, if a rather hefty one, in Kitty's limelight. Sitting there in that picture, I might be the confidante of the heroine in a French classic tragedy, a solid Oenone to a rashly confiding Phèdre.

Kitty had always seen her coming-out year as the culmination of our upbringing and education, as the moment when she was expected to burst, in dazzling colors, from her crysalis, and she had prepared for it with a certain deliberation, but without any noticeable enthusiasm. If she didn't seem to consider it of prime importance, it was always clear to me that she didn't hold anything else to be more so. At Miss Polhemus's Classes, as our school was somewhat primly known, where she and I were a grade apart, we were obliged to wear the ugly school uniform — green blouses and bloomers, and black stockings — four days in the week, but on Fridays we were allowed to dress as we chose. Kitty would seize the occasion to sweep into class like a movie star, having helped herself generously from Mother's copious wardrobe. Her weekly performance almost induced Miss Polhemus to abort the privilege.

One of the reasons I loved Kitty so dearly was that she never considered that her advantage in looks, or in popularity with boys, gave her any reason to feel my superior. I was the only person, she always maintained, with whom she could really talk. We two were a family within a family; Mother and our Tracy demi-siblings, though important, were on a different plane. And Father, after his and Mother's divorce, was rarely there. Though the elder, I was the less sophisticated, and much less cynical than Kitty, who was always making remarks such as: "Oh, Alix, can't you *see* what an ass So-and-So really is?" But she gave me the feeling that I cherished above everything else: that she and I shared a world between us that had little to do with other, perhaps illusory existences. You might almost have called us a pair of solipsists.

But not entirely. Oh, no. There was an exception so important that it became in time almost the rule. The first and greatest thing that Kitty did not share with me was Ted Shaughnessy. What happened with Ted happened in a Bar Harbor summer, on Mount Desert Island in Maine, when Kitty was sixteen.

Mother used to rent a large shingle villa at the end of a little wooded peninsula just outside the village which faced the charming little islands called the Porcupines. There she launched us solidly in the summer colony society with rather wonderful children's parties on the lawn, with potato races and little silver cups as prizes and a trickman who made the girls scream by taking rubber spiders out of their ears. Mother differed from some of the more conservative parents by including the children of the new rich (particularly of the new *very* rich), who came to Bar Harbor in the hope of cultivating families whose doors were closed to them in Boston and Philadelphia and New York but whom the more relaxed atmosphere of summer and the easy commingling of their young might make more hospitable.

Mother made a good thing of her availability to the "Ostrogoths," as she privately called them. While not quite so directly mercenary as the duchess in *The Gondoliers* who charged five guineas for attending a "middle-class party," she obtained plenty of yachting excursions, tickets to charity galas, valuable market tips and winter bids to luxurious southern resorts while we children were included in all the expensive dances and sports held in the lavish estates of the new people.

Mother's particular protégé was the richest of them all, Patrick Shaughnessy, a Boston Irish textile manufacturer who had competed successfully with Lowells and Lawrences in their own field and now occupied a great Italianate villa and a garage filled with fancy European cars. He had a silent, moody, rather stupid but quite handsome son, Teddy, just eighteen, for whom he had no end of ambitious plans that the unhappy lad was obviously not qualified to fulfill. Teddy was too shy and awkward to be very popular with the younger set, but as the estate boasted a steam yacht, a couple of sailboats, a well-equipped gymnasium, a tennis court and a mammoth swimming pool, they all ran like mice to it whenever invited, and frequently when not.

Kitty made an immediate conquest of the son and heir. He followed her about like a poodle. But she professed a low opinion of him.

"I suspect he's one of those guys with nothing above the waist," she told me crudely. Kitty could be very crude when we were alone together. "But of course we're all tied up in this elaborate mating ritual. Really, we're no better than a savage tribe. Worse, actually, for at least the savage tribe makes no bones about it."

"And Teddy's old man, I suppose, is the chief."

"Well, he'd like to think so, but he's not there yet. And he's got his sights fixed on something a lot grander than Kitty Whelan. Besides, it's far too early, not only socially but time-wise. Teddy-boy must finish college and maybe law school — if they can buy him into one — before he can even think of a squaw. And by then his papa may be ready for a Cabot or a Lowell."

"Well, I guess they can be bought, too," I said with a sniff. It was 1935, and we were still climbing out of the Depression. "But if you ever wanted him, which I gather you don't, I think we could bet on Mother to bring his old man around."

"These people are not dumb, you know, Alix. I mean the ones who've made the dough, not their callow kids. They can be had by someone as shrewd as Mother, but not for long. I think old Shaughnessy is already on to her. He sees that her social position is not quite the dizzy altitude he at first imagined. There's the old scandal of her first divorce and the gossip of all she does to make ends meet. No, you watch. He'll drop her in time."

"He wouldn't dare." I could hardly repress a little shudder at the prospect of Mother really aroused. "Don't you think he's just a bit scared of her?"

"Like you?"

"And you too, dear."

"I *am* scared of Mother," Kitty replied thoughtfully. "Because she doesn't believe in anything."

"What do you mean, in anything?"

"Oh, in God. Or right or wrong. Or love. Or even hate. She believes in satisfactions, I suppose. She certainly looks for them."

"But she goes to church."

"To see and be seen. She sweeps into her pew and bows her head in prayer like the leading lady in a play making her first entrance. I had a dream the other night that I had died and was all alone in an empty room. And I heard Mother's voice saying that in another minute I should be erased, nothing, zilch. And then she laughed. But it wasn't a mean laugh. I knew that she expected the same fate."

"And then what happened?"

"I woke up."

"And you weren't scared?"

"Horribly."

Kitty continued to be haunted by Ted Shaughnessy at parties, at the swimming club, in the village, everywhere, and at last she came around to a seeming toleration of him. She accepted his expensive presents, went sailing with him and let him come to the house pretty much when he wanted. Her only explanation to me for her change in attitude was that he was useful: he had tickets for everything that happened on the island and provided elegant transportation to any part of it to which she expressed any desire to go. Besides, he kept off the swarm of importunate admirers.

And he was pleasant enough, if not very interesting; his temper was equable. I suspect he resembled his mother in character, but Bar Harbor didn't see much of that dark, dim little lady who was supposed to be too ailing to be included in the parties given by her large, flamboyant, noisy mate who was known to keep a mistress in a camp across the island in Pretty Marsh. When Mr. Shaughnessy came to one of Mother's dinners, it was always alone.

And then came the terrible night when Ted took Kitty to the movies at the Star Theatre in Bar Harbor and didn't bring her home. At midnight Mother called the Shaughnessys; they were not there. At six in the morning she and I drove to the Italianate villa, where Ted's father had already summoned the police.

The guilty couple were discovered that same day in a cheap hotel in Bangor, where they had spent the night in the same room. They had taken little pains to disguise their escapade and returned meekly to their respective abodes. Mr. Shaughnessy contributed a considerable sum to the police welfare fund in the hope of stemming loose talk, and he and Mother spread the word that Ted and Kitty had spent the night at the Shaughnessy camp on the mainland, where they had been properly chaperoned by a maiden aunt who spent her summers there, preferring the woods to the social life of the island. There was gossip, of course, but Mother and Mr. Shaughnessy were a fairly formidable combination, and the matter died away. Think what a bagatelle it would be considered today! But for a sixteen-year-old girl of such a family as ours to lose her virginity under such circumstances could have been fatal to her reputation in 1935.

Kitty offered Mother no excuses or apologies; she maintained a sullen silence under the terrible harangue to which Mother subjected her in my presence.

"You can be a slut if you want, but not in my house or on my money. You must learn once and for all that the good things of this world — and there are such — are to be had only by observing certain rules, however arbitrary those rules strike you. I'm not going to waste my time justifying those rules. It must be enough for you that they exist. Maybe one day you'll achieve a status where you can ignore them, but that day is a long way off, my girl. So don't come to me yapping about how Mrs. X has done this and Mrs. Y that, and nobody cares. You're not Mrs. X or Mrs. Y. You're a sixteen-year-old girl who would be known from one end of this island to the other — if I hadn't lied in my teeth to save you — as a tramp whom every respectable mother would go to any lengths to save her son from. So remember that! I've bailed you out once, but I shan't do it again!"

Shrewd as always, Mother exacted no response. She had

delivered her threat, and she never repeated it. Thereafter she treated Kitty exactly as before. It was most effective.

But Kitty had a strange reaction to Mother's warning. Once alone with me, she emerged from her sullen stupor; she was suddenly angry, angry as if she had been cruelly misjudged.

"She's so cold, Alix! She doesn't feel anything at all. If she'd tell me I was wicked, perhaps I could see it. Perhaps I could even understand it. But in her world there are no rights or wrongs. There are only rules, senseless rigid rules. And if you break one of them, you're dead. It's like those Mayan games the guide told us about when we were down in Yucatán, do you remember? Where they drowned the losing team? And the terrible thing is that she's probably right. That *is* the way the world is."

"Mother ought to be more understanding about love," I suggested. "It's not as if she hadn't had her own experiences."

"What has love got to do with it?"

"Well, aren't you in love with Teddy?"

"Oh, Alix, dear, you can be such a goose. Of course I'm not in love with Teddy. How could I love someone as dumb as Teddy? But he's rather a dear, and he wanted us to elope and get married in some state where we didn't need permission, but I knew his father would never forgive him, and I didn't want to anyway, but he'd done so much for me, given me presents and all that, and he said he'd die if he couldn't have a night with me, and really it meant so much to him and so little to me . . ."

"So little to you, dear?" I interrupted reproachfully.

"Yes, so little," she affirmed defiantly. "You don't know anything about these things, Alix."

I sighed. "And I guess I'm glad I don't."

Kitty became thoughtful. "And I guess I'll have to learn to adapt myself to Mother's world. If it's the only one there is."

"It may not be as hard as you think."

And it wasn't. Kitty was soon enough a great success.

What Mother never told anyone, but which I found out from her years later, in her loquacious last illness, was that she had extracted a large sum of money from Mr. Shaughnessy. She had not had to be so crude as to hint that his son might be prosecuted for seducing a minor. She had only to intimate that a spanking big debutante party might go a long way to drown any ugly rumors about the Bangor caper, and Teddy's father was only too happy to underwrite the expenses of Kitty's and my debut, and indeed the whole cost of our debutante year.

Teddy was sent out west for the rest of the summer, nor was he ever allowed to set foot on Mount Desert Island again while the Whelans were in residence there. How he would have fared in the afterlife we were never to know, as he enlisted in the Marine Corps in the war and perished on Iwo Jima.

The planning of my and Kitty's coming-out party was typical of Mother's approach to life. I had not wanted to come out at all and had persuaded Mother to stake me to Barnard College only by agreeing to live at home and not in a dormitory (she was always afraid of my becoming a *bas bleu*) and by agreeing to share a party with Kitty, which would reduce expenses. It meant that I would be a year older than the other debutantes, but that made little difference. As Mother put it:

"You mustn't allow yourself to get too different from the class you were born in. You don't want people to think you're a freak. Being a debutante is an experience expected of you. It won't do much for you, but not doing it might be worse.

For Kitty, it will be essential to the success her looks are apt to bring her. You will share some of her reflected glory. Make of it what you will."

Kitty and I had what was considered one of the more brilliant parties of the season, and she became the debutante most in view. To say that she relished her success might be going too far, but she certainly accepted it as her seeming due, and Mother was unfeignedly pleased. Kitty, of course, had many beaux, but she took none of them too seriously; she gained the reputation of being charming but cool. Mother claimed that this was a sure preliminary to a great match.

"A man likes to feel that he may be the one to light the flame," she told me. She always talked to me as though I were her contemporary; she assumed that my size and bookish interests had exempted me from girlish frailties. "And a cool demeanor signifies to him a pure heart. Or at least an untouched one. So he can have the satisfaction of believing himself the first, the conqueror."

"Mother, do you think *all* men are fools?"

"No, but enough are."

I had tried to persuade Kitty to do something with her mind and had induced her to audit one of my courses at Barnard, on the English poets, but her attention soon faded, and she gave it up. Her only serious concentration was on clothes, which she chose with an expert eye and wore with the style of a professional model. When I complained to Mother that her mind was too good to be wasted on such things, she reproved me. "As long as she's doing something really well, why worry? The next thing she does may be more important. Sloppiness is what I object to. Speaking of which, Alix, may I point out that your slip is showing?"

The year following our debut saw the beginning of the

war in Europe, which, while it did not at first much alter the routine of our lives, did put a question mark over the future of our men friends. They were already applying for commissions or going off to training camps, and the feeling among some of us girls, particularly in Kitty's faster group, was that if one was going to catch the right man, now was the time to grab him. If they were all to be off fighting, it might be better to have an absent husband than none at all.

It was in such a mood, I believe, that Kitty entertained the attentions of Oswald Carey. The Careys were rich — not like the Shaughnessys, but buttressed by venerable trust funds — and they lived on a rolling spread of verdant acres in Westbury, with a farm and stables and a beautiful rambling old white manor house. Oswald and his three brothers played polo at Meadowbrook and were squash champions at the Raquet Club in New York. Their father had made a minor name for himself as an explorer of African jungles, and he and his lovely, graceful wife, skilled equestrians, never missed a fox hunt. They were the kind of people who thought they were democratic because they were down-to-earth and outspoken and disdained the tinselly ostentation of Newport and the vulgar new wealth of the Hamptons. But their north shore society was still a closed one, as the money couldn't be too recent, the muscles had to be strong and the language purged of any affectation. To be "fancy pants" was to be beyond the pale. That they and their friends were "real people" was their only faith.

Oswald had the charm of ruddy good looks, a cheerful temper and the desire to please and be pleased. He was certainly not intellectual, or even particularly bright, but he made up for this with his candor, his honesty and the kind of good manners that can only come from the heart. He worked in a brokerage house, but he made no secret of the fact that he lived for his weekends in the country, and one was sure that with his first substantial inheritance he would chuck all gainful employment and devote himself to farming and rural life. And do it well, too.

Oh, yes, you can see that I would have fallen for Oswald, given half a chance. But that I never had. I was only Kitty's sister from the beginning, and he danced with me at parties in order to talk about her. But unlike other blind lovers, he made a point of trying to entertain me; he would get me to talk about myself and my interests, as if he really cared. Perhaps he did. He was nice enough to.

It bothered me that he tended to regard Kitty as a kind of goddess. I didn't want him to put her on a pedestal that she might fall off.

"I hope you don't think I'm downgrading my darling sister when I point out that she's made of flesh and blood."

"But do you think she could ever really go for an ordinary guy like me? Am I just eating my heart out and wasting my time? Be frank with me, Alix. It's only kind."

"And why shouldn't Kitty like you? I'm not saying she does, mind you. But I'm sure plenty of girls regard you as rather a catch."

"Kitty's not 'plenty of girls.'"

"But she's not that different, Oswald!"

Of course, I could see what was troubling him. Did Kitty's difference from other debutantes mean that she had no heart? I knew that she had one, and a very warm one, but I did *not* know that she had one for a lover. She had been willing to give up the whole idea of a lavish debutante ball if Mother would have spent the money on sending *me* to pursue culture in Europe. And when our half-brother had suffered a nervous breakdown and left college, it had been the thirteen-year-old Kitty who spent her weekend afternoons with him and helped to shake him out of it. It was Kitty in Maine who always fed the dogs and let them sleep in her bed when they were sick. But it was also Kitty who accepted her forced parting with Teddy Shaughnessy without a visible sigh or uttered protest. It sometimes seemed to me that she could have tossed away her very life, in Emily Dickinson's phrase, "like a rind."

There was someone else who shared my doubts about my sister, though she did not share my love for her, and that was Oswald's mother. Cornelia Carey was revered by her husband and four sons, although — or perhaps because — she appeared to be made of finer material than they. It was not that she was unathletic; as I have said, she rode to hounds and was a graceful figure skater. But where they were inclined to be bulky, she was elegantly slender, smoothly coordinated, with a noble straight nose slanting from a high brow, like the busts of Queen Nefertiti. She wore on her left wrist a jangling bracelet of miniature squash raquets studded with tiny rubies, each the championship token of a triumphant son. Mother used to say that bracelet was the envy of every social climber on Long Island. It marked an inaccessible peak.

Mrs. Carey, however, had none of the easygoing give-and-take of the males of her family. Though her manner was soft and reserved and coolly polite, it covered a force of steel. She was not called Cornelia in vain; the domestic Lares and Penates were hers to guard, and guard them she would, with her life. Had she married a politician or a financier, her values might have been different, but married to a sportsman and explorer, she had adopted his values unquestioningly, accompanying him to arctic climes and tropical jungles and centering her social life in hunting, golfing and fishing circles. So long as her sons had enough money to support their sporting interests, enhanced modestly by ten-to-five jobs in city banks or brokerage houses, and so long as they had beautiful, loyal wives and little boys or even girls to throw balls at, and so long as they enjoyed the robust Carey health, she asked for nothing more. The gods were smiling. But she kept her eyes on Olympus. She knew how quickly it all could change.

She looked askance at Kitty from the first, and she did me the dubious honor of confiding her doubts to me. It was Oswald who had told her that I was a person with whom one could be entirely frank without fear of betrayal, and I can see now that she had really nowhere else to turn. Her husband and other sons were sympathetic with Oswald's passion; they had no subtleties in their evaluation of women, and Mrs. Carey knew Mother well enough to see that the welfare of a son-in-law would hardly be a factor in the acquisition of an eligible spouse for a daughter. And so she called me one morning and asked me if I would join her for lunch at the Colony Club. It was like her, I reflected later, to make no secret of our conference, even if, observed by a common acquaintance and related to Kitty or Mother, it could be interpreted as bearing on matters from which they had been deliberately excluded.

It was like her, too, to put all her cards on the table.

"Does your sister want to marry Oswald? Because if she does, she certainly can. I've never seen one of my boys so possessed."

I had steeled myself for something; I didn't know what. Anyway, I rose to the challenge.

"Let him propose to her then, and we'll find the answer to your question."

"We'll find if she wants to, yes. But will we find out why?"

"Wouldn't it be because she's in love?"

"But would it? Your sister strikes me as a cool personality. I don't say that's a bad thing. But does it go with a warm one like Oswald's?"

"Cool people can become very passionate."

"All the more reason not to marry until they are."

"Why do you think Kitty would marry a man she didn't love?"

"Oh, come now, Alexandra, you're not being frank with me. Surely you know that lots of girls marry simply not to be unmarried. Or to get away from their families. Or because they're bored. Your mother must be a very strong presence in the home."

"You don't like Mother, I know." I was becoming defensive.

"I think it's more a matter of her not liking me. And I'm not sure that she and I wouldn't agree about Oswald and Kitty. I think your mother may hope that Kitty's place will be in the 'great' world. With people who run things. My Oswald's never going to be one of those. He's going to go 'downtown' as little as he possibly can, and he'll certainly never run anything but a polo team or a country club. But he'll be a pillar of the local community and a loving husband and father. *Provided* his wife is happy."

"I can only think you underestimate Kitty."

"Or overestimate her. Look, Alexandra. If you will try to convince your sister that Oswald may not be the right man for her — and I wouldn't have gone this far if I didn't suspect that you agree with me — I will undertake to get hold of Oswald and somehow induce him to swallow his disappointment."

"Oh, Mrs. Carey, I couldn't possibly do that!"

And I couldn't. Besides, it was already too late. Two days after our talk, Kitty came to my room early one morning to tell me that she and Oswald were engaged. She was very cool, very much in command of herself. It was obvious that our little scene had been rehearsed.

"I know just what you are going to ask me," she said immediately after imparting her news. "So ask it now, and you and I can get it over with and never have to discuss it again. Ask me if I'm in love with Oswald, or is it Teddy Shaughnessy all over again."

I met her stare resolutely and asked the question just as she had put it. She nodded.

"I don't suppose I'm quite in love with Oswald in your romantic sense of the word. But I think we'll rub along together well enough. He's a sensual man, and I'm not nearly as cool as some people think. *That* part of the marriage should be all right. And if I'm occasionally bored with the rest of it, I shan't be any more bored than I am with life as it is."

"Oh, Kitty, darling, wait, please wait! You'll find something better. I don't mean just a better man — for I think highly of Oswald — but a better life. I *know* you will. Dear sister, you have so many gifts!"

"But there's something else. Something you don't know, Alix. A darker side, if we wish to be dramatic. Ever since I made up my mind to live by Mother's little rules — I shouldn't call them Mother's — I mean *the* rules — I've been haunted by a certain low attraction to those who don't. You know what I mean. The losing team."

I recalled her old analogy. "You mean the ones the Mayans used to drown?"

"Just so. Except now we're less merciful. We leave them to flounder. To put it bluntly, I have found myself drawn to some very *louche* types."

"*Louche* in what way?"

"In every way. Socially, morally, even physically. I've decided it may be a good idea to remove myself from temptation. I've shown that I could turn myself into a perfect debutante. Maybe I can now turn myself into the perfect society wife."

I didn't know what to say. The poor darling appalled me. "At any rate, Mother will be pleased," I muttered.

"In a pig's eye! She just told me I could do much better than the Careys! Isn't that like her?"

Kitty's acceptance of Oswald and the almost immediate public announcement of their engagement was hailed as the most romantic of matches by all their friends, and a speedy wedding was planned. It appeared that a small but charming Federal house was available near the Careys' estate, and Oswald's father snapped it up for them as soon as Kitty had given her approval. It was evident that the young Oswald Careys were going to be the darlings of north shore society.

And so indeed did their married life start out. The first two years seemed idyllic. Even Mrs. Carey appeared to be satisfied; she and I, at any rate, had no further meetings like the one at the Colony Club. Kitty's pretty likeness, stylishly garbed, appeared regularly in fashion magazines, including *Style,* where I was already working; Oswald beamed contentedly when he was not on a horse or hitting a ball, and in due time a dear little girl was born to them, named Alix, for her aunt. And Kitty on the whole seemed at ease. Apparently satisfied with her amiable spouse, she was never a threat to the young matrons of her circle, who accepted her gratefully. Only Oswald himself seemed to sense that all might not be as well as it appeared. Taking me aside at one of their parties, he confessed his concern.

"You know, Alix, I sometimes think Kitty hasn't enough to do. The nurse takes care of little Alix, and the cook doesn't relish any interference in her kitchen. I have to keep in practice on weekends for the squash championship, and sometimes, when I get home, I find Kitty just sitting in the living room, staring out the window. Not even reading a book. Didn't she used to read a lot? Hasn't she as big a bean as you, old girl?"

"Or bigger."

"Well, there you are. Can't you get her to use it?"

"What would you suggest?"

"Oh, hell, how should I know?" His handsome brow puckered at the cloudy prospect of female things. "Don't you belong to a book class in town? Couldn't you get her to join it?"

I laughed. "Oh, she thinks we're much too dowdy. There must be some charity work down here. I'll talk to her."

But when I next lunched with Kitty on one of her frequent shopping trips to the city, I failed to educe any enthusiasm.

"Oh, those female committees," she retorted. *"Don't!"*

We were in 1941, and England was fighting for her life. I was suddenly irked by her lassitude. "How about Bundles for Britain? They need people there."

"Oh, they're all too shrill. I can't abide women a thousand miles from the smallest danger clashing their shields like Valkyries. Why can't you leave me alone in my doll's house?"

I pounced on the reference. "Is *that* what you call it? Do you consider yourself an Ibsen heroine?"

"Well, aren't I?"

"No! Because there was no way that Nora could get out of her doll's house unless she stayed out for good. Whereas you can come and go as you please, slamming doors that *aren't* heard all over Europe. Why, your own husband thinks you should do something more with your spare time."

"Does he? Perhaps I should take up squash. Or even polo."

"Kitty, be serious."

"Oh, don't ask me to be *that*. You might be sorry."

What did she mean? She refused to enlighten me. It was not for another year that I plumbed the full depths of her discontent.

By then, of course, we were in the war, and Oswald, who had a reserve naval commission, had been promptly called up and was off in the Atlantic on convoy duty as the executive officer of a sub chaser. Even Kitty now agreed to do some war work, and she moved with the baby to Mother's apartment in town, where she served as a hostess at an officers' club. I had become a Wave, and worked in naval headquarters at 90 Church Street as assistant to an old admiral in personnel. My hours were long, and I saw Kitty rarely (I had my own apartment now), but I gathered from Mother that she considered her duties to include the accompanying of officers on leave to nightclubs. Neither of us quite liked this, but Kitty, the matron, did not relish advice from her family.

One morning I was told that a Mrs. Carey was in the reception hall asking to see me. I walked out to find Kitty's mother-in-law, an odd figure among the many waiting military figures.

"I wouldn't have come if it wasn't important," she told me, rising quickly. "Where can we talk? I'll make it as brief as possible."

It was noon, so I took her to the cafeteria, where we sat in a far corner. Mrs. Carey refused even coffee; she sat up stiffly as she talked, enunciating her words as if she had memorized them.

"You must act immediately. Your sister is having an affair

with an Argentine naval officer. You needn't ask me how I know. I *know.* I was warned by a friend of Oswald's who had seen them at a nightclub, and I hired a detective. Enough said. You must tell her to break it off at once. On that condition I won't inform my son. I need not tell you that only my feeling for *him* controls my sense of outrage."

"Mrs. Carey, I can only hope and pray . . ."

"That I'm mistaken. Of course you do. It can't be agreeable to have a sister who betrays a man risking his life for his country with an oily Latin American neutral. I know that you and your sister have nothing but blood in common. That is why I can trust you to act. And you and Oswald have the bond of being fellow officers. Would to God he had married you!"

And without allowing me to say another word, she rose and left the cafeteria. Her hatred of Kitty was so intense that uttering that brief speech had probably made her ill.

Mother was out when I went to the apartment that night, and I had the luck to find Kitty alone. She seemed at once to know what I had come for, for she rose to mix herself a stiff drink and then settled resolutely back on the sofa to hear me.

"Of course, she's had me followed, the old cat," she said coldly when I had related my brief altercation with her mother-in-law. "I knew she'd been snooping around."

"But is it true?"

"Oh, it's true enough. I know what you're going to say. How could I? With Oswald braving the storms of the North Atlantic and the U-boats of the Hun. And with . . . what did she call him? . . . an oily Latin American neutral? I love it! It's so like Mrs. Carey. To get the 'neutral' in, too. Shouldn't a girl like me be chased out of decent society?"

"Which is just what you will be if you don't shape up."

"Oh, I'll throw Cesar over, don't worry. I'm not completely foolhardy. And don't try to understand me, Alix dear, for you never will. You could never imagine the temptation, nay the *yearning,* to outrage every tenet of our sacred little society with one glorious screw!"

"Oh, Kitty, please! Stop trying to shock me."

"Well, that's what it was. And that's all it was. Cesar is divinely handsome — though you're probably too Nordic to see it — and he makes stupendous love."

"Are you in love with him?"

"Are you kidding? A jerk like that? Who seduces the wife of a fighting man? Or *thinks* he's seduced her. I despise him."

Desperately, I seized this straw of consolation. "You have more of the old values than you admit."

"Indeed, I do. For *others.*"

By the time I left, I was breathing with some relief. At least we were over that hurdle. Mrs. Carey, of course, would loathe Kitty for the rest of her life, but she would impart her knowledge to no one, not even to her husband or sons. She would be too afraid that they in their wrath might blurt it out to Oswald. What I would have to do was dream up a way of keeping Kitty from doing it again. And how, with her despair and her recklessness, was I to do that?

I knew I would get no help from Mother; moreover, it was imperative that she should be kept in the dark. To offend not only against the moral code but against the deepest patriotic emotions of an excited era would have been to her a folly for which there could be no redemption. I could visualize the shrug that would accompany her dry comment: "What can you do with someone who shouts *Vive le Roi* to a gallery of *tricoteuses?*" But I did receive aid from the last quarter from which I should have expected it. Kitty may have tried to dismiss her mother-in-law as an "old cat," but she still brooded over the image that Mrs. Carey must have of her.

"I suppose Oswald's mother is made of the same stuff as the old martyrs," she told me bitterly. "I'm sure she never suffered a moment's doubt in her life. It must be delectable to be that way! To go through life like a horse with blinkers on! If her right hand ever did offend her, she'd stick it in the fire, like Cranmer, to have it burned off first."

I suppose that Kitty, who had not been able to attach herself to any faith, or even to any system of ethics except such as were prompted by the sentimental impulses of her basically generous heart, had never encountered an opposition to her will or whims that she could not discount as either hypocritical or motivated by worldliness. Mother was a power, but she reeked of Mammon. Our old headmistress, Miss Polhemus, had been a manifest prig. Father was charming but a deep cynic. I had principles, it was true, but Kitty had always been able to take advantage of my devotion to her to get around me. The Episcopal Church had been to her only an empty form, drenched in sanctimoniousness. To put it in theological terms, she saw no one qualified to offer her the blood of the New Testament for the forgiveness of sins.

But Mrs. Carey had judged her; Mrs. Carey had damned her. Her sins were as scarlet, and there was no way they would ever be as white as snow. Kitty had never known what it was to be hated; her beauty had always offered an effective bar to any serious hostility. It was not so much that she had dreaded any such ill will; it was more that she had not believed it could really exist — at least in her respect. And now she was discovering that she did not relish her sudden loss of immunity.

At any rate, she gave up her Argentine officer and did not replace him. Why am I so sure of that? Because she told me so, and never in her life did I catch Kitty in a lie. She had silences — oh, yes — but when she made a statement — to me, anyway — it was always true. I informed Mrs. Carey that Kitty had ceased to see the man in question and that in the future she would confine her entertainment of officers to the clubhouse where she worked. Mrs. Carey simply nodded and offered no comment.

When Oswald came home on leave, all was apparently as usual between them. But Kitty admitted to me that one of the principal chords that united their tender relationship had been severed. Oswald had heard of her having been seen with "Cesar" at nightclubs, and, without jumping to conclusions, he had been deeply upset. It had shaken forever his belief that Kitty's coolness was basic to her temperament and that the kind of love she had shown him was all that she had to offer any man. When he was transferred to temporary shore duty at naval headquarters in London, word came back to us through the usual "dear friend" that he was having an affair with a flamboyant peeress. Kitty exhibited neither surprise nor any particular indignation.

"He has to reassure himself that he's a good lover. He's got to convince himself that it was *my* fault, not his, that I didn't respond to him more ecstatically. And no doubt it was."

After V-J Day the Oswald Careys returned to their home in Westbury and resumed the life they had led before the war. They even had another baby, a boy. Oswald was as ruddy and cheerful as ever — none of us ever mentioned the English lady — but he was fleshier and noisier, and he drank noticeably more. Kitty never reproached him for this, even when he became rather tiresomely boisterous, nor did she make any scenes, so far as I could make out, when he took up with Linda Terhune, the sexy blond wife of Jack Terhune, one of his polo pals, both charter members of the Careys' smart younger set. Kitty's attitude seemed to be one of cool disdain.

I had been coming down to visit Kitty at this time more often than usual, not because of the Linda Terhune business but because I needed my sister's backing in reaching a decision as to whether I should marry Dan Powers. Dan was a dozen years older than I, a widower with two children, a plain man of sterling character, a brilliant but almost too scholarly lawyer, who in Mother's candid opinion was "a man of no charm, a pedant, a bore." I was beginning to rise on the ladder of *Style,* and Mother was actually wondering if I might not yet make what she called a "great match." She would lecture me: "You've always considered yourself a wallflower, child, but in spite of yourself you may turn out a lily. Try to live up to your future!"

I loved Dan, and there was really never a time when I seriously thought of rejecting him. But my nerves were frazzled by Mother's cruel gibes at him, and I even began to wonder if someone who took her mother that seriously was worthy of him. Kitty was a tower of strength. "Do you want to marry Dan," she kept repeating, "or do you want to marry Mother?" It eased my neurotic throes to be with her, and on one of these weekends, at the private beach of the Piping Rock Club on Long Island Sound, I witnessed the remarkable scene between Kitty and her mother-in-law that was to have such a profound effect on all our lives.

It was on a Saturday at noon, the cocktail hour, sacred to the denizens of the north shore. The Oswald Careys and their little group of beautiful people with all their small wriggling offspring, clad in bathing attire, were seated on the sand, partially shaded by gaily-colored umbrellas, drinking from glasses occasionally replenished by a boy in white ducks operating from the beach house bar. The lovely Linda Terhune was seated placidly by Oswald, while Jack Terhune, long and white-skinned, with a fine profile and a mean jaw, the "intellectual" of the little band and to me the worst philistine of them all, was making up to Kitty, who responded with a small fixed smile that he probably hoped was enigmatic.

And we were being watched. On the shaded terrace by the ladies' bath house, overlooking the sloping beach and the umbrellas, seated alone but sitting up straight in a wicker chair, was Mrs. Carey. The formality of her light blue dress, even of her tightly fitting blue beret, seemed to announce her resolution not to go near the water, as the unopened volume in her lap advertised her desired freedom from company. Why had she come? The beach, a mere adjunct of the distant club, was not, as in the Hamptons, a social gathering place for morning gossips; it existed primarily as a bathing facility. If Mrs. Carey had not come to swim, it could have only been to watch, and there before her was the promiscuous gathering of her son's little group.

I was soon aware that Kitty was seeing herself and her friends through the pitiless vision of her mother-in-law: all those healthy muscular tanned torsos, except for Jack Terhune's, whose ivory whiteness seemed to cast a question over the others; all the golden locks of the babbling children thrusting their pails and shovels in attention-seeking gestures at smiling parents nonetheless more concerned with keeping their drinks unspilled; all the laughter, the peals of laughter, the homogeneousness, the closeness of it all, like a romantic painting of a golden age when everyone was young and beauty-bodied and concerned with love, a love that tumbled over borders like an irresistible flood and brought

flesh to flesh in warm contact that would have been Edeni-
cally innocent had it not been seen by . . .

By Mrs. Carey.

Kitty suddenly appealed to Jack Terhune. "Do me a favor,
will you? Take little Alix and dump her in the water, would
you? I want her to swim before she has her sandwich."

When Terhune had complied by scooping up her daughter and lumbering down to the water's edge, Kitty turned to
me with an angry shrug.

"He thinks we ought to have an affair, just *because* of
Oswald and Linda." We were slightly on the edge of the
group. No one could overhear her, though I wondered if she
would have cared if they had. "Just to show them! As if they
cared! As if they probably didn't imagine we already *were.*
I'm sure the others do. And I'm certain *she* does." She jerked
her head in the direction of her mother-in-law. "She sits
there like God in an old painting of the Last Judgment. I
could never redeem myself in her eyes even if I went out to
a Pacific island to work and die in a leper colony."

"Oh, Kitty, why don't you *tell* her?"

Kitty stared, astonished. I felt immediately that I had
stumbled upon something in her own mind. "Tell her what,
for God's sake?"

"Tell her what you haven't done. What you haven't even
had any idea of doing since . . ." I paused.

"Since *then,* you mean? But she'd never believe that.
Nobody but you, my dear, would believe that."

"Try her!"

Kitty looked up at the terrace where Mrs. Carey was
sitting. "You mean now?"

"Well, why not?"

Kitty debated this. "Will you go with me?"

I had not bargained for this. But I was game. "Sure."

Minutes later, having pulled up two chairs on the terrace to either side of Mrs. Carey's, we formed a conversational trio with Kitty's surprised but formally polite mother-in-law. After some routine comments on the lovely weather, Kitty leaned closer to Mrs. Carey.

"I feel a sudden urge to be very frank with you, Mrs. Carey. Alix has encouraged me."

The older woman looked at once reserved. "It is not always an urge to give in to."

"But there are times, aren't there, when there seems nothing to be lost?"

"Does that mean you have something unpleasant to tell me? That is usually when the urge comes."

"I'm afraid you won't find it so much unpleasant as unbelievable. It is suddenly important for me to tell you that ever since a certain episode that came to your knowledge during the war I have been entirely faithful to your son. And that I have every intention of remaining so as long as he wishes to continue to be married to me."

Mrs. Carey for a long minute looked intently into her daughter-in-law's unblinking eyes. Then her expression changed. She seemed to show something like fear. Or was it awe? "What makes you tell me that *now?*"

"You mean why didn't I tell you before? Because I thought you had condemned me so utterly that it wouldn't do the slightest good. And I still feel that may be so. But today it came over me that I had to have my day in court. Even with a judge who had already made up her mind!"

Mrs. Carey's voice now broke. "Oh, my dear girl, you mustn't think me so hard! I'd give anything in the world to have you and Oswald happy again. May I embrace you now as his loving and faithful wife?"

Kitty rose. "Of course, you're just doing it for him."

"Kitty, my dear, give me a chance! I'm not the only one who's being hard."

Mrs. Carey also rose, and Kitty, flushing, let her put her arms around her. I shall never forget, as I turned tactfully away from the scene of their reconciliation, the look on the face of Oswald, down the beach, who had just stood up and turned around in time to witness this strange act of intimacy between his wife and mother. His expression was dazed. I think it even showed betrayal.

❀   ❀   ❀

What happened in the next few years to Kitty and Oswald is a dreary tale best quickly told. Oswald seemed unable to adjust to the sudden alliance between his wife and mother. I am sure that my sister and Mrs. Carey never made scenes, or that even Mrs. Carey ever went so far as to reproach Oswald for his infidelity, but together they must have created an atmosphere of silent but implacable disdain for his indulgences. And it could not have made matters easier for him that Kitty, as if deriving some mysterious sustenance from the support and love of a woman clad by her quixotic imagination in the raiment of near sainthood, seemed to grow in a kind of spiritual grace and loveliness. Her cheeks thinned out, and the perfection of her features was enhanced by the cool pallor of her complexion. Kitty's beauty, and the new ease of her bearing and gestures, the whole wonder of her slim, trim figure always so faultlessly clad, vulgarized Linda Terhune's noisier blondness. "How could he prefer *that?*" you could almost hear people murmur at any gathering as they compared the two.

Oswald's drinking grew worse. He hurt his back in polo

and had to give up the sport. He lost his job. Kitty supplemented their unearned income by wearing designer dresses at conspicuous parties for a private fee (there was something of Mother in her despite the elevating influence of Mrs. Carey), and I boosted her value in the fashion world by positioning her photograph advantageously in *Style*. But two grave and almost simultaneous events at last shattered the Careys' marriage. Jack Terhune, who had found someone other than Kitty to pursue, sued his wife for divorce, and the sudden death of Oswald's mother of a heart attack removed Kitty's last reason for clinging to her union. When Oswald, shamefaced, told her that it was "his duty" to wed a mistress "stained" by her husband's legal onslaught, she agreed to let him go with merely a shrug. Dan, however, to whom I was now securely and happily married, saw to it that she got a good settlement and custody of the two children.

Mother insisted on seeing it all in the most favorable light.

"After all, the Careys and their lot are essentially down the drain," she told me briskly. "Kitty will do much better without Oswald. If a woman has looks and a little money, she really doesn't need a husband in society today. And anyway, why shouldn't she snag one of these tycoons who's made a fortune in dog food or smut or children's games? Won't one of them see the advantage of having a real lady to grace his board?"

"Would he know one if he saw one?"

"Of course he would! Those men aren't dumb, you know. Besides, it sticks out all over Kitty. You can't miss it. Particularly if he looks at his own wife chewing bubble gum or eating with her knife or whatever she does."

"You admit, then, that he may have a wife?"

"Oh, they shed them the way snakes shed old skins." One would never have supposed, to hear Mother castigating the morals of the new rich, that she herself had been twice divorced. "Read your history, Alix. Wasn't Attila the Hun bedazzled by Honoria, the sister of the Roman emperor? Even the barbarian knew style when he saw it!"

Kitty's Attila, however, did not have a wife when she met him; he had already shed that skin. Or rather, she had divorced him for escapades that he had supposed his wealth would induce her to swallow. Instead, he had had to fight desperately to preserve his wealth from her legal attack. Reading of that redoubtable court battle had been my first introduction to the saga of the "unbeatable" Frank Dickson. Dan had been his lawyer. That is, one of his lawyers. The Frank Dicksons of this world need many.

He had been humbly born, the son of the foreman of a corset factory in Roanoke, Virginia, one of those sterling lads who won every school prize, every available scholarship, rising steadily through ranks from which he seemed to take no characterizing marks or even accent, arriving at a Wall Street success at age forty as a smooth, darkly handsome, impeccably clad investment banker, who had used his facile mind and copious imagination, and his utter freedom from any prejudices, loyalties or creeds, to take advantage of every opportunity that fate, stingy at his birth, had been subsequently obliged to open up to him.

Dan had been one of the first to assess accurately his client's genius as an analyst of companies and an expert, if ruthless, acquirer of them, but, a consistent realist, he saw no reason to admire him as a man.

"If you had to bury someone in a time capsule to show the

man of the future what our era was like," Dan explained to me once, "I'd stick in Frank. You might call him the soul of the capitalist system. For him there is nothing but profit. Whatever he has, he must double. It's a process that never lets up, no matter how long he lives. Men like that may even turn to religion in old age. As time runs out they look to their profit in heaven. In the past they might pay for Masses to be said for their souls. Now they make charitable bequests. Or set up huge foundations like pyramids or tombs filled with gold objects."

Frank, however, was a frequent guest at our apartment and a very desirable addition to any dinner party, as he was witty and bright, well turned out and of a pleasant disposition, despite an air of self-assurance that seemed to contain the threat of arguments in store or even lawsuits that could be called upon to strike you down if you should offer a serious resistance to his points of view. He and I had developed an amusing relationship of playful rivalry that sometimes just bordered on the acerb. He treated me with the respect tinged with sarcasm that he reserved for women whose intelligence he acknowledged but who did not attract him sexually. I was entirely frank with him, and he pretended to be so with me.

Mother, learning that he was now single, pestered me to invite him to meet Kitty at dinner, and I at last somewhat reluctantly complied. I invited Mother as well, and seated her by Frank, placing Kitty at the other end of the table. But of course he spotted her the moment she entered the room and monopolized her during the whole of the cocktail period.

After the meal he followed me into the living room and waylaid me before I could reassemble my guests.

"You've been holding out on me, Alix. Why haven't I met your lovely sister here before? Have you been hiding her?"

"Hiding her? I should have thought she was very much in view."

"In the society columns, yes. But I had no idea she was your sister."

"And we're told you know everything!"

"I wasn't raised in your little hothouse, where everyone knows everyone else's mother's maiden name."

"But you've caught on quickly, haven't you? Now you can even distinguish between a Van Rensselaer and a Vanderbilt. But you're also smart enough to know how little it any longer matters."

"Unless a gal can *look* the part. That can still be something. And your sister looks like a princess. That's almost the same as being one. Certainly your mother seems to think so."

"How did you and Mother get on? She has a weakness for tycoons."

"How like you to call it a weakness. Well, she didn't go overboard about me."

"That's one of her principles. She says the new rich can only be 'had' once. So you mustn't sell yourself cheap."

He mimicked a look of shock. "Sell yourself?"

"That or whatever you happen to be peddling. In her case, it's more apt to be a museum or a hospital."

"Not a daughter?"

"We haven't come to that yet, *Mister* Dickson."

"Oh, tell me, Alix. Is the beautiful Kitty's heart free?"

"Why don't you ask her?"

Which is just, I suppose, what he did, for he went directly to where she was sitting and remained with her for the rest of the evening. I noted that no other man attempted to join them. Frank, without being offensive, managed to create the impression that the area around Kitty had been somehow licitly staked off.

Mother, leaving the party, beckoned me to follow her into the foyer.

"He's on the hook," she murmured with a shocking satisfaction. "I never saw anything so fast."

Anyone who saw Kitty and Frank together in the next few weeks could have understood that the courtship would not have to be long. It was like a television serial: all glittering nightclubs and suave good looks and gleaming jewels and bright shiny limousines, enough to make a puritan out of the most acrid cynic. Kitty hardly saw me at all during this time; I think she suspected that I would be seeing it as I have just described it and wanted no cold water dashed over what may have been the first really exciting experience of her lifetime.

But serious words between us had to come, and they came indeed on the day she arrived at my office to tell me that she was engaged.

"Here we go again," I told her with as much of a smile as I could muster. "Tell me, are you in love with Frank? Or is it Ted Shaughnessy and Oswald all over again?"

"No, it's neither of them. I'll be very frank with you. Why not? Who else have I ever talked with? Except Mrs. Carey, and she'd *never* have understood what I'm doing now. She'd have hated Frank. But then, she lived in a different world. I have to live in this one. Do you remember what I told you, back when I was engaged to Oswald, about my being attracted to low types?"

"Vividly. But surely you're not going to tell me that Frank is *that*."

"But he is, darling! He is! He's terribly low. Brutally low."

"Kitty! How can you?"

"Because it's just what attracts me. But the difference between him and others is that he's on the winning team. This terrible world, this chaos with no moral values, is *his* world! With him it makes sense. Sense as nothing has ever made sense to me before. I have a place with Frank, a position with Frank, a job, if you like, with Frank."

"Tell me, Kitty. Does the man have a heart?"

She only hesitated a moment. "No, I don't really suppose he does."

"What'll your job be? To give a lot of parties?"

"If that's part of it, yes. You see, Alix, Frank *believes* in what he's doing. That's what gives him vigor. And reality. You and I grew up in a world that was disillusioned with its own past but not yet ready to accept its dismantlement."

I could hardly believe that anyone could adopt such a creed. "And so you're content to become the beautiful, the ravishing Mrs. Dickson? The best-dressed woman in town? The reigning queen of the fashion plates?"

"Don't knock it. Where would *Style* be without the likes of me? Isn't it more than I've done with my silly life so far?"

❀   ❀   ❀

And that is Kitty's story. She became exactly what her husband wanted her to be, and she took him with her, right up the ladder. They became the shining lights of New York society. To be invited to the Dicksons' for a weekend at their huge seaside villa in Southampton, or to their hunting plantation in South Carolina, to be asked to go yachting with them in the Bahamas or skiing at their lodge in Idaho, was to have attained the summit of the social mountain whose trails and precipices were no longer easy to define. But at least one knew when one was on the top.

Kitty's beauty endured into her late thirties and forties with an almost eerie persistence. People assumed she had her face lifted, but I knew she didn't. She did, however, take infinite care of her looks and body, with unguents and powders and every kind of massage and exercise. And her clothes! They were a miracle. Even her two Carey children (she and Frank had none) were in awe of her, and her friends tended increasingly to treat her as a dryad who had escaped from Mount Olympus to wed a mortal. Only that mortal failed to recognize her role.

It was not that Frank was ever a brute. He was too intelligent not to be outwardly decent to her, the way he was outwardly decent to everyone so long as they were of use to him. But he made no more effort to conceal from her his many love affairs than would a great director have from the leading lady in the film he was producing. Kitty never complained to him or to others. Taking a man without a heart had been part of her bargain, and she was always willing to live up to it.

Perhaps it was just as well that she didn't outlive her utility to him. After the diagnosis of her fatal cancer, she told me that now her worst fear would never be realized: she would not survive her own beauty. She did, of course, in that the ravages of the disease destroyed it before they did her, but this was only a matter of months, and she made Frank promise that he would never come to see her in the hospital. He never did.

The Ancient Greeks

LEWIS TOWER was perfectly, even complacently aware
that his physical appearance was not what would initially
attract the interest of his fellow travellers on the Mediterra-
nean cruise of the *Hellas* in the summer of 1950. His belly
was a bit of a pouch and his limbs were too slender; his
reddish sandy hair on the sides of his head did not rise to
cover a pink dome, and his more pleasing, even rather finely
sculpted features were minimized by small, darting green
eyes and the gold-rimmed glasses that he usually wore halfway down his nose. What he counted on for such social
attention as he needed (which was no great amount) was his
reputation as the brilliant, caustic but popular head of the
classics department at Pulver Academy, the New England
boys' boarding school that attracted the kind of Boston,
New York and Philadelphia parents who were drawn to such
expensive and discreetly advertised cruises as the one on
which he was embarked. Tower was not one to suffer fools
gladly — at Pulver he was the terror of the slower-minded
boys — but on the other hand, he would not tolerate socially the acutest intellect at the cost of a vulgar manner or a
cracking of coarse jokes or even an overeagerness for intimacy. Tower liked people to be like himself: quick, sharp

and to the point. A private school and a restricted cruise were his natural bailiwicks.

He had chosen as his travelling companion a fellow master at Pulver, a young Latin teacher, Edwin Breese, twenty-eight, almost of an age to be his son, a handsome enough fellow with wavy black hair and friendly blue eyes, but of a reserved and scholastic manner, unmarried, like Tower, but not, like him, a long-time widower. He was also, like his senior, possessed of ample independent means to allow him a costly vacation. He had shown at school a gratifying admiration for Tower as his department head; indeed, the relationship went further back, for Breese, as a boy at the school, had learned at the same source his passion for the glory that was Greece and the grandeur that was Rome. And Tower, after due consideration, had decided that he might prove the perfect partner for the cruise: interested, punctual, respectful, handy with luggage and tickets and not always chasing after girls.

The cruise had started well. The *Hellas* had sailed from Marseilles and stopped briefly at Corsica and Sardinia, on neither of which islands had Tower condescended to set foot. Edwin, of course, had gone ashore on each and been bused about with the other passengers, but he had not, despite urgent invitations, joined any of the frivolous younger groups aboard, seeming quite content to confine himself to the company of his fellow teacher and the few distinguished older individuals, including a Pulver trustee and some Pulver parents, who invited them for cocktails at the bar. Edwin had brought along a complete Gibbon in which he immersed himself as he and Tower reclined on adjoining deck chairs.

But en route to Naples, on the morning they were to

enter the famous bay, Edwin suddenly closed his book and introduced a jarring note.

"We're going to be two nights here, you know. One of them I'm planning to stay ashore, in the apartment of a cousin. I hope you don't mind."

Tower was not only surprised; he was surprised at being surprised. Why shouldn't Edwin stay ashore if he liked? What did he think his young friend was? A valet?

"I didn't know you had relatives in Naples."

"I don't, really. It's just a young nephew of Mother's who's decided to spend a year here and see if he can paint. He's got a couple of rooms in some old *pensione* and says he can put me up."

"And has he talent as a painter?"

"I'm afraid I rather doubt it. He's just an amateur. But he wants to see what he can do, giving it full time."

"*Is* that what he gives his full time to?"

"Why do you ask that?"

"Because Italy is full of young Americans who come here to do things they can't do at home. Your cousin, I suppose, has independent means."

"Far from it. He's related on Mother's side and not a bloated Breese. As a matter of fact I've had to help him out. He had a bad marriage and a messy divorce and lost the job my old man got him in the family bank. I thought he needed a chance to think his life over and maybe find himself."

"Or lose himself," Tower commented with a frown. "It seems to me, my dear Edwin, that you're taking quite a chance with this young man. You may be encouraging idleness. And who knows? Perhaps even vice. What is his name?"

Edwin noticeably hesitated. "Adrian Mount."

"But wasn't he at school? Isn't that the name of a boy who would have been in the class of 'forty?" Tower had every Pulver name and date at his fingertips.

"Would have been if he hadn't been kicked out."

"Precisely! I'm sorry to say it if he's your cousin, but he was hardly a reputable youth. He was sent away, as I recall, because of his lamentable grades, but his case was not ameliorated by what we learned from his dormitory master about his morals."

"There were episodes that are not uncommon among boys, confined as ours are to a monastic life."

Tower glanced more keenly now at his younger friend. What was this new note of sympathy that he detected in his tone? Tower detested all sexual irregularity. To tell the truth, he had little enthusiasm for sexual regularity. The latter had not been responsible for much joy in his own life. His dull, dear little wife, who had died of meningitis after only five years of wedlock, had caused him traumas of guilt. He had thought he had loved her, but he had known he had never satisfied her, though she had never uttered even a murmur of complaint. She had bored him, and he had hated himself for being bored by her, and even more for being relieved at her demise. A rigid school routine, informed by a religious faith he did not share, had given him the scaffolding to support the life that his marriage had almost shattered, and he clung to it with a desperate resolve.

"I don't suppose you're suggesting that Pulver go coed?" he inquired testily.

"Would that be the end of the world?"

This was very bad. Tower had not dreamed that Edwin could be so innovative. He had known him as a boy in the school, silent, serious, gracefully conformist, fitting in with the Pulver spirit, never loud or difficult, the son of a rich, dry little father who had contributed a dormitory to the campus and a beautiful, amiable, very social mother without a brain in her head. Edwin, an adored only child, had shown no interest after Harvard and a few dutiful years in the family bank in any other business or profession; his sole desire had been to return to Pulver to teach and perhaps to recapture permanently the security the place had given him as a boy. His every interest had seemed to be in keeping the school just as it had always been.

"It might be the end of *a* world, if not *the* world," Tower responded now to Edwin's question. "With girls at Pulver we should have to turn the place into a police state or a brothel. You cannot put the two sexes together, night and day, at their highest point of sexual curiosity and not court trouble."

"Trouble?"

"Well, what would *you* call it?"

"Oh, I might call it life. But anyway, Lewis, the problem is not before us. Nobody's propagandizing for a coed Pulver as yet. And you may very well be right. I can't compare my two years on the faculty with your twenty."

But Tower could not accept this. Edwin *was* comparing his two years with that longer term, and very likely with the notion that time had simply encrusted the older master in his errors. He was startled to realize, in this suddenly charged moment, how much he had already come to value Edwin's outward subservience to his influence and opinions. It seemed to give him an added luster to have a kind of disciple, making up a picture, in Tower's secret but nonetheless perfervid imagination, of a plump and princely, richly robed Renaissance cardinal behind whose gilded chair stood a silent hooded Zurbarán monk.

And what would happen to the monk in the hands of a dissolute scamp like Adrian Mount? What did Edwin know of the world that awaited him in Naples, that stinking cistern of writhing, copulating snakes?

"Don't stay with your cousin, Edwin. Ask him to dine with us; we'll take him to the best restaurant in Naples. That's all he'll care about, believe me. And you and I will rent a car and spend a night in a lovely hotel I know near Herculaneum, which will give us a whole morning to inspect the new excavations. I have a letter from Dr. Caldi, who's in charge of the works, and we'll get the red carpet treatment!"

"Oh, Lewis, that is nice of you, but Adrian would run a mile if he knew you were even this close to Naples — he's still very bitter about that school business. No, I've got to see him and spend a day and a night with him; I'm really responsible for his being here at all. There's no way I can get out of it."

Tower was about to plead with the young man not to let his wicked cousin lead him into any trouble, but he suddenly realized how ridiculous this would sound, and he shrugged as if the subject were of no further interest to him and picked up his copy of *The Sea Kings of Crete*.

"Bring me back one of his sketches," he muttered. "We'll see just how much talent he has."

❀   ❀   ❀

Edwin Breese had always, however suspiciously, envied the ease with which his cousin Adrian had treated life as he ambled through it. This envy was by no means shared by any other members of the Breese or Mount clans, who had written Adrian off as a kind of bad debt. But if Adrian was useless and perpetually broke, he was also perpetually cheerful, with messy blond hair and bold brown eyes, round-chinned, thick-lipped and graced or cursed with what Edwin's father described dryly as a "kind of disgusting charm" for women. Adrian professed to admire the handsome but reserved and diffident Edwin; he liked to shock his slightly older cousin with salacious stories and to lure him to expensive and *louche* night spots where the nonparticipating Edwin — if it came to going upstairs — always paid. Their friendship became even closer when Edwin decided to underwrite Adrian's proposed expatriation, which the indignant family regarded as watering the primroses on the prodigal's downward path. But Edwin was that rare type of anchorite whose sympathy for those who had strayed beyond the walls behind which he had encased himself was large and generous. Adrian to him, if never quite redeemable, was always forgivable.

It was an old game of Adrian's to be always hinting that behind his cousin's reserved exterior there lay a cauldron of seething lusts. "You don't fool me for a minute, old fella" was his cheerful retort whenever Edwin pretended to wish to change the subject from one of his scatological tales. He maintained that Edwin secretly enjoyed his stories of sexual adventure, and didn't really even mind Adrian's knowing this. The burden of his discourse was usually women, but in Italy he extended the field.

On the evening that Edwin had agreed to be his guest at the *pensione,* as the two cousins were drinking brandy at a veranda table of a street café near the docks, Adrian warmed to his new theme.

"What I like in Europe, dear coz, is the catholicity of tastes. As you go to one restaurant for its sole meunière and another for its omelette au jambon, so in Paris it's the *femme* above all while in Naples it can be the beautiful lad."

"You mean you go in for lads!" Edwin was too astonished to disguise his immediate and tense curiosity.

"Do I shock you, dear coz? Are my lurid schooldays so

soon forgotten? You thought I'd left all that behind? Very well then, I must shock you. For I see no earthly reason to confine myself to the charms of a single sex. I can be, if I choose, as Greek as Alcibiades. Last night, let me tell you brashly, after you had gone back to your stuffy cruise boat, I went out on the town. Ah, you should have been with me!"

"You mean you were with a *man?*"

"I was with a delightful youth. And he had a charming companion who would have been just your affair. I had thought of asking you to join us. But then I thought, no. I pictured a pilgrim's black hat over your censorious features. I saw you grimace as you would turn away. Was I wrong?"

Edwin did not answer for a moment. His heart was pounding and his lips were dry.

"But you thought I might have been tempted?"

"Oh, tempted, yes. Even pilgrims are tempted."

"What made you think I had . . . those tastes?"

"Dear coz, everyone has them, at one point or another. But you particularly. You have such a passionate nature. All locked up though it is. Oh, if you'd only let it out, what a ball you might have!"

Edwin beckoned the waiter to bring him another brandy. He knew now that he was helplessly in the grip of his violent curiosity. "But what have I ever said or done to make you feel that I was interested in the kind of thing you did last night?"

Adrian smiled, and Edwin was only too aware of the shade of malice behind his smile. But it was too late for him to care now.

"Really, Edwin, your library alone would be a dead give-away. All that Oscar Wilde and Swinburne and Aubrey Beardsley and John Addington Symonds. And your pictures! All those photographs of handsome school chums in scanty rowing pants and drawings of nude males!"

"I had only two such drawings, and they were by our uncle Ned! They were works of art!"

"Tell that to the marines. Though maybe you'd better *not* tell it to the marines. Though even they . . . but let's not get into *that*. More to the point, can you deny that you've been eyeing that inky-haired youth who's twice sauntered by our table? He's just waiting to be picked up. Shall I ask him to join us?"

Edwin abandoned the last pretense.

"Where would you go with someone like that? Not to a hotel?"

"Well, you might, if you gave the desk clerk a big enough tip, but they don't like it. It's better to let the boy take you where he wants. He knows all the places."

"But I speak so little Italian!"

"Am I such a linguist? You'll find him very accommodating. Just indicate by gestures what you want him to do."

Adrian took in his cousin's look of acceptance and burst into a mocking and triumphant laugh. Then he turned and roughly beckoned to the Italian lad to come over.

۞   ۞   ۞

Edwin had learned, in his last two years as a student at Pulver, to maintain a rigid wall between his sexual fantasies and his activities, or, more accurately, his nonactivities. In his fourth year at the academy, at age fifteen, he had confided the former in a friend, with unhappy results. Not that the immediate result had been unhappy. He had invited Bobby Catlin, to whom he was strongly attracted, to visit his family in Maine in the summer, and on a hike up one of the mountains of Mount Desert Island he had summoned up the courage to suggest that they engage in what he had heard described at school as "mutual masturbation." Catlin

had had no objection, and the incident had passed off to
Edwin's intense satisfaction. But that fall, back at Pulver,
Catlin had blabbed it to a ringleader of the class, largely to
refute the latter's allegation that Edwin was a "little plaster
saint," and Edwin had had the mortification of a group's
dogging him in the locker room with the chant "Ooo-la-la,
we hear it's whoopee in the woods of Maine!" It was not that
the boys were in the least shocked; they were simply paying
off Edwin for what they had taken to be a hypocritical pose
of virtue. But to Edwin, what had happened on that beautiful mountainside had been a deeply romantic experience,
and now it was forever stained with vulgar winks and chuck-
les. In ancient Greece, a friendship such as he had contemplated, even with a boy as shallow as Catlin, might have
been a respected, perhaps almost a noble relationship, and
now they were only a pair of smutty schoolboys who, if they
didn't pretty soon turn from each other to the girls, would
become social pariahs. And justly so. Edwin did not challenge what he saw as the law. Was it not the law of the
school, of his mother and father, of the great world? He had
tried to get away with making a secret reality of a secret
fantasy. Well, he had learned his lesson.

His and Adrian's uncle, Ned Mount, whom Edwin deeply
admired, an exquisite bachelor of New York social circles
and a popular portrait painter of Gotham, had been charm-
ingly broad-minded in his discussions of life with his favorite nephew. He had little use for the reprehensible Adrian,
whose bold manner offended his taste, but he cared very
much for Edwin, who he saw was in danger of being pushed
too far in the opposite direction by his awe of his ultra-
conservative parents. Uncle Ned was anxious that Edwin
should not develop any "hang-ups" about sex. He himself
had lived with a mistress in Paris when he had been a

student at the Beaux Arts, and even now he still used nude models of both sexes; he had a broad and healthy appreciation of what he called the "glories" of love, but it was always perfectly apparent to Edwin that these glories were confined to what went on between men and women, and that his uncle deemed all forms of inversion the results of psychological disturbance, to be treated with benign toleration or, if possible, medical therapy.

And that was the most that these "unfortunates" could hope for. His uncle, after all, was an artist, and to some extent his genius exempted him from having to subscribe to the moral law which required that all such offenders be branded. Indeed, had they not once been burned alive? Was that not why they were still called "faggots"? Edwin remembered as a lad an ancient night watchman in Bar Harbor, a dear, friendly, sensitive old soul, who had been hired largely out of charity by the summer residents with villas on Bar Harbor's shore path to patrol their lawns and gardens after dark, who had been arrested in the village for soliciting an indignant minor in a public washroom. Edwin remembered his beautiful mother's horrified exclamation: "To think all these years we've been at the mercy of an armed pervert!"

Why should he have been born with a larger share of original sin than others? The fact that it was larger he had no doubt — why otherwise would he not have taken the jeers in the locker room as easily as did other mocked classmates? Edwin had little religious faith, but he hugged to his heart the puritan heritage of sin. How could he deny the conviction of his passionate senses? But there was one consolation, a gleam of hope born, of all places, in a class in French literature. The master, in lecturing on Racine and Jansenism, had made the point that sinful thoughts in the former's tragedies were at worst venal and that damnation came only with their communication. The sin of Phèdre, for example, was not so much in her guilty passion for her stepson as in her avowal of it to Hypolite, which generates all the "facts" of the tragedy. Silence, then, was as close as one could come to innocence.

If some of Edwin's friendships at school were now tinged with romance, it was only in his mind and heart and imagination. A monk could not have behaved more circumspectly. A perfect self-control in manners, in dress, in deportment would ultimately carry one through to the fulfillment of the role that his heritage, his parentage, his whole background required him to play. And in later years, at Harvard and in the family bank, he began to wonder if the best place for him to spend his life might not be as a teacher at Pulver.

For the episode with the boy on the mountain and the jeers of his classmates had been, after all, a very small part of a male world of young scholars and athletes still trained in the languages of an ancient culture that had not seen sin in things that were beautiful to Edwin, however forbidden to modern youths. Pulver was infused by its deeply religious and inspiring headmaster with an atmosphere of moral idealism in which Edwin thought he might be able to live in a kind of serene monastic content.

And so indeed it had proved until that night at Naples.

⊗   ⊗   ⊗

It had not taken Lewis Tower long to observe, on Edwin's return to the boat after the time spent at his cousin's *pensione,* that something had occurred to alter radically the young man's usually equable disposition. He looked haggard, as if he had not slept, and he answered Tower's inquiries in clipped monosyllables, quite unlike his usual manner of deference. This continued all during the next two days on their voyage to Sicily, and at the temples of Girgenti he refused to join the passengers who followed the special guide provided by the *Hellas* and wandered from fane to fane by himself. At last he seated himself moodily on a rock before the best preserved of the façades and contemplated it with eyes that seemed to take nothing in. Tower decided to join him.

"You scorn our learned pedagogue?"

Edwin shrugged, as if in slight irritation. "I want to let the temple do its own talking. Isn't it eloquent enough?"

"I think it should be." There was a pause. "But tell me, my friend, what's wrong? You've hardly smiled or talked since that night in Naples. What did that scamp of a cousin do to you?"

"You don't really want to know, do you, Mr. Tower?"

The unexpected formality of address, added to the roughness of the tone, made Tower stare. It also restored the academic rank between them. "I think I do, Mr. Breese. Otherwise I shouldn't have asked. When we agreed to take this trip together, I thought it was understood that we should have confidence in one another."

"Very well, then. Adrian arranged for my deflowering. Assuming I had ever been anything as pretty as a flower."

Tower struggled to play the man of the world. He even managed a wink. "Maybe it was something long overdue."

"It wasn't with a girl."

Tower started as if he had been spat at. The snakes in his imagined cistern seemed suddenly to slither about. He closed his eyes; he sighed. Then he cleared his throat. "Well, this is Italy."

"Where such things don't really count, is that it?" Edwin was now excited. "Where people go to get it out of their systems? But I'm that way, all the way, that's what I've learned, Lewis! I can't go back to Pulver! I'd be a menace. I should put an end to myself like the man in the Housman poem. Do you remember? 'Shot so quick, so clean an ending? Ah, that was right, lad, that was brave.' Mine was not an 'ill for mending. 'Twas best to take it to the grave.'"

"But, Edwin, my friend, your case is not that uncommon. If you only *knew!*"

Edwin shrugged as if in even greater disgust at himself. "Oh, don't worry. I shan't do anything violent. But I've got no appetite for this cruise. Aunt Leonie is Father's maiden sister. She lives in a converted abbey near Fontainbleau. I think I'll disembark at Taormina and join her. I can be quiet there and think out what to do with the rest of my silly life."

It was time, anyway, to rejoin the others who were returning to the boat. Tower rose, and Edwin sluggishly followed him. That afternoon the older man paced the deck alone as the vessel sailed towards Syracuse and considered his options.

Edwin's proposed visit to his aunt was one solution. Tower could then proceed comfortably on his cruise, freed of the unattractive and messy complications of his friend's physical obsession and mental turmoil, restored to a happier world where his contemporaries, liberated by age, only looked at each other and talked. He could explain Edwin's absence in lowered tones to those who inquired by saying he had suffered a mild attack of nerves which a couple of quiet weeks in the Gallic countryside was bound to cure. Would it not be best?

But then he remembered the presence on board of the Pulver trustee. Would he want sufferers of nervous ailments on the faculty? And suddenly gripping the railing as he faced the sea wind, he realized that Edwin *must* come back to

Pulver! For Tower's own sake, if no one else's! The prospect of walking to chapel in the morning after breakfast in the great school dining room without this sleek, faithful hound at his side was of an instant dreariness. He needed him. How? Why, as the Renaissance cardinal of his imagination had needed the austere young monk who might indeed be his son, as the Roman senator of old had needed the togaed youth to escort him from his marble chair in the *curia* to his *lectica,* as anyone needs somebody, as he had needed the poor little wife who had failed him and whom he had failed — but so much more warmly, in such a more heartfelt manner.

He went to the bar, which was empty of passengers, and surprised the man behind it by ordering and drinking a double scotch.

Going to Edwin's cabin, he found his friend sitting up in his bunk, clad in a blue wrapper and staring at the bulkhead. He pulled up a chair beside him and started to talk.

"Listen to me, Edwin, and don't say a word until I have finished. There was nothing wrong in what you did that night at Naples. Your cousin's inveigling you into it was wrong, very wrong, but that does not make what you did wrong. How can a thing be right for Plato and wrong for you? No, don't answer the question. It was purely rhetorical. But you opened a kind of Pandora's box which can never be closed again. So the question is how to live with the opened box. You could leave Pulver and live quite openly in New York or any major city with a love life of your choice, so long as it was conducted with a certain tact. We all know men who do that and move in the very highest social circles. But I don't see you in that role." Here he held up his hand to ensure continued silence as Edwin nodded his head in sudden violent accord with his last statement. "You have too strong a regard for your parents and the whole orthodox world. Indeed, your principal trouble is that there's a side of you that agrees with them. Oh, you see I've studied you, my boy. You don't really like the wretched Mount or the life he leads. It intrigues you and disgusts you at the same time. Where you really belong is Pulver. You need Pulver, and Pulver needs you. Very well. What you must do is divide your life rigidly in two. I suggest that you let the Atlantic Ocean be the dividing line. In America you will be chaste as the driven snow. But on trips to Italy in the summer, nobody need know what your diversions are. Of course, there are always people who will suspect such things, but the difference between suspicion and knowledge is what we all in one way or another live on."

Edwin was now so still that Tower wondered if he was taking his idea in. He decided to try a lighter note.

"I assume your Neapolitan cousin will continue to live over here as long as you support him. No doubt he could be your caretaker and guide on your summer excursions."

"You mean my pimp. I wonder, Lewis, if what you think of him isn't what you really think of me."

Tower was encouraged by this abruptly more matter-of-fact tone. "No, dear boy, never. You must know, deep down, anyway, that you have a true friend in me."

"I think I do know that." Edwin reached over to give Tower's hand a smart little pat. His whole mood seemed to fall away, to be replaced by an exuberant hope. Tower wondered that anyone could be so simple. "Would you really help to keep me on the straight and narrow if I came back to school?"

"You could always come to me if you felt trouble ahead. We could talk it out."

Edwin was silent again for some moments. "Perhaps I'll try it," he said at last. "Perhaps I really will."

❦   ❦   ❦

They finished the cruise without further incident, and Edwin flew home to spend the balance of the summer vacation with his parents. Tower was considerably relieved when he showed up at the opening of the fall term at school, seemingly relaxed in appearance and revived in spirits. They did not discuss what had happened in Naples; Tower assumed that their silence represented a tacit agreement that Edwin had taken his senior's good advice to heart and was determined to act upon it. And all during the ensuing school year he manifested a new enthusiasm for his courses and pupils and even took a more active part on the athletic fields in supervising the sports of the younger boys. Indeed, in the spring the headmaster took occasion to speak to Tower about Edwin's progress.

"You know, Lewis, the assistant head and I have had some doubts as to whether Pulver was really the right place for Breese. He seemed so quiet, so diffident, not the type for boys to admire and emulate. But I pointed out that you had taken him under your wing. 'Let's see what Tower makes of him first. He couldn't have a better guide and mentor.' Well, my friend, you seem to have done it! Breese this year has really come up to snuff."

Edwin was off to Italy the very day after the spring term ended. Tower had suggested that they meet in Venice in July for a two-week motor tour of the Palladian villas, and Edwin had agreed, but not with the enthusiasm that Tower had expected and with the irritating condition that the trip be limited to a single week. The younger man's summer in Italy, it appeared, was filled with commitments the nature of which he didn't offer to divulge. Tower, however irked, decided to overlook this lapse in their intimacy, and when they met in Venice and embarked on their excursion he tried to behave as though nothing had occurred to disturb what he considered their former accord that Italy intrigued them solely as the preserver of beautiful antiquities.

But then, one night in Vicenza, something happened that upset Tower deeply. Edwin announced, without a word of excuse or explanation, that he was "engaged" for the evening and left his friend to dine alone in their hotel. Tower waited up for him until midnight and then went to bed, too angry and fretful to do more than doze until dawn. Descending for breakfast, he found Edwin, shiny-faced and cheerful, already at their table.

"Did you enjoy your evening?" Tower inquired stiffly.

"I enjoyed it very much indeed, thank you. I was sorry to leave you alone, Lewis, but a friend of mine had told me that he'd be visiting his parents in Vicenza and wanted me to join him for dinner. I didn't think he was exactly your cup of tea."

"I daresay not. A young Italian, I suppose? A boy, perhaps?"

"Not a boy, Lewis. I'm not a threat to minors. And, anyway, you know about these things. You know all about *me,* God knows. And so long as we're in Italy, maybe you can take off your New England hat long enough to let me tell you about Julio. His is really an interesting story . . ."

"Which I am not in the least interested in hearing!" Tower found that he was trembling all over with anger. Anger? It was more like fury. "Nor do I need any scatological details about your life over here! I told you to keep the Atlantic strictly between your two lives. Well, leave me on the other side of that *cordon sanitaire.* I close my eyes firmly on your Italian escapades. Be sure you don't try to open them. Or anyone else's who has anything to do with Pulver School!"

Edwin took the rebuke very well. He offered no retort; he simply nodded his head as if accepting what was said and poured himself more coffee. But there was a kind of serenity in his manner which struck Tower as that of a deeply convinced convert to a new faith. It was as if, his old doubts and fears allayed, Edwin had soared too high above the heads of his old coreligionists to care what they had to say. He felt for them only a regretful good will, a kind of misty benevolence. It was maddening.

Nor was there any difference in this new independence of Edwin's when they were back in school in September. He was never remiss with his older friend; he was polite, respectful, attentive, but he was no longer the disciple. Edwin had little need of Tower now. He was becoming one of the more popular of the younger masters, inspiring some of his Greek students to read more of Euripides than actually assigned, joining in games of basketball as well as coaching them, acting as a literary adviser to the editors of the school magazine. Boys came to him now with their personal problems; he was seen as a sympathetic link between the faculty and the student body.

Tower became increasingly resentful. How had Edwin's new confidence and self-assurance been formed except by his unspeakable summer activities? Hadn't this newfangled ease of his relations with students been learned in illicit Neapolitan entanglements? Tower's mind was inflamed with the pictures that he conjured up of a naked Edwin engaged in every kind of carnal conjunction with swarthy Italian youths. The wretched young man had descended from the high, dry, windswept plateau of his friendship with Tower to this cesspool of lechery and sin! And he exulted in it, shamelessly! He made it seem a lush lake in which all might luxuriously wallow. He was a menace! Tower seemed to hear the Venusberg music from the first act of *Tannhäuser.*

The school year passed, and Edwin returned to his beloved Italy, not this time followed by Tower, who took himself to a lonely hotel chamber in the chastity of the White Mountains. The following fall term found Edwin back in better spirits than ever. He was even beginning to be spoken of as a possible candidate for successor to the headmaster when that exalted figure should step down in a few years' time. Tower was appalled. Could so flawed a creature really step from the stews of Naples to the principal's chair?

And then it happened. Not precisely what Tower had feared — or in his not so subconscious thoughts may even have wished — but something very like it. Tower was summoned to the headmaster's study and in that grave presence was asked to peruse a letter that Edwin had written to a sixth former during the summer. The letter had been found by the boy's mother on his bureau after his return to school, and she had read it and shown it to her husband, who had forwarded it indignantly to the headmaster.

The letter was certainly warmly affectionate; it went beyond what any schoolmaster should write to a boy of seventeen. But there was nothing indecent in it. Written by one teen-year-old to another it might have passed for a slightly overdemonstrative expression of affection. But what had shocked the boy's parents and obviously the headmaster was Edwin's exposition, written evidently to answer a question put to him by the boy as to his summer reading, of Socrates' theory of friendship or love between men and boys. While it was true that Edwin, like a bowdlerized Plato, took the position that this love at its purest and best needed no physical incarnation, he nonetheless gave as his own opinion that it occupied a higher level among the emotions of history than any that love between man and woman could reach, and he ended the letter with what he evidently considered the inspiring picture of two warriors, man and youth, marching arm in arm out of Athens to battle its besiegers.

"The assistant head feels that Breese should be let go," the headmaster observed weightily when he saw Tower look up from his reading. "I am less sure. His record here is excellent, and we haven't a scrap of evidence to indicate he ever laid a hand on a boy or suggested an indecency. I think a stern warning might be enough. If he will give me his word of honor that he will never again discuss with any boy his theory of Greek friendship (I will not contaminate the word "love" by using it in this context), I think we can let him stay. But I must have your agreement on this. I must first have your assurance, as one who knows him better than anyone else in the school, as one who has even travelled with him in summertime, that to your knowledge Breese has never been guilty of an act of sexual perversion."

Tower tried to look as if he were thinking. And actually he was thinking. If the head should learn that, knowing of such an act, he had allowed Edwin to return to school, would it not affect his own status at Pulver?

"No, sir, he has not." But then he paused. "Certainly not at school."

The headmaster's bushy eyebrows soared. "Not at school? Do you imply he might have elsewhere? In Italy, for example? For you have travelled with him in Italy, have you not? Examine your conscience, man! Think of what you owe the school!"

"Well, sir, there was a night, the summer before last,

when he and I were in Vicenza, when he left me to join a young Italian man who met him there and they were gone all night. He never explained this or offered to introduce me to his friend, who I rather suspected was not altogether respectable. I didn't like this, but it was very little to go on, and I hesitated to inform you and ruin the man's career here on what may have been only a vague suspicion."

"I can see that, Lewis. You were put in a hard position. I'm not sure what I should have done in the same case. But I am perfectly sure what I shall do now. That episode, plus the letter, is enough to convince me that Breese is not the man for Pulver. I shall show him the letter and ask for his resignation at the end of the school year. If he gives it to me, which I have little doubt that he will do, I'll tear up the letter, and no one need ever know that his leaving Pulver was not entirely of his own free will. Your name need never be mentioned in the matter."

❀   ❀   ❀

Edwin placed his leaving Pulver on the ground that he was going to move to Rome to write a novel. This was the reason that he offered to Lewis, who professed to accept it and even made a plan to call on him when he himself should next visit the Eternal City. And Edwin did write a novel, a rather daring one for the early 1950s, about the romances of various young American expatriates abroad, which obtained some excellent reviews and was nominated for a National Book Award.

So Lewis did not feel too bad about the way things had worked out. He still believed in the ocean as a kind of *cordon sanitaire*. He was even amused when he heard one of Edwin's aunts, a highly sophisticated New York lady whose husband was a Pulver trustee, quoted as saying of her now much talked of nephew: "No, he's only gay in Europe. Over here, I'm told, he's square as a cube."

Tower lived on to become a living legend at the school. Exotic rumors began to circulate about him among the boys. He was a Jesuit priest in disguise. He had a secret fortune that he would never spend but that he might one day leave to the school. He disappeared to Europe in the summers where he might be involved in strange vices. It was even whispered that he had initiated the novelist Edwin Breese in the life that the latter now openly adopted.

Tower shrugged in amusement when a friend on the faculty told him of the existence of these stories. Did they not at least make him more interesting?

Geraldine:
A Spiritual Biography

"SOME PEOPLE say that no one will survive an atomic war. But I doubt that. There are some forms of life that can survive any holocaust. Take my dear wife. Out of the rubble of our capital city, out from under the fallen bricks of this very house, I can see crawling a haggard Geraldine, peering about to find how many of her Georgetown pals are still extant. Will there be enough to give a party? A coming-out party? Oh, very informal, of course. Come just as you are, in rags and tatters. We'll see if there aren't a few bottles of wine left in the cellar!"

These words of Rex resounded in Geraldine's mind for minutes after their scornful utterance to embarrassed guests at what she had hoped would be one of her better dinner parties. Never before had he been quite so nasty, though he had been getting nastier by the month. She had a giddy feeling, almost as if she were going to faint, and then, as with a drowning man, a swarm of events passed through her seething mind. One thing anyway she was sure of. She was sure that her marriage was over. Like broken glass, the pieces were all over the floor of the dining room.

Was there any way she had deserved it? She was only two years away from the dreaded half-century mark, but her figure was slimmer than when she'd been a girl. And her hair, her fine auburn hair, had almost no grey, and her heart-shaped face, unlined, and dark eyes had still their appeal to men, even if they had lost their charm for Rex. Oh, yes, she knew that, even if she, unlike him — oh, very unlike — had remained faithful to her nuptial vows. Certainly she was more attractive today, as a woman, than he, balding and fattening, was as a man, which had not been so when, to everyone's surprise, she had "caught" him, the big blond god of a naval hero in the war, on the rebound from his unhappy affair with her beautiful friend Corinne. Ah, Corinne! Why had she given him up?

The things he found fault with in her would have been assets to a more civilized man! Had she not chosen and beautifully decorated their enchanting red-brick house in old Georgetown? Had it not been photographed in *House and Garden* and was it not the most popular of the residences annually opened to the public for charitable benefits? Were not her dinner parties the smartest and most elegant in town, and had they not been sometimes attended by the Kennedys themselves back in the Camelot era? There had been no detail of household arrangement too small for her immediate attention: a stain on a rug, a crack in the ceiling, a faded flower in a bunch, a dish the least bit overcooked or under-chilled. She could rightly say that when Saint Peter asked her what she had done with her life she could reply: "Well, at least I've made one man very comfortable." But had she?

Anne, of course, thought all that was the bunk. Anne had broken with both her parents, her mother because she deemed her "snobbish and trivial," and her father because he was in the Central Intelligence Agency and "persecuted" radicals. She lived in a loft in lower Manhattan with a pornographic (at least in Geraldine's opinion) photographer and wrote for a leftist sheet.

But what really did Anne and Rex have in their lives that was so much better than hers? Weren't they both engaged in tearing apart a world that she simply strove to make more livable? Rex had changed in his years with the Central Intelligence Agency. The cheerful blue-eyed blond hero that she had married, the decorated naval veteran of the Coral Sea and Wake Island battles, had become impatient and hypercritical. There was a hard ring now to his too continuous laughter, and she hated the way he snarled "Don't be so wet" to anyone who suggested that it was wrong to plot the assassination of an unfriendly dictator or to incite undefendable small nations to rise against their communist oppressors. Ugh! He had become a barbarian; that was the long and short of it.

And had not all their friends in Washington always complimented her on the perfection of her arrangements? But they were probably all her detractors underneath, like Rex and Anne; they may have thought her a fool for her pains. Yet how they came to her — oh, how they came — voraciously eating, copiously drinking, talking so brightly, seizing everything that she so blithely offered them! The time had clearly come for Rex to marry his mistress of two years' standing. God knew, Ellen Slater was vulgar enough for him!

The drowning creature came again to the surface. Geraldine remembered her duties as hostess. The curator from the National Gallery should have been talking to the lady on his left. She caught his eye and slightly raised her voice to make it carry three places down.

"You must ask Mrs. Halsted to loan you her Lancret for your French eighteenth-century show." And seeing how quickly he now turned to the owner of the coveted canvas, she continued her conversation with the deputy secretary of defense on her right as though no interruption had occurred. But as the butler leaned down to serve her, she murmured in his ear: "That new girl you brought is asking people if they want red or white wine. I told you both were to be served. Tell her to fill all the white wine glasses and put the red bottles on the table so that people can serve themselves." And she went on to her neighbor: "But you must have *some* jet lag. Can you really sleep in those army planes?"

"Oh, yes. The only tiring thing about travel is worry about tickets and reservations, and waiting in airports. All that is done away with when you fly officially."

The conversation, except for Rex's outburst at her down the table, was in pairs until after the roast, when, according to her habit, it became general. The theme, somewhat to her dismay introduced by Rex, was whether the antiwar protests would shorten or actually prolong the conflict in Viet Nam. But Rex, showing the effects of the cocktail hour, turned it more into a one-man harangue in favor of the second alternative.

"The shouters and screamers are really getting the country's back up. We hear the Pentagon is flooded with letters from people who up till now hardly knew there was a war going on and now want us to drop the A-bomb on Hanoi. These stupid kids have never heard of such a thing as backlash. And can you beat it, my own daughter has given away every penny I've settled on her to crazy, radical antiwar causes? And you *know* that money's going straight to Moscow! So much for all that fancy estate planning we go in for today. From now on I'm turning a deaf ear to my tax lawyer. What I have, I'll keep, thank you very much."

Geraldine, distressed by this uncouth revelation of family affairs, but seizing it as a means of changing the subject from a topic as party-destroying as the Dreyfus case in France of the *belle époque,* retorted in a tone of the mildest reproof: "But you make it sound, my dear, as if you'd settled a fortune on Anne, and of course it was no such thing. I think it's an excellent idea for parents to give modest sums to their children, not merely for tax purposes, but to see what they do with the money. If they blow it all, why then you know to put the next gift in trust. It can be a valuable lesson."

Leonard Holmes, the suave bachelor New York lawyer who was visiting them, Leonard, her oldest friend and adviser, the brother that she, an only child, had never had, came now to her aid by embroidering on the new topic. He amused the table with the account of a client who had kept his children from contributing to antiwar causes by threatening to expend double their gifts in hawkish propaganda. This was followed by a general discussion of the virtues and vices of excessive estate planning, a subject of interest to all, but which was roughly interrupted by Rex, who wanted to get back to the war.

"These idiotic kids call us imperialists, but I ask you, has any great nation ever entered a war with *no* intent to acquire *anything* for itself? It's a goddam crusade, that's what it is!"

Even now Geraldine sought to broaden the topic from just the war to the broader question of youth. "But it's not just the war they're against. It's what they call the establishment. They're looking for what they see as a better world. Do we really want our children to *start* as conservatives?"

"But you, of all people, should be resisting them!" Rex

almost shouted. "Isn't it you and your kind they're basically trying to destroy?"

"My kind?" she murmured wonderingly.

"I mean the last generation of women who care more for the looks of things than things themselves! Who go in for fancy trimmings and etiquette and who sits by whom and matching colors and everything just so divinely perfect!"

The shocked silence around the table was broken only when Leonard, smiling gravely, rose from his seat and said to Geraldine: "Do you mind terribly, my dear hostess, if I take my plate and finish it in the living room? I find the air in here a bit stifling."

"Not at all, Leonard. In fact, I'll join you."

Standing together by the fireplace in the other room, they waited in silence to see whether they would be joined by the guests or whether the latter would take their embarrassed leave.

"Geraldine," he said, "the time has come for you to leave that man."

"I think you are quite right."

❦   ❦   ❦

Geraldine's mind, in the dreary months that followed, with all their cloying content of the legal paraphernalia of divorce, went often back to an afternoon in the fall of 1939, just after the outbreak of war in Europe, when she and her two best friends had sat on a rocky peak in Mount Desert Island in Maine, contemplating the incomparable view of forest and sea and discussing their futures, or what seemed to be left of them.

She and the beautiful blond Corinne Bruning were nineteen, post-debutantes and noncollegians who planned shortly to go to work on *Style,* the New York fashion magazine. Leonard Holmes, black-haired, pale of countenance, lean and cerebral, was slightly their senior, now a law student, the kind of man who could be an intimate friend of women without the question of sex ever arising. Geraldine and Corinne had discussed whether he was what they called a "pansy." Corinne thought he was but didn't care; Geraldine thought he wasn't because she did care. She had not yet reached her friend's modernity.

Leonard was expressing his disgust that world conflict should interfere with his plans.

"You think you're all ready for life. You're booted and spurred. Your ears are still ringing with the golden words of graduation addresses. There is nothing to stop you. And then, bang! The upstart Austrian house painter rings down the curtain before your blinking eyes!"

"What'll you do, Lenny?" Corinne asked. "Apply for a commission, like everyone else we know?"

"I think I might try for naval intelligence. It seems a pity not to use one's bean at all."

"You won't mind people criticizing you for wanting a desk job?"

Geraldine knew that nothing would ever stop Corinne's bluntness. She watched with unexpressed sympathy the slow flush on Leonard's cheeks.

"There's such a thing as combat intelligence, you know," he retorted. "And anyway we're not in the war yet. And may never be."

"Though the smarter people think we ought!" Corinne exclaimed warmly.

Geraldine was sure that Leonard, with his great intelligence and sense of political channels, was never going to be exposed to enemy fire, but what of it? That was Leonard. And Leonard understood her as no one else ever had, even her doting old parents, who deemed her a miracle of smartness and "chic."

"It does seem as if we were all stopped dead on the threshold of our careers," she observed, to get back to the original theme. "And it may not be a bad thing for us women. Here we are, Corinne and I, preparing for lives where marriage is the great culminating event. Maybe the war will change all that."

"You mean you'll take over men's jobs?" Leonard queried. "And become dreary lawyers and doctors and insurance salesmen? I guess that's in the cards. But for some time to come I'll wager a woman's best road to power will still be through the man she marries."

"You must make yourself more available to us, Lenny," Corinne suggested.

He ignored this. "Look at Mrs. Roosevelt."

"Well, we've certainly come a long way from Madame de Pompadour!" Geraldine exclaimed with a laugh. "My trouble is that there aren't enough great men to go around."

"There may not be enough for most," Leonard agreed. "But there ought to be enough for you two. Corinne has the beauty and charm to choose pretty much whom she wants. And you, dear Geraldine, with a subtler kind of beauty and charm . . ."

"Spare me the subtle," she interrupted. "I know what you mean."

"With a subtler kind of beauty and charm," he repeated, "you have what it takes to assist a man of any first-rate ability to get to the top."

"And how, pray, am I to do that?"

"My dear, you were born to be a great *maîtresse de maison*, a splendid hostess, with a brilliant salon, a whole sphere of influence!"

"I see. Corinne is to do it with her blue eyes and melting smile, and I with my tea and *petits fours*."

"You may laugh at me, both, but you know what I mean." He was gazing now over the landscape and talking as if he were addressing it and not the women. "Corinne will always be the more popular one. She will accept the world for what it is. Indeed, she will epitomize it. She will always be young, like Freia, and bring youth to the other gods in Valhalla. But Geraldine will never be satisfied with the world as it is. She is too much the artist. She has to change things, rearrange them to better advantage. That little lake down there, the one so close to that tiny village, would look better, wouldn't it, if you cut a channel to the sea and made it an inlet? And isn't that rocky peak over the valley on our right a bit too short? Almost stubby, wouldn't you say? Geraldine might add a hundred feet to it."

"Oh, stop it, Lenny. You're making me out such an ass!"

Geraldine got up to stand apart from the others, afraid suddenly that she was going to weep. There were times when it was almost unbearable to be condemned to be what everyone thought she was. She took in the view now, that infinite, unbelievable view, as if she were gasping for air that could never sufficiently reach her lungs. Below and then beyond the sweeping richly dark green of the cascading pine forest, edged by the grey rocky coast and the white line of the breaking surf, was the glittering expanse of the blue and green ocean, under a pale cloudless sky, dotted with green and rocky islands and the alabaster triangles of sails. In the far distance, almost at the horizon, she could make out the tiny round tower of the lighthouse on Egg Rock. The beauty of it, which she had known and loved since her childhood, was what made life worth living.

·

"And you think I'd touch a square inch of that?" she exclaimed, waving to the view as she turned back to the other two. "How little you know me, even you, Lenny."

"But, darling, I meant it as the greatest of compliments! I'm calling you an artist, and art to me is all. If I'm studying law, it's only because I know I can never be a writer — a great one, that is, and what other kind matters? At least in the law I can play with words."

"But I've never written a thing, and I can't draw anything but a square house with a balloon of smoke coming out the chimney. And I can't play a single instrument or even carry a tune! All I can do is take in what I feel!"

"Maybe that should be enough for any of us," Corinne suggested.

"Do you really think so, Corinne?" Geraldine asked earnestly. "Well, let me read you something then. I was planning to anyway, when we reached the summit, but then I got cold feet. I thought you'd think me pompous."

"Oh, go ahead and read it, Gerry," Leonard urged her.

"I warn you it's a passage from Wordsworth. *The Prelude*. I copied it out this morning. It's not long."

She produced a piece of paper from her pocket and read:

> . . . if, in this time
> Of dereliction and dismay, I yet
> Despair not of our nature, but retain
> A more than Roman confidence, a faith
> That fails not, in all sorrow my support,
> The blessing of my life; the gift is yours,
> Ye winds and sounding cataracts! 'tis yours,
> Ye mountains! thine, O Nature! Thou hast fed
> My lofty speculations; and in thee,

For this uneasy heart of ours, I find
A never-failing principle of joy
And purest passion.

"But that's beautiful!" was Corinne's simple comment.

"I still maintain you're an artist," Leonard insisted. "In the same way, essentially, that Wordsworth was. Nature gave him the idea that he tried to copy. It's like Plato's ideal forms. We try to reproduce them on earth in our own crude way. Your material is life, Gerry! You look at life and can't keep your hands off it. It needs a twitch here and a twitch there, maybe even a yank; it has to be straightened out or pushed a bit farther back or even tilted to one side. Look what you've done to that hideous old shingle pile your parents have on West Street, with all its Victorian horrors! It's absolutely charming now, and the miracle is that you've managed to keep the lesser horrors they couldn't bear to part with and made them blend with the new things! So that the whole interior still reflects their personalities. Now *that*, I claim, is decorating raised to Olympian heights!"

"Oh, but I loved the Cartright house as it was!" Corinne protested. "Nothing should have been touched. It was the perfect shingle villa of the 1880s."

Leonard winked at Geraldine, who had put away her poem and had definitely nothing more to say. "As I said about Corinne, she's like Margaret Fuller. She accepts the universe!" He glanced at his watch. "Come on, girls, we'd better start down the mountain."

❦　　❦　　❦

Geraldine's plans for her future, vague as they were and like those of many women, had long been frustrated by her infatuation with Rex Boyle, never in the least her type, nor

even remotely the sort of man she had envisioned as needing a modern version of Madame Récamier to preside over
the salon of which he would be a principal decoration. She
had wasted countless summer mornings going to the Swimming Club on the chance of watching his lithe brown body
descend in a graceful arc from the high dive and his torso
plough the length of the long blue pool. He was friendly
with her; he was friendly with all their summer gang, and
he came to the little parties that she induced her elderly
and somewhat reluctant parents to give for her — shabby
affairs, really, she feared, compared with what the tycoons
gave, but well attended because the Cartrights were as
much a part of the Bar Harbor scene as the rocky shore and
the cries of the seagulls. But he would never come to her
house unless he knew that Corinne would be there.

There was no getting him away from Corinne, but there
was always the chance that Corinne might tire of him, and
this she did, and just at the time, too, when no one would
have expected it, right in the middle of the war and on one
of his leaves, when everyone fell over themselves to be nice
to heroes. Of course, that was like Corinne. She and Geraldine worked at an officers' entertainment bureau and
lunched together whenever they had a chance.

"I've suggested to Rex that he take you out," Corinne
informed her blandly on one of these occasions. "He needs
a shoulder to weep on, and I think yours might be a consoling one."

Geraldine had never discussed her passion with anyone,
even with Corinne, but of course she knew that her friend
was well aware of it.

"Will he want to?" she gasped.

"Oh, I think so. He asked me if you had anyone else."

"And what did you tell him?"

"I said I thought there had been something between you and poor Tommy Aspenwall."

"Oh, Corinne, you didn't!"

Tommy had been killed at Guadalcanal. He had been one of the less notable of their summer gang, shy, inhibited and rather sweet, supposedly hiding a crush on Geraldine.

"Why not? It makes you seem prettily sad and romantic to have lost someone in the war. Rather the way Rex sees himself, having lost me." Anyone else's laugh, at this point, would have seemed cruel, but Corinne's was simply pleasant. Obviously, she had no faith in the depth of Rex's emotions. "Don't you want him, dear? Now's your chance. He's up for grabs, and if you don't take him, someone else surely will!"

"Oh, Corinne. Are you sure you want to let him go? Why?"

"Several reasons. But one will do. He likes the war too much. In fact, he dotes on it. He goes after submarines the way he used to go after tarpon and swordfish. The idea of what it might be like to be trapped in a sinking U-boat, descending slowly to the depths of the ocean, miles down, would never cross his mind, and if it did, he'd shout with glee!"

"But that's war, Corinne! Men have to make themselves think that way to get through the horror of it. How else are we going to win? And you yourself from the beginning were all for fighting for Britain. I remember!"

"I was. But I still can count the cost. Unlike Rex, I have *some* imagination. Of which quality he hasn't a grain."

"Then why do you think he's so right for me?"

"Because you want him, my darling! It's as simple as that. And you don't have to *marry* him. Take it from me, he's a very handy lover. It wasn't *there* that he failed my test."

Geraldine, like many of her contemporaries, had never had an affair, and she was impressed and excited by Corinne's freedom and sophistication. She took her advice, however, and it was not long before she found that her friend's assessment of Rex's amatory capability was exact.

It was all very fast and unbelievable, and when he had to return to the Pacific, in only a few days' time, fearing he might have impregnated her, he insisted that they marry. After all, he pointed out, he might never return, and she would be left in a very awkward situation. She agreed, but when he came home, a year later, there was no baby, and she found what thousands of war brides later discovered: that she was wed to a stranger.

Rex had at first considered staying in the Navy, his ample inheritance compensating for the relatively low pay, but Geraldine, appalled but resigned at the prospect of a life in seaports and on Pacific atolls, had been greatly relieved when his friends had convinced him that if he really wanted to work for the defense of his country, the new CIA offered a more exciting and adventurous career. And she had been excited by the prospect of life in Washington. Had the great Henry James not once described it as the "city of conversation"? It seemed the true field for her talents.

There was conversation enough, it was true, but not of the sort she had expected. In the first place her husband and his colleagues were bound by strict rules of confidentiality; there was no way that a spouse could share in their plots or activities. Secondly, she found that they were more and more bound up in a form of crusade, or holy war, against communism; it lent to their social gatherings and talk a note of heated conviction, even of violence, that hardly fitted with the kind of cool, witty, terse and detached French eighteenth-century salon give-and-take that her readings in history had taught her to believe was the very essence of civilized life.

And it was unhappily true, too, that Rex's work tended to accentuate a certain streak of brutality in his character that she had begun to detect under the golden crust of the war hero. The only way she could think to combat it was to use all her arts to make their home as different as possible from what he had in his mind all day. To counteract death, so to speak, with beauty. Beauty, of course, as *she* conceived it. How else could she operate?

But it was only too evident now that she had only made things worse. So much worse that all she could do was tell him: "Keep your money. Keep the house. Keep your mistress. Just let me *go!*"

Corinne, as expected, had gone way ahead of her. She had married Adam Cabot, one of the brilliant young men most in view after the war, not only, like Rex, a hero, but a passionate Democrat (though a Boston Brahmin) who got himself elected to Congress and made a great stir in his vigorous opposition to Senator McCarthy. Corinne seemed in her element, but her luck suddenly changed when Cabot killed himself in an utterly unexplained fit of manic depression, leaving her, as he was a poor Cabot, with little but glowing memories. Always unpredictable, she then, in an astonishingly short time, became the second wife of Bruce Shellpacker, a dour little multimillionaire with a fortune in pharmaceuticals who was twenty-five years her senior.

❀ ❀ ❀

Corinne was there when Geraldine returned to New York to live, after her divorce, as generous as ever and all ready to launch her in the changed society of the great metropolis. She and her husband occupied a huge, handsome apartment in the Waldorf Towers, modern and gleaming and white and gold, which had the cool look of a place decorated entirely by the best professionals, without a single personal touch. Corinne obviously didn't give a damn. She sought distraction among people she could both impress and despise; she dressed superbly (*that* she still cared about) and spent her husband's money in a way that alarmed his heirs, all dreary nephews and nieces who had no reason, she told Geraldine with a sneer, to think they would even be mentioned in his will.

Leonard Holmes, who was Bruce's lawyer, described him to Geraldine with his usual freedom (among his intimates) from conventional ideas of loyalty.

"When he was in college in Chicago — his father was a moderately prosperous undertaker — he bought half the stock of a pharmaceutical business started by two enterprising friends for ten grand. They never got rid of him, even when the thing had waxed into an empire. I won't bore you with the legal details of how he managed to hang on to his percentage through thick and thin; just take it from me that he did. The man has the tenacity of a bulldog or should I say a snapping turtle. Sometimes I think all he can do is cling; he has raised that capacity to the level of genius. Other than that he's a simple enough soul. He has a passion for fishing and elegant ladies. Of course, he's always been afraid of being married for his money, and of course he has been — twice. They always are."

"Oh, come now. Corinne?"

"Corinne indeed. She's the most lethal type of gold digger, the one who doesn't know she is one. She thought she could *do* things for Bruce: bring out the 'human' side of him, turn him into a philanthropist, maybe even a Democrat. Of course, she found him immovable. Again, they always are."

"But she and he still get on?"

"It depends what you mean by getting on. They're to-gether, yes. But I gather Corinne leads a very independent life. In every sense of the word."

"And he puts up with that?"

"That remains to be seen. I've had considerable experi-ence with his sort of rich man. He seems meek and quiet and unexpectedly tolerant, but, deep down, there's a mean, hard, rocky little ego. Beware!"

"Why need I beware?"

"Because he likes you. I could tell that the other night at dinner. He'll want you to help him with Corinne."

"And shouldn't I?"

"If you want. But remember, nothing can change him."

Geraldine found herself in a society very different from the one she had left. Many of the old names had survived, and she found plenty of familiar faces at her club, the Col-ony, but the makers of new fortunes — as had always been true in New York — the media giants and investment bank-ers, dominated the scene; and the charity ball, with tickets so dear as to exclude most of the old brownstone group, with all its lavish display of jewels and designer dresses, its hot crowded ballrooms, bad service and harassed waiters, its crush and its noise, and, above all, its glaring publicity that ensured that it would be more read about than enjoyed, was the order of the day.

Corinne was very much in the center of things, and her picture (she was as photogenic as she was beautiful) ap-peared regularly in the evening papers, sometimes at a table of smiling guests, sometimes on the dance floor in the arms of a dark and handsome man, sometimes at one of those posed ladies' "teas" for a ball-organizing committee. She invited Geraldine to all her parties and was indefatigable in finding gentlemen to pick her up and take her home. She seemed to enjoy everything in her life but her husband.

"Bruce is simply hopeless in social life," she complained to Geraldine. "He won't dance; he hardly talks; he won't even drink. I've done everything in my power to amuse him, and he won't be amused. I've tried to get him to go on this board and that, to get him to take a little interest in the life of the city, but he won't budge. His idea of heaven is to sit in his study and watch some stupid sport on TV."

"A lot of men are like that."

"Well, they'll have to learn to do it alone. Not that they'll mind that, I don't suppose. But Bruce resents my activities. He says nothing, but I feel it. What can I do? No woman could cope with him." There was a pause, in which Geraldine felt that she had been leading up to what she now said. "Except possibly you."

"Me? I didn't do so well with Rex, did I? He seems blissfully happy with his new wife."

"Ellen? She's dumb enough to make any man happy. Do you know what was wrong with you and Rex?"

"I have some ideas, but I'd love to hear yours."

"You were up against something you couldn't possibly lick. He was up to his ears in all kinds of ghastly secret operations, murders and I don't know what — Adam Cabot told me about some of them when he was in Congress — and he had to have some conflict with the basic puritanism with which we were all brought up. So he comes home every night with that on his conscience — though he has to be jaunty and defiant in self-defense — and he finds you giving one of your perfect dinner parties with everything so gorgeously arranged. Bloody days and elegant evenings. The contrast was just too much. He flipped."

"Corinne, why didn't you tell me this at the time?"

"Because I didn't figure it out until afterwards. You never complained. You just suddenly up and left him. But anyway, what could you have done? He was beginning to hate you. You couldn't have known it was really himself he hated."

"How horrible!"

"Never mind that now. It wasn't your fault. You showed the patience of Job. That's why I'm wondering if you couldn't even handle Bruce."

Geraldine had not found Bruce Shellpacker nearly as difficult as Corinne made out. In fact, she rather liked him. It was true that he was round and dumpy, with very thin grey hair and a bland, expressionless countenance, but he had large clear blue eyes, quite beautiful really, dimly lit with a mild perennial suspicion. And he was a wonderful listener; he never seemed to be thinking of his answer but only of what you were saying. Yet when he talked about himself, he had the rare gift of almost persuading you to share in his own self-pity.

"I suppose a man of my age and appearance has no right to expect devotion from such a beautiful woman as your friend," he told her one night when they were sitting away from the other guests in a far corner of the great living room after one of Corinne's dinner parties. "It was hazardous on my part. As it was hazardous for me to marry my first wife. I try to give women what they want. But if it isn't precisely what they want, one might as well spare oneself the trouble."

"And what is it precisely that they do want?"

"My dear lady, I'm perhaps too delicate — or too prudish — to tell you. But I've heard there are only two kinds of women in the world: those who are nice to you when they get their own way, and those who are still not nice to you, even when they do. I seem to have encountered only the latter."

"But the former *do* exist!" Geraldine exclaimed, a bit surprised by her own vehemence.

On another evening, arriving at Corinne's at what she had supposed would be another grand dinner, she met her hostess in the lobby below, swathed in furs, escorted by a strikingly handsome man, vaguely familiar looking (was he a movie star?), and two other couples, all obviously en route to some gala at a place other than the Waldorf Towers.

"Oh, Gerry, my love, *here* you are at last!" Corinne paused to embrace her. "We're off to dinner at the Plaza. But Bruce is waiting for you upstairs. You and he should have a much better time alone. I know how you feel about charity balls! And I can guarantee you a very fine dinner. I ordered it myself."

Geraldine took her friend firmly by the arm and led her beyond hearing distance of the others. "Look, Corinne, I'm not a call girl!"

Corinne threw back her head in a peal of laughter. "My dear, you're the one who's calling yourself that! And I must say, it hardly becomes you. The idea was all Bruce's. He said he'd take three tables at the ball at a tab of thirty g's if he could dine quietly with you. How could I refuse? And he's not a beast, you know. Your virtue's entirely safe."

And on she swept, followed by her gay and tittering group, for all the world like Blanche Ingraham of Ingraham Park leaving poor little Jane Eyre to the clutches of Mr. Rochester!

Geraldine decided to smile. Some minutes later, having cocktails with Bruce in his paneled study lined with standard sets, she could not help thinking how she would do the apartment over if it were hers.

"I don't like being thrust at people," she warned him.

"How else is one to get at you?"

"Call me up. Ask me directly."

"You'd never have come here if you'd known Corinne was going to be out."

"I might have. I do things very much my own way."

"Corinne quoted you as saying that you regarded it as a worthy accomplishment to have made one man very comfortable. Mightn't it be twice as good to be able to say you'd made *two* men very comfortable?"

"And Corinne? Where does that leave her?"

"Oh, don't you know? I thought you girls told each other everything. Corinne wants to marry that actor you may have seen her with in the lobby. She knows it's folly and that it will never last. One thing you have to give Corinne is that she doesn't kid herself. She has asked me for her freedom — as if she'd ever lost it! — and her financial demands are reasonable, to say the least. She says I'm just the same as I was the day she married me, so she hasn't earned much."

Geraldine had listened to him with intense interest. Now she nodded. "How like her. But I suppose you settled something on her when you were married."

"Only a million. She says with that and what she's asking for she can make do."

"Oh, she could make do with anything." Geraldine reflected for a moment. The atmosphere that this curious little man created around him was oddly relaxed. She felt she could say anything. Anything at all.

"I have something more than a million," she heard herself remark. "But it doesn't go far these days."

"I'll give you another if you marry me. I might even give you two!"

She laughed. "But why should you want to, in God's name? With your track record? Why aren't you better off alone?"

"Because you strike me as the kind of woman who would be nice to me even after you'd got what you wanted."

"And how do you know I want all this?" Her eye took in the study and the view of the long living room beyond.

"I don't. I'm taking a chance, that's all."

Again she laughed. He certainly put her in a remarkable mood. "I'm not in the least bit in love with you."

"Of course not. How could you be?"

"And I haven't the least desire to sleep with you."

"Forget it. Since my prostate operation I'm zilch in that department. Your bedroom would be strictly off-limits. Think it over. It's not a bad proposition, all things considered."

"How can I not think it over? I'll need some time, of course. But here's your man telling us that dinner is ready. Let's talk of other things."

That night, back in her own little apartment, she sat up late by the fire, which she kept lit, mulling over Bruce's proposition. How many opportunities were there for a divorced woman, only decently well off and pushing fifty, trained for no career but that of a hostess? Here was a chance, at the earnest invitation of a rich man, with all cards face up on the table, to amplify and enrich what appeared to be his wasted life. It was true that the brilliant Corinne had failed at the same task, but it was also obvious that the brilliant Corinne had not really tried and had despised the unfortunate man to boot. And didn't she begin to see a way to turn his life around in a way that *both* would enjoy? For she had certainly learned that if marriage was not teamwork, it was nothing. Wasn't Bruce Shellpacker what she had been waiting for?

@ @ @

After Geraldine and Bruce had agreed to marry, he sent her downtown for a legal talk with Leonard Holmes. She knew, of course, what it would be about. She was to sign a waiver of her rights as a widow to make any claim against her husband's estate should he leave her by will less than the share she would have taken in intestacy. This was routine procedure in the case of very large estates, and she had no question about it. But Leonard looked very grave.

"I think I wouldn't sign it if I were you, Geraldine."

"Why on earth not?"

"Because I know your husband-to-be; I know him up and down. I wasn't at all sure this marriage was the best thing for you, but I decided that if anyone could make a go of it, you could. And Bruce is devoted to you; there's no question about that. But he has a shrewd, stubborn, suspicious streak. Once he gets the idea he's being taken advantage of, he never forgives."

"But I haven't the least idea of taking advantage of him! Everything I do as Mrs. Bruce Shellpacker — with his money, that is — will be with his knowledge and consent."

"I'm sure of that. What I'm talking about is that if he develops doubts, even *unreasonable* ones — doubts you might never know about — he'd be quite capable of writing you out of his will altogether. And never tell you about it!"

"Well, let him!"

Leonard looked pained. "But, my dear, it's *such* a fortune, and his blood pressure is *so* high. Let's face it, Gerry, your betrothed may not make very old bones. And please don't look at me that way. I'm only trying to see that you get fair treatment!"

She made an effort to control her indignation. "Very well. I know you're a true friend. But do you think for a minute, if I *don't* sign the waiver, he'll marry me?"

"He might. He's awfully keen on you. And he understands people who won't sign things. He doesn't like signing them himself."

"I'm finding it hard to remember you're *his* lawyer."

"I may still be acting for his best good. Viewed broadly enough."

"Would *he* think so?"

"If he knew I was advising you not to sign that waiver? He'd fire me like a shot."

Geraldine at this got up. "Give me that waiver, Lenny. I'm going to sign it. And then you can take me to lunch."

After her marriage Geraldine started her new program slowly and tactfully. At least so she thought. Bruce made no objection to her total redecoration of the vast apartment, which she accomplished, one room at a time, in such a fashion that he was never bothered with movers and painters. When it was finished, it was true, he said hardly a word to commend it, though it was hailed by all who saw it, but he did allow it to be photographed for a glowing article in *Architectural Digest*.

They certainly seemed to get on together very nicely. If they were alone in an evening, and there was no sports program on TV, they would sit comfortably by a fire, reading books or magazines and occasionally exchanging chatty reminiscences. It was rather like living, she decided, with a silent, friendly and adequately generous uncle. He allowed her to give as many parties as she liked, and she strove to ask persons who might amuse him, but he didn't seem to care very much whether the guests were total strangers or old acquaintances.

Lunching with Corinne, who was already having trouble with her movie star, she waited until the complaints had subsided and then reported her own progress with Bruce.

"Oh, you're doing fine," her friend lightly assured her. "Everyone's talking about the 'lovely' Mrs. Shellpacker's 'lovely' parties. So much more taste than that rather garish Corinne. But don't do it *too* well, my dear. Don't let him start thinking people are calling him *Mr.* Geraldine Shellpacker."

"Oh, dear, you sound just like Leonard. What am I to do? What does Bruce really want?"

"He wants to be nothing. And to get all the credit for it."

"It sounds as if I were going to have my experience with Rex, all over again!"

Corinne shook her head, more serious now. "I don't think so. I think you'll come through. Hang on, and you'll be the girl who gets the brass ring."

"What do you mean?"

"Don't you remember the old merry-go-round? The lucky one got the brass ring. You'll be one of the great women of the town!"

"You mean when Bruce dies?"

"Of course I mean when Bruce dies! If old friends like you and I can't be frank with each other, who can? You have the perfect training for an heiress. For years you've had a front-row seat to watch how badly the rich dispose of their riches. You'll know just how to spend and, equally important, how to give it away. You can be a power in philanthropy, in society, even in politics. You can buy an ambassadorship! Oh, you'll be great! You'll be what Leonard always said you'd be."

"Leonard?"

"Don't you know he always predicted that *you* were the one of our old threesome who'd be the biggest star?"

"How silly."

"But he's right."

Geraldine became reflective. "I married Bruce, of course, because I wanted to be secure and comfortable. We were entirely frank with each other. It was a perfectly reasonable and honorable transaction. But I was determined to do what I could for him. He wanted me to make him comfortable. Well, I've tried my best."

"Perhaps you've made him too comfortable."

"What should I do then?"

"Do you really want to know? Then I'll tell you. Don't touch another thing in the apartment. And I hear you're about to do over his horror of a house in Long Island. Leave it be. Don't give any more dinner parties. Stay home alone with him. You might even watch TV with him. Go out for a good lunch with friends. That'll give you a recess, and he won't mind it. But make that your only one."

"My God, what a life!"

"It shouldn't be too long. With his heart. And the rewards may be phenomenal."

"Corinne, you're awful!"

"I'm a realist."

"Well, I couldn't treat him that way. I guess I'll keep on the way I've been going."

❀   ❀   ❀

Corinne was right about its not being too long. Only a year later Bruce slumped in his armchair before the TV; the end had come. The day after the memorial service Geraldine sat in Leonard's Wall Street office while he gravely read her the dispository clauses of her husband's will. He paused after reading this one: "To my wife, Geraldine, on whom I have already made a substantial settlement, I bequeath the sum of one million dollars for having executed to the best of her abilities her pledge to make me comfortable."

Geraldine found herself reflecting that it was probably exactly what she deserved. "To the best of her abilities," she repeated musingly. "How nicely put. Well, is that all? I mean as far as I'm concerned?"

"The furniture in the apartment, of course. That was in the personal property clause."

"And that's very valuable. With the million he gave me when we married, I'll be fine."

"Maybe. But it's pretty small potatoes compared to a hundred million dollars!"

"Is that what the estate's worth?"

"Approximately."

"And where does it go? To the nephews and nieces?"

"Oh, no. To a foundation for research in heart diseases."

"Nothing to the family? Oh, Lenny, how could you let him?"

"I finally induced him to leave each nephew and niece a cash bequest of fifty thousand. They'll sue, of course. And they'll lose. The will provides that if the new foundation consents to any settlement with the family, the entire residue passes to the Red Cross."

"Well, Leonard, there we are. Are you taking me to lunch?"

"Wait a bit, Gerry. 'There' is not exactly where we are. You have an election to take against the will. Your intestate share, Bruce being childless, would amount to half the estate. An election will entitle you absolutely to fifty million dollars, free of estate tax!"

"Lenny, what are you talking about? You know as well as I do that I waived that right!"

"But Bruce destroyed your waiver two years ago. In this very office, and before my very eyes. And I dictated this memorandum, which he and I both initialed." He handed a paper to her. "That, of course, is a Xerox. I keep the original in my safe."

Geraldine now read the document.

"Mr. Shellpacker came to my office on the above date to make his annual check of his papers in my safe. When he found the waiver executed by Geraldine Cartright Shellpacker just prior to their marriage, he informed me that he had no further need of it, as he now fully trusted his wife not to oppose any of his testamentary dispositions, and he wished to destroy it. He then tore it up in my presence and asked me to destroy any office copies that I had."

Under the text, in the middle of the page, were what certainly appeared to be her husband's initials and Leonard's. After several moments of reflection she observed: "It seems incredible. Why should Bruce have destroyed it? Even supposing he had decided to leave me his whole estate, the document would have been simply surplusage. And if, as he did, he decided to leave me only a small fraction, it would have been vital. Tearing it up was like tearing up a paid-up insurance policy. It makes no sense."

"Perhaps he wanted to show you how totally he trusted you."

"Then he would have told me what he'd done!"

"Are you absolutely sure he didn't?"

"Absolutely."

"Well, the foundation's lawyers will certainly make your argument. But I don't think they'll get anywhere with it."

"When will they make that argument?"

"Why, when I file your election, of course."

"But, Lenny, I'm not going to file any election! If Bruce trusted me not to contest his will, I shan't."

Leonard was really excited now. Indeed, she had never seen him so moved. He jumped up and walked to the window. "Gerry, Bruce's will was the product of his last few weeks. It's the product of a mind diseased with suspicion and resentment. Believe me, I know how that mind worked at the end. It's up to you to take the money his better nature meant you to have and spend it gloriously, magnificently. The other half of the estate is plenty for research, and you can will them more if you wish. You can even sweeten the legacies of the shorn nephews and nieces! Oh, my friend, you can't just let a chance for greatness slip by you for a silly scruple!"

"Is honor a silly scruple?"

He raised his hands to his temples in exasperation. "Look, Gerry. Don't decide anything today, or even this week. You have plenty of time. Go home and think things over. Talk to Corinne."

"I'll go home and I'll certainly think things over. But I don't think I'll talk to Corinne. I have an idea that you and she have already talked."

Geraldine decided not even to have lunch with him. She wanted to be alone, utterly alone. That afternoon she walked for a mile in Central Park and settled at last on a bench facing the Bethesda Fountain to watch the pigeons pecking at crumbs. She had a strange, rather eerie feeling that a vision of something, a recollection, perhaps, of a forgotten or neglected event, an action perhaps trivial or barely noticed at the time, was going to flash on the screen of her mind if she could only make it blank enough. If she could relax enough.

And then, just as she was about to rise, it came, with startling clarity, and she sank back on the bench. What she saw was her late husband sitting at a table in Leonard's law office on which were stacked the long printed forms of leases to various loft buildings that Bruce had purchased in lower Manhattan, each page of which required the landlord's initials. She and Leonard were chatting on a sofa in a corner of the room; she remembered that she had accompanied Bruce on his mission downtown, lured by the prospect that all three would lunch afterwards at Leonard's club.

But now she saw why she had remembered the occasion. Bruce's pen had run dry, and he asked Leonard for another. Leonard went to his desk, picked a pen off the stand and gave it to Bruce, who tested it by scribbling his initials on a blank piece of paper, nodded and resumed his work on the leases.

So that was it! Had Leonard, finding the initialed page on the table that afternoon when he returned from their lunch, conceived the sudden notion of its tremendous utility in his projects for his friend Geraldine? Had he typed the words of the revoking memorandum on that page over Bruce's initials and added his own? And then placed the memorandum with the waiver in the safe so that after the death of his client he could produce the one he thought most appropriate, in view of whatever new will his client should have subsequently executed?

She felt a lump in her throat at the thought of the risk that Leonard was taking in what he thought were her best interests. Perhaps it was not a great one, but discovery would lead to certain disbarment. Was it right for her to reject a gift of such sublime disinterestedness? And wasn't he right? Hadn't her husband, a small man in every way, treated her with extraordinary shabbiness? And, after all, maybe he *had* destroyed that waiver. Maybe he *had* wished her to be free to take the percentage of his estate to which she regarded herself as entitled. Maybe he had meant to leave the decision to her!

But no. She was absolutely convinced that Bruce could never, never have torn up her waiver. It was simply too unlike him ever to give up even the lowest-ranking card in his hand. When she rose to go home, she knew there would be no court action, because she would never file the election against her husband's estate. And the inward struggle and decision would be hers alone and would always be hers alone. She could never tell another human being, because it would put Leonard at risk. She could not even tell Leonard, for it might make him nervous that she had guessed. After all, she might talk in her sleep or lose her mind and blab!

But everything was basically all right. She would have no commendation in the world, and she wanted none. She simply wanted to be sure in her own mind that the forms of beauty that she had tried to reproduce in her daily life bore some true relation to the perfect forms above — in the sky? did it matter? — of which Plato had made so much. And if these forms did not have a moral as well as an aesthetic beauty, then what were they? The tinsel on a Christmas tree, lampshades in a decorator's shop window, a roll of sample chintzes. In the end one had only oneself to live with, and it had better be a comfortable self. She smiled at her use of her and her husband's word.

When she next saw Leonard and told him of her decision, he knew at once by her tone and look that it was irreversible, and he abandoned further argument. But she couldn't resist one further passage.

"Tell me something, Lenny. You remember the plot of *Portrait of a Lady*?"

"Of course."

"Then you recall that Ralph Touchett induces his father to leave Isabel a fortune because he wants to see what she will do with it."

"He wants to see her do great things with it. But she's a fool. She falls victim to a clever fortune hunter."

"And Ralph dies of disappointment."

"Are you implying that he deserved his fate? That that is what should happen to voyeurs?"

"Oh, voyeur is a harsh word. After all, he loved her. No, all I'm saying is that one mustn't get too close to the lives of others. We must all live essentially by ourselves. Anyway, I know how dear a friend you've been."

"Ah, Geraldine, what you're throwing away!"

"It's nothing to what I'm keeping," she assured him.